# Be Careful Who You Marry

## LIZZY MUMFREY

🐦@iamselfpub
www.iamselfpublishing.com

Dedication
To my Godmother Cookie who lived at the real
Hoathly Farm.

# Contents

Acknowledgements....................................................................1

Prologue 1 ............................................................................3

Prologue 2 ............................................................................6

Prologue 3 ............................................................................9

Lilli 1–29.........................................................................10–85

Mouse 1–40................................................................86–202

Lizzy 1–42 ................................................................203–320

Epilogue 1 ......................................................................321

# Acknowledgements

Thank-you so much for reading Be Careful Who You Marry. I love to hear what people think of my writing so if you have any thoughts on the book that you'd like to share you can find me on my Facebook page @LizzyMumfreyAuthor or on Goodreads. I would also be most grateful for a review on Amazon so that other people know what you thought about it too. If you enjoyed this story, you might also enjoy Fall Out my first novel which shares the same characteristics of exploring relationships and how one straightforward choice can change your life and that of those around you.

I would like to thank all those who encourage me in my writing especially Bob who puts up with me disappearing into another world for days on end and my daughters Pop and Francesca for their support and inspiration including coming up with the giveaway name tape on "Alan's" hat. Thanks to my sister Diana for her beta reading and sage suggestions.

As a mark of years of friendship I have included the names of three schoolfriends and their spouses for key characters and stolen aspects of their lives. This is with their permission with the proviso that I haven't made them nasty or weird. I hope I haven't but they do have a habit of becoming very much their own characters while I write. Thank-you Tina, Liz and Nikki for your lifelong comradeship.

Be Careful Who You Marry is set on the Kent and Sussex border where I grew up and I have unashamedly referenced real institutions, people, places and establishments but please note that the novel is purely a work of fiction. Names, characters, places, and events are either the product of my over active imagination or are used entirely fictitiously.

Thank-you to I Am Self Publishing for their editing, proofreading, cover design and turning the ideas that swirl inside my head into the reality of a published novel.

# Prologue 1

**"I am totally convinced that your entire life depends on who you marry."**

The sixth form science girls of Uplands Community College, soporific after a carbohydrate heavy school lunch, slumped on chairs, some perched on desks, skinny adolescent legs dangling in all directions, ties skew-whiff.

"What on earth brought that on, Liz?"

"Well, it is Halloween 1987 this weekend. Mum is fifty and has been married to Dad for twenty-five years. Imagine if they had married someone completely different it would all be… well, completely different."

"Your dad might have married my mum!" piped up Tina. "We'd be sisters."

"Don't be daft, Tina. You wouldn't exist."

"Yeah, and if my mum had married someone rich, instead of my obnoxious dad, then we wouldn't be living in a council house out in the sticks," moaned Nikki, running her hands through her mad, bushy hair.

"So girls, where on earth will we be when we are fifty? Where will we be living? An exciting city or stuck in this rural backwater? Council house or mansion? Richer or poorer… In sickness or in health?"

Liz looked around the group challengingly.

"Who will we have been married to for twenty-five years? What will our kids be like? It is clear to me that you have to be very careful who you marry, girls!" Heads nodded in agreement.

Tina interjected. "For a start, I wouldn't touch any of the boys here at Uplands with a barge pole. Just so puerile, so unworldly. We should be looking at older, mature boys."

A cheerful, round-faced girl, Charlotte, piped up, "The only eligible boys living round here in this stupid country idyll seem to be Young Farmers. Let's face it, at fifty I will be with my ruddy husband, in our messy farmhouse, with two boys called Will and Olly and piles of smelly dogs – oh and you lot can come round for a mug of tea and home baked cake with fifty candles on top."

"Sod that. I am going to get out of here. When I am fifty I want to be drinking champagne, wearing an amazing designer dress, with our delightful sons, William and Oliver, note that their names will be in full, we will be so posh, because I am going to marry someone like Patrick Shepley-Botham – handsome, rich, adorable…"

This provoked snorts of laughter.

"Well out of your league, Elizabeth."

"An unrequited love, I would have to say."

Liz retrieved control. "Where shall we start if we are to hunt for a suitable husband? Let's commence our mission this very weekend! The best place to seek out the talent has got to be the Young Farmers' Halloween Disco. It's at the Commemoration Hall."

Tina nodded. "With a bit of luck there will be more than just agricultural yokels on offer. One advantage of living in the middle of bloody nowhere is that all the eligible young men should gravitate to any local party that offers both booze and birds."

"Yeah – and it is half term. Perhaps even Patrick Shepley-Botham and his plummy, public school chums might be there."

Liz clapped her hands decisively. "Young Farmers' Disco it is…"

"Hey, can we all stay at your place, Liz?"

"Yeah, yeah, can we? It is literally just up the hill."

Liz knew that her parents wouldn't mind. They seemed to be pretty tolerant of a gaggle of giggly teenage girls dossing down.

"As long as no-one throws up on the carpet this time."

Miss Churchill popped her head round the door. They all automatically sat up straight at the sight of a teacher, the conversation stopping dead.

"Elizabeth?"

"Yes," chimed all the Elizabeths in the room, at which point they all laughed.

**"Just too many Elizabeths in this class," said Miss Churchill.**

# Prologue 2

**They all dressed up as witches – sexy ones of course.**

They took it in turns to smear green body paint on to each other's faces, arms and chests. Tina backcombed Nikki's wayward hair so it all stood on end in a giant afro halo, making her look even taller than she already was. She wasn't overly pleased but was too acquiescent to say anything.

Liz, minutely petite and very pretty, managed to look alluring despite a tooth blackened with poster paint, which, it turned out, tasted disgusting. Her skirt barely reached the bottom of her bum.

Tina, blonde and with her tiny waist and respectably proportioned boobs, had managed to purloin a bottle of mead. It was sickeningly sweet but had a good strong belt of alcohol, even more powerful than their usual staple, sherry. When each came to their turn they gulped at it to make sure of a copious portion – some managing to down more than others – before the bottle was snatched away by the next in line.

"Right – time to go, girls!"

"When witches go riding, and black cats are seen, the moon laughs and whispers, for 'tis Halloween."

Tina interjected. "What on earth is that crap, Elizabeth!"

An indignant face turned to glare at Tina. "What are you going on about?"

"No, not you – that other Elizabeth." Tina wafted her broom vaguely at the espousing poet.

"A poem – Robert Burns."

"Ooh – get you!"

The coven scampered down the hill with suitably witch-like cackles, past the genteel shops and tidy houses that lined Wadhurst High Street to the Commemoration Hall, to hunt for husbands.

The disco was in full swing as they made their entrance self-consciously through the heavy old wooden doors. Their awkward asides of "You first…", "No, you…", accompanied by shoves and dodges, manoeuvring Liz to the forefront, Nikki hanging back at the rear, tumbled them inside; out of the crisp clean air and into a warm, noisy fug.

Farmers' wives, as elderly as their own parents, sat behind trestle tables, perched on metal framed canvas chairs with ingratiating smiles on their faces, eager to take their ticket money. Their farmer spouses, equally ancient, were behind the table that served as a bar.

Their unctuous "Thank you so much, ducks" was drowned out by 'Whenever You Need Somebody' belting out from enormous speakers. The DJ was on the stage, headphones on, cueing up the next song on his CD deck. Behind him psychedelic blobs of light swirled around, looking incongruous against the functional background of the old-fashioned, utilitarian hall.

A few pipe cleaner spiders hung apologetically from the window furniture, ironically propped against real cobwebs, above a roughly carved pumpkin, providing a hint of the theme. At least everyone seemed to have made the effort to dress up. A ghost or two were at the bar, chatting to a Frankenstein clutching a half pint tumbler and a mummy puffing away at a cigarette. An incongruous cow was swigging out of a bottle. Swarms of witches swished around.

"Eyes right, girls. I spy with my little eye – Patrick Shepley-Botham. And eyes left, girls, there are the more mature farmers that we had in mind."

"Don't stare so obviously, Liz!"

Liz cackled.

The whole coven started prancing about as alluringly as they could while surreptitiously perusing the dark corners. Any potential spouses? Their alert eyes scanned the room, weeding out potential targets while trying to look as if they were actually focused on their dancing.

**You have to be patient when seeking husbands.**

# Prologue 3

**At exactly midnight the bar closed and the DJ said a firm goodnight.**

The dance floor was empty, except for a few mismatched monsters and sorcerers entwined and swaying to their own tune. Patrick Shepley-Botham was one of them, managing to hold a glass, smoke a cigarette and yet still trail his hand over the back of the blonde dancing partner draped over him. Misshapen bundles could be vaguely made out to be zombified piss artists.

A scandalised Liz, returning from a 'walk' around the recreation ground behind the hall, otherwise known as a crafty fag and a passing snog with Daniel, yelled unnecessarily into a tipsy Nikki's ear, "Bloody hell. They are all at it like rabbits out there! There are witches everywhere and it is not broomsticks that they are riding." A quick glance round showed numerous members of their coven missing. Liz and Nikki exchanged widened eyes and stretched eyebrows.

"I am sure one of our lot was wrapped round James Arbuthnott."

"Who?"

"That farmer bloke – quite cute actually."

"No, I meant… never mind. We'd better round them up and get back to Tina's and discover how successful our husbandly mission was."

**Had they met the one they would marry?**

# Lilli 1

**"For God's sake, Elizabeth."**

Mum only called her Elizabeth when she was angry. Ninety-nine percent of the time it was Lillibet, very childish. She thought of it as Lilli inside her head; when she said it, it didn't seem so juvenile.

"You have so much potential, you can't just throw it all away. Why on earth didn't you say something before now, while we could do something about it?"

Lilli didn't know what to say.

"You are so bright and have such an amazing future, if only you would take it. You can't give it all up. What about your university offers? What about your dreams of a career in computing?"

Her mother had materialised ominously in the doorway of her bedroom and just would not stop hammering on. She'd obviously been chewing things over with Dad, become rather over excited and been sent on an unaccompanied mission, armed and dangerous. Lilli, prone on the floor, imprisoned awkwardly by her beanbag, trying to revise for her Physics A Level, felt at a disadvantage. Her mother loomed over her. She decided to keep her lips firmly pressed together.

*How many times must we go over this? I wish I'd never told you.*

"Please, darling, just think hard about this. We can just sort this out for you. It isn't too late yet. It is easily done these days, and it can be all over before you take your A Levels."

Lilli waited stubbornly silent.

*A pregnant pause. Ha-ha. Very funny.*

Lilli was getting increasingly irritated.

"You have the rest of your life to think of. You can have any number of babies in the future. Now is not the right time. For heaven's sake, you are nearly eighteen. You barely know the father and he is just a local farmer. How is he going to support you both? Please, darling."

Lilli couldn't look at her. She felt intimidated and at a disadvantage with her mother hovering over her and she was just beginning to get to the rolling boil stage of anger. In her head, her real thoughts agitated.

*Who cares what he is and what he does? I wish I hadn't told you who the father was. I'm not bloody telling you what he thinks of the whole thing.*

Mum caught the look on Lilli's face and advanced again. "Please, darling. The world is your oyster."

*Stupid, stupid expression. What did that mean anyway? What do oysters have to do with anything?*

"You are by far the brightest... you are just so clever... we had hoped... better things..."

*Here we go – blah, blah, blah – old stuck record – or should that be CD these days?*

Her mother's pleading was starting to descend into a pitiful, defeated whine. Lilli was just not giving in to this emotional blackmail. It was her life, not her mother's. She focused on her mother's pathetically mournful face, glared and flared her eyes. She was so angry that her brain felt as if it was trying to escape from her skull.

*Here goes, Mum, bloody listen to this. You asked for it.*

"So, mother, you would like me to slink off secretly, without showing you up in front of your friends of course, and discreetly murder your grandchild. Is that what you want?"

Her mother gasped, shocked, speechless.

*Oh God, that's done it.*

Lilli instantly felt guilty. It was malicious, but it was the only way she could make her wishes understood. Surely even her buttoned up, uptight mother would understand now. Her mother stared transfixed at a spot somewhere on the wall. Rigid. One of her very best death stares was on her elegant face.

Lilli waited. She'd stopped breathing.

After forever, Lilli's mother took a deep breath and let it out dramatically. It sounded ominous. She spoke very quietly, which made it scarier, with her teeth clenched.

"If you feel like that, Elizabeth, then you might as well **pack** your bags…" The pack was spat out, and it made Lilli jump. "Get out, you slut. Move in with one of your friends, or how about moving in with the father? Just get out of my sight." She was shouting now.

She retreated in a flurry, without looking at Lilli, letting out a gasp that might have been a sob. Lilli was trembling. She wrestled her way awkwardly out of the beanbag. Her stomach churned with horror and guilt.

*Oh my God. Oh my God. She means it. What shall I do? She can't mean it. Where can I go? I will have to go to James. Will she let me stay if I apologise? Oh God, what an idiot I am.*

She stood tall, unconsciously cradling her belly, and promptly burst into inconsolable sobs. She desperately needed her friends right now, but she couldn't go downstairs and ask to use the phone after that dramatic confrontation.

*Where can I go? What shall I do? I suppose that I'd better get in touch with James once Mum has had a chance to calm down.*

**Her stomach would not stop churning.**

# Lilli 2

**Moving in with James was weird.**

It hadn't struck Lilli that, having decided to have the baby and move in with James, she would actually be going to live in his house with him and sleep in his bed. She had never shared a bedroom, let alone a bed, with anyone before.

It was ridiculous because she didn't know James at all well; actually she didn't know him at all! She felt so shy with him. But what else could she do? Did she have any other choice? He sweetly scooped her up and even asked her to marry him, but she knew he was putting a brave face on it.

Having been unceremoniously thrown out by her mother, she was going to have to go into school every day from James's house. In her uniform. While it still fitted her. Thank God they had months of study leave before A Levels when she could hide from everyone, and thank God their summer uniform was a loose, belted dress. It was bizarre. She hadn't dared tell anyone at school about this latest development, only Nikki. They might expel her.

*Can I be expelled for living with a man who is going to be my husband?*

It was a nice house, a big stone farmhouse with a friendly face settled into a neat garden with an attractive, fancy, iron fence. It was surrounded by old wooden byres with low ceilings and cosy barns sheltering a multitude of beautiful, relaxed, brick red cattle. A purebred herd of

Sussex, as James explained; he was obviously exceedingly proud of them. It was peaceful.

As they went into the house for the very first time, through the back door, no-one ever used the front door, James's mum scuttled past them. "Damn, I was hoping to be out of your way when you arrived. Have a good look around your new home, settle in. I'll see you later, ducks. I'm Barbara by the way, James's mum." She scooted out of the door in a flurry of patterned apron, bouncing curls and a broad, friendly smile.

Grabbing her hand firmly in his, James took her for a tour of the house, every room, one by one. There seemed to be an awful lot of them: larders, cloakrooms, boot rooms, store rooms. It all looked completely different to home. Thick textured wallpaper in the dining room that she was itching to touch, three ducks flying up the wall. The lounge was cosy, with ornate plump armchairs that exactly matched the sofa. Each sported white, lace-edged aprons along their backs. Home was simpler, less frilly, more constrained.

*But this is home now. This is my home…*

The kitchen was enormous, almost a complete house in itself, with an archetypal farmhouse scrubbed pine table. A scruffy sofa seemed to be upholstered in a blousy flowery fabric and, grubby with dog hairs, it came complete with a huge, black Labrador.

"And this is Wellington. Say hello, Wellington." Wellington politely wagged his tail in greeting.

She spotted an Aga. She knew what it was but had never used an Aga. In fact, she hadn't cooked anything at all using any sort of oven.

*Am I going to have to do all the cooking? Oh God, what am I going to cook? Will I have to do the shopping? What else am I meant to do?*

She hadn't had a dog either. She wasn't quite sure what you were meant to do with dogs. He looked very friendly, grinning at her.

*Would she be looking after him – taking him for walks?*

Upstairs, she was shown three bedrooms, all decorated with fancy, flowery wallpaper. Then two bathrooms, an amazing walk-in linen cupboard that was as warm as a sauna.

*All that linen. I suppose I'll have to look after it all. Ironing?*

She had ironed the odd shirt but never tackled anything like a sheet.

"This is, or rather was, Mum and Dad's room." It looked very empty and abandoned. James sighed, looked sorrowful and explained. "Dad passed away six months ago from sepsis. It was stupid, unnecessary. He ignored a cut that he made with his own pen knife. It slipped when he was cutting some baler twine." He took a deep breath. "Mum was devastated. She has become obsessed ever since with any small cut that I get and drowns me in TCP. I was shattered; it was so sudden, and he wasn't old enough to be dying. He was only fifty." James shuddered. "It hit me hard, but life goes on. The cows still needed to be milked even on the day that he died."

It seemed a bit rude to break into the sadness, but Lilli was wondering where Barbara was sleeping if she wasn't in here. James read her mind.

"Mum insisted on moving out of the farmhouse the moment she'd heard you were moving in. Next generation and all that. We had a barn that we converted to a flat for students and she moved in there. She seems quite chirpy about it: 'A granny annexe because I am going to be a granny!' I think it feels like a new start for her. Don't worry – she loves it."

*Was this going to be their room? Apparently not. I'm quite relieved, in a funny sort of way. Too melancholy.*

At last they came to James's room. "Da-da – last but by no means least – here is our room! I sleep on the left, unless you have any objection." Lilli blushed and couldn't think of a thing to say.

*Oh my God. I am going to be sleeping here tonight – with James. Do I wear pyjamas? Does he wear pyjamas? Am I expected to make love tonight – every night? I am going to be sleeping here forever!*

"Well now, that is the grand tour. Let's go and have a cup of tea. Mum has baked her legendary coffee and walnut cake in your honour." He patted her bum, grabbed her hand and led her downstairs.

**Phew, I can at least do that. I know how to eat cake.**

# Lilli 3

**Lilli and James's wedding in Lamberhurst church was small but beautifully formed.**

Her mother still wasn't speaking to her. Not a word. Her father was acting as a go-between. Her sister seemed to be on the fence.

Lilli had second guessed her parents' wishes and agreed to get married at church in the hope that her mother might relent a bit. Lilli insisted on wearing white; she was only going to get married once and she had dreamt of this day since she was a small girl. Her attempt at getting a blousy dress to hide her bump had the opposite effect – the silky polyester billowing over her bump made it seem even bigger than it was, but she was not going to hide it for anyone.

Her father offered to pay for the absolute basics – but that was it. Dear, kind James stepped in and wrote cheques for everything, it seemed, but she didn't feel it was right. Her father seemed unwilling to cough up for bridesmaids' frippery for Lilli's choice of Nikki from school as her bridesmaid, probably her mum was behind that. She decided not to have any at all, which then put her sister's nose out of joint, apparently.

*Good – she isn't being very supportive. Why did everything have to be so bloody fraught with difficulty? I am trying to put things right by marrying James. Please meet me halfway.*

Mum reported via Dad that it had been "too far to come and at such late notice" for various uncles, cousins, aunts, old family friends, even her godparents. She even said that Granny was apparently a little under the weather at the moment and wouldn't be able to make it. Lilli thought that, in all honesty, Granny would be livid to be missing it.

*Mum, why do you have to keep punishing me?*

Dad picked her up from James's house. They arrived at the church, Dad driving the family Austin Metro, Lilli in the front clutching her bouquet of lilies. They filled the car with scents to compete with Dad's cigarette. They parked with all the guests, spotting James's Land Rover, spotlessly clean and bedecked with white ribbons, ready for their onward journey. They awkwardly wandered up the path, not knowing what to say.

The vicar greeted them at the door with enough gusto and much jollity to change the funereal tone. As the door opened to let them in, Lilli heard the burbling organ playing some wandering unknown tune, alongside the burr of voices, and glimpsed a riot of colour; she felt warm happiness emanating like fresh bread.

"Righty ho then – are you ready?" boomed the vicar.

"Ready, Lilli? Lamb to the slaughter!" added Dad.

Lilli grimaced but held her tongue.

Her dad awkwardly held out his arm and Lilli slipped her hand behind his stiff elbow and they stepped up to the door. At a deft signal from the vicar, "Here comes the bride all fat and wide" bellowed out enthusiastically, another concession to convention. She and James had wanted something up to date and came up with all sorts of hilariously inappropriate hits from the charts: 'With or Without You', 'It's Not Unusual' and 'Nothing's Gonna Stop Us Now'. It had been fun. He was so funny. He made everything seem so much better.

The warmly delighted faces of her stalwart friends from school were there to wish her well as she emerged from the quiet of the porch. Nikki beamed at her affectionately from a great height, her mad hair tamed into a very sleek style. All the others grinned and waved and mouthed "Wow!" and "You look fabulous!" As she stepped into the start of a new life, in fact new lives, and started down the aisle, she smiled for the first time.

The right-hand side of the church was heaving. James's family were out in force, all in their wedding finery, shiny suits and hats. They seemed to be as delighted with the occasion as her own family were not. James's mum, Barbara, was peering excitedly out of her pew, a feathery chicken creation perched on her curly-haired head and her kindly, round face looking thrilled with the whole thing. It was sad that his dad had died last year and was missing the marriage of his only son, but Barbara was a stoical widow and seemed delighted with the whole occasion. She was just one of those wonderfully positive people. She saw the good in everything, and anyone.

Lilli's father walked her down the aisle with a fixed rictus grin, her hand tucked into his resistant arm. Despite all the despondency emanating from her family, her heart ballooned in her chest; she could feel her own pulse thudding. She cleared her throat, swallowed heavily and sniffed all at the same time to keep a surge of emotion in check.

Despite her father's reservations, now kept firmly behind a closed face, she knew that this was absolutely the right thing to do and patted her bump gently with the fist clutching her bouquet of lilies. A flurry of pollen stained her pristine, white dress.

James stood solidly, glowing from the summer sunshine streaming through a magnificent blue church window, looking as if he had just shared a joke with his best man, Daniel.

When James turned and looked at her, she gulped. She'd never seen him dressed up before and he looked so incredibly handsome in a black tailcoat. His blue eyes crinkled at her, full of encouragement. His unruly dark curls tamed for the occasion, he was freshly shaved and looked squeaky clean. She found herself grinning. Her cheek muscles stretched painfully with the vigour of her smile.

*I am actually very happy. This is going to turn out okay.*

She was amazed to see her mother standing bolt upright in the front left pew. Unfortunately, she was looking like a mournful Eeyore, stolidly repressing her tears, sadly not of joy, comforted by her sister. Both were wearing ludicrously posh hats and looked like something out of *Country Life* that had strayed into the *Farmers Weekly*. At least they had come.

*Thank you, God. I am so grateful. Perhaps we can redeem our rift.*

The vicar barely smothered his smirk at the "Marriage is ordained for the procreation of children" bit. Her father seemed very happy to relinquish her to James when the vicar asked him, "Who giveth this woman?"

Lilli stuttered and nervously giggled her way through her vows. She was conscious of her mother's eyes drilling into the back of her head. She didn't know what she was saying, but she was very impressed by James's solid, deep-voiced responses that resonated with belief in what he was saying. "In sickness and in health, for richer, for poorer…" He didn't take his eyes off her as he expounded his solemn promises. "Until death do us part."

"I now pronounce you man and wife." Mrs James Arbuthnott. Elizabeth Arbuthnott.

*Wow – how grown up.*

**Her mum and sister declined to join them at the Chequers for the reception.**

# Lilli 4

**Lilli went into labour on the same day that the A Level results came out.**

Lilli became aware of something happening as she half-dozed, wondering what had woken her up. She lay in bed, carefully listening to her body. What was that? She lay wondering when the next twinge would come. Had it started? Was she going to have a baby today? It came again. And again.

She lay, stiffly, tuned in, as if listening out for a burglar. The twinges that pinched and squeezed were actually very bearable and she was wondering why everyone made quite such a fuss about this whole business.

After about an hour of indulgently listening to this new phenomenon, she decided to get up. She cocked her head on one side as she cleaned her teeth, tuning in to the next spasm, stroking her belly and feeling it ripple and squirm. That seemed to be it for a bit. She got dressed on full alert to any further upheaval.

Gingerly stepping down the stairs, her antennae twitching for further activity, she suddenly remembered that today was A Level results day. It was a bit odd because she seemed so far removed from schooldays. Ridiculous, childish school days dressed in tartan ties and rolled up skirts, uniformly dressed and uniformly conforming to a set of rules. None of it mattered anymore.

Her results didn't make any difference to anything… but she was still a bit excited. She scooped up the important-looking envelope from the mat, bore it into the kitchen as if it were on fire, stuck the kettle on the Aga and sat down in James's carver chair at the head of the scrubbed pine table.

*Ooh, another contraction, I think.*

She sat carefully observing it, her hand pressing her tummy. It passed.

She opened the envelope, suddenly in a hurry, pulled out the contents and found the important bit. She was sort of pleased at an adequate BBC. Being pregnant when you are sitting your exams is a distraction, but she'd hoped to do a bit better – at least one A would have been nice.

*I mugged up so hard on Diffraction Gratings and Newton's Rings. I thought I might have got an A for Physics. Damn.*

She wondered how all her friends had done. She bet Tina and Nikki had done better than her, particularly in Maths. Her grades wouldn't get her into her first-choice university but would have earned her a place at East Anglia, but did it matter? It was irrelevant now.

Thoughtfully, she levered herself up and made a cup of hot Ribena; she hadn't been able to face coffee and tea for ages. As she lifted the kettle and closed the lid of the hotplate, another contraction started. This one seemed more urgent. More uncomfortable.

Should she wait for James to come in from milking? Should she go and find him? She rummaged around on the dresser and found the notes diligently taken at antenatal classes. She suddenly realised that, despite everything that they had said in the sessions, no matter how many books she had avidly studied, in reality she just didn't have a clue. She certainly wouldn't get an A grade in child birth.

**She decided to go and find Barbara – she was only across the yard.**

# Lilli 5

**Why the hell has no-one told me how much giving birth hurts?**

She had thought that the expulsion of a giant, oversized object from her vagina was going to be the worst of it, but it was the contractions that led up to it. Jesus. They went on and on, hour after hour. Agonising. Gripping. Searing.

It didn't help that the midwife kept simpering at her, patronisingly telling her that she was "doing very well", "this was all absolutely normal", that she was such a "healthy young mum that she didn't need pain relief". This was absolutely normal! They had to be joking. It was bloody agony. She needed anything that was going for the torture. Were they deliberately trying to punish her? They were very uncooperative despite her pleading, and by the time she was finally allowed to suck on gas and air, ravenously, it was quite frankly pretty useless.

Thank God for James, who let her crush his strong, leathery hands when the clutching contractions built up and up relentlessly, worse and worse. He laughed and complained, "Steady on, old Moo!" (his pet name for her), and his genial face crinkled into a cheerful grin. He didn't help quite so much when he started telling the midwife about a difficult calving, at which point Lilli wanted to punch him in his mouth.

The final push and slithering rush of baby Arbuthnott, as his body finally slid from her fanny, was as releasing as an orgasm. The rapture of hearing this new little person immediately letting out a healthy bellow, as good as any calf's, was ecstasy. They bustled off with him, leaving her feeling redundant; all attention abruptly shifted away from her, her arms and her womb flaccid and empty, on tenterhooks as she strained to see him. They gave her a jab, she wasn't sure why.

After forever they gave him to her to hold, all bundled up in a towel, and she thought that she would burst with pride. She stared at this new little face, a stranger; he didn't look anything like she had imagined he would, the reality of her beautiful, perfect son. He looked so like a mini-James! His tiny immaculate fingers were minute and pale against James's leathery, stained farmer's hands. The heat in the delivery room was exacerbating James's familiar background smell of cow poo. Their son would always recognise his father.

"Well, my boy, welcome into the world." He hesitated for a moment. "Moo, can we call him William, after Dad?"

"Of course, James, of course…"

She felt the weight of William in her arms, the little pressures as he snuggled and moved his head in instinctive search of nourishment, the movements outside her instead of in. She grinned at James, her husband, this new person's dad.

**How could anyone have ever, ever wanted to murder this little man?**

# Lilli 6

**Lilli very soon discovered that when you are pregnant they tell you all about the mechanics of birth but they don't tell you what to do with this new dependent little human being afterwards.**

Suckling came easily to Lilli, obviously the experience of being a farmer's wife had its benefits, and she enjoyed those peaceful moments when she was bodily reunited with her son. She was proud to make it look easy when everyone else from the antenatal group was going on about the difficulties of latching on.

William was so solemn and she loved the way he stared at her. He would abruptly break off from his wet and messy nuzzling, accompanied by a strange high-pitched crooning sound, then his head would loll back and he would watch her intently, the milk oozing from his pursed, cooing little lips. He would suddenly dive back in for more and re-engage with gusto.

*They don't tell you about the sore nipples either. Ouch.*

It was the times when he continuously whinged and moaned that were harder to take. He cried, actually more like screaming, a lot. She changed his nappy, offered him more boob, offered him water in a carefully sterilised bottle, jiggled him up and down gently, jiggled him up and down more vigorously, put him in his bouncy chair and bounced him up and down, sometimes rather too rapidly when she was getting really wound up.

She put him in his pram and wheeled him off down the lane, striding along to release the horrible tension that seemed to grip her continuously. If it was too wet to go out, she would put him in his pram and pull him back and forth, back and forth, teeth gritted, until her arm was about to drop off. He would go quiet. She would stop, relieved. He would instantly start squawking again. It made her head feel as if it was in a vice, some sort of Elizabethan torture.

He never slept for more than five minutes. She put him in his bed, plugged a dummy in his mouth and tucked him in. She patted him a lot. Plugged the dummy back in when it dropped out. He would scream some more and wave his arms about, puce in the face and clearly very angry. As the tension escalated and the pats became more vigorous, she would leave the room, the tears streaming down her face – he was safer that way.

She could get him off to sleep if she put him in the car and drove around. Just being in the car with the engine on wasn't enough. She drove miles and miles through the narrow, deserted back lanes, aimlessly, endlessly, desperately trying not to fall asleep as she too was soothed by the gentle vibration and hum, with no screaming for a blissful change.

James was fantastic, when he was in the house. Farming was a full-on occupation. He encouraged her, told her she was doing a great job as a mum. "Cheer up, silly Moo. You are doing so well!"

Thank God he came in for lunch every day, always followed by his faithful shadow, Wellington, the black Lab. It broke the monotony of waiting hand and foot, and boob, on their son. When she sobbed into his chest in frustration and inadequacy, he patted her and stroked her, a bit like how he comforted the dog.

In the evening, after milking, clean and fresh from a bath, although he could never quite lose the smell of the cows, James jiggled and danced around the kitchen with William in his arms, seemingly able to ignore his high-pitched, colicky cries that stabbed her brain and made it whirl. He would sing totally inappropriate songs learned from the rugby club, horribly off key, but in time with William's roars, which at least made Lilli smile even if William just carried on.

Barbara came bearing earthy casseroles, cottage pies and delicious cakes. "I am so used to cooking for crowds I couldn't resist doing one for you." Bless her, except that the cakes were not helping with her burgeoning waistline.

Lilli only wished Barbara wouldn't turn up unannounced. She felt so inadequate, still in her dressing gown at half past eleven, the kitchen littered with yesterday's debris, dried washing spilling out on to the floor all getting mixed up with the pile of dirty stuff waiting to go in.

Barbara was sweet and would get stuck into clearing up as if she still lived there. It made Lilli feel a bit guilty, but it was done with such kindness and lack of fuss that it was bearable. She actually looked as if she was enjoying the ironing. She said that she did.

Her family visited just the once, all formally arranged. It involved tidying up, better known as shovelling stuff into any cupboards that would take any more, laying on a meal which was exhausting and made Lilli prickle with tension.

Lilli wasn't experienced in the cooking department, her mother had never taught her, but she knew how to rise to expectations, finding napkins and the best cutlery and laying up in the, until now unused, dining room. It meant leaving William squawking to himself in whichever place of safety she had chosen to plonk him to free up her hands – and her mind.

Dear Barbara anticipated the stress of the occasion and, much to Lilli's relief, her mother-in-law managed to pass off one of her own delicious homely casseroles as Lilli's, although she knew that her own attempt at mashed potatoes were more than a bit lumpy, which was a bit of a giveaway. Her disastrous attempt at a lemon meringue pie was swiftly replaced by Barbara's chocolate roulade. Were her mum and dad fooled? She wouldn't know and quite honestly was too knackered and tense to care.

Dad was fine but Mum was cagey with Lilli and with William. With James too in truth. It was as if she thought William knew her previous murderous intentions. Lilli most certainly did but kept trying to push it to the back of her mind. It wasn't working.

James chattered away, giving Dad a rundown on the latest calves, the outrageous price of milk and the meanness of the supermarkets. He was utterly and completely his normal self, fondling her bum, an annoying habit, and giving her smacking kisses, accompanied by his catalogue of loving remarks. These included such remarks as "Let me at you, my gorgeous Moo" and "Just look at the size of your udders". It was all very embarrassing and incongruous in front of Mum.

Mum cuddled William, ignoring his screaming protests, and changed his nappy and sang to him. She had a good voice, but there was something held back. Lilli caught her looking at her uneasily, as if hoping that Lilli was noticing what a good grandmotherly performance she was giving.

*Will we ever get over this? Can we?*

Obviously not, she never came again, not even to say goodbye when they moved to "A very pleasant retirement flat with marvellous views", according to her dad.

**Lilli cried herself to sleep that night.**

# Lilli 7

**Lilli was so excited when some of her old friends from school dropped by at Christmas.**

They were down from their various universities. They bounced in, energy fizzing around them, looking fresh and clean, shiny and vibrantly young, and well kempt and carefree. Lilli's excitement fizzled out as she realised that she was totally the opposite: knackered, grubby, scruffy, put upon, old.

They chattered eagerly about Freshers' Week, parties and amazing drunken exploits, new friends, dates with unknown boys from unfamiliar places and exciting new intellectual challenges. Visits to each other's university had already been made so they had met each other's friends. "You must come and see us – you will love it!"

It seemed that they all "just didn't do a stroke of work". Oh yeah, Lilli bet they worked very hard, they always had. They all had. They were clever girls destined to get their degrees – unlike herself.

Lilli found herself smiling, nodding mechanically, somewhat glazed by the lack of sleep. Their chatter seemed muffled, distant. All sensible or interesting thoughts and responses on her part were stultified by being a too young mum in her unimportant, withered, small world. Who could get excited by milk yields, consistency of poo and mastitis – for both herself and the dairy herd – her only areas of expertise these days?

When they arrived, William was actually asleep, a rarity in itself. They insisted on handing him around, despite her pathetic protests, cuddling him clumsily, his unsupported head falling back, which then woke him up and made him cry. At this point they handed him back to her.

The front of her shirt was soaked from breast milk, it always happened when William cried, it just seemed to gush out. She tried to look happy as she frantically tried to jiggle him back to sleep as they escaped the hideous noise with promises to come again.

She put a brave face on it, but sometimes she could actually see that what her mother had said held more than a glimmer of truth.

*Have I made the right choice? What have I become?*

# Lilli 8

**James made sure that her twenty-first was a suitably fabulous occasion.**

He booked dinner at a seriously upmarket restaurant in Tunbridge Wells and then planned to stay overnight at a little hotel on the Pantiles. It was to be just the two of them, which was a treat, and also avoided any awkwardness about her absentee family. They had never visited again. Her family seemed to have wiped her out of the family history. Ostracised.

More than anything at all, she was thrilled that she would be able to get a good night's sleep, uninterrupted, and a long lie-in in the morning – that still never happened with William, even though he was a busy toddler. They might even make love in peace and quiet without interruption. She found it embarrassing that she enjoyed it with James so much. Was she meant to or was she really a slut?

Doting Barbara was a very willing babysitter for the night. She had been named Nanny Bap by her adoring grandson. She had bustled in and taken over a jam-smeared William, Nanny Bap's homemade jam of course. He didn't protest when it was Nanny Bap who briskly and efficiently wiped his face and hands. He shouted and squirmed and yelled "No" when Lilli did it.

William's whole approach to life was to destroy things and make a lot of noise, but more than anything, he wanted to be with his daddy on the farm or with Nanny Bap. *Not with me.* He threw himself joyously at Nanny Bap when she arrived in the kitchen, hugged her hard and dragged her off to play.

She tried so hard to engage him herself. If she tried cooking or craft things with him, he would chuck the ingredients or the paint or whatever all over the place, often deliberately at her. If she popped him on her lap to read, he would pull her hair and fidget and wriggle off.

Getting him dressed every morning was a nightmare. Getting him undressed for his bath every evening was a nightmare. Getting him to eat anything was only achieved by saying that Nanny Bap made it or that Daddy had grown it in the garden.

It was exhausting. It was so hurtful. After all that she had gone through and given up to save him and actually let him live. She knew it wasn't his fault, but it would be easier if he showed that he liked her, even just a little bit.

Lilli was soaking in the bath, all by herself for a change, no William leaping in and splashing her in the face and pouring water over her head. She was surrounded by copious bubbles and an equally bubbly glass of sparkling wine that dear Nanny Bap produced like a magician from a Safeway carrier bag. Very decadent. It went straight to her head and made her feel like a grown-up.

Lilli was worried about what on earth she was going to wear. She spent a horrendous half hour feebly going through her wardrobe, trying to find something that would fit. She had never managed to get rid of her baby weight. It is hard not to eat when your husband is shovelling in giant platefuls at every mealtime. On top of that, she hoovered up William's leftover sandwiches. "Mustn't let things go to waste!" she could hear her mother saying.

*Oh, Mum.*

She nibbled on sweet things, and the fruits of Nanny Bap's baking, to keep herself awake and to give her energy, she convinced herself. It had taken its toll. It had gone to her waist.

The only thing she could fit into that was suitably posh was a dress she bought from Topshop for Nikki's twenty-first a month ago. She loved the dress when she bought it and Nanny Bap had been super flattering when she tried it on, but when she arrived at Nikki's party, she felt like Nellie the Elephant compared to all her classmates. They were all willowy and thin and fashionably dressed, with the latest shoulder pads and Princess Diana hair.

Thank God for James, who held her tight, his hand possessively on her bum, and sang along into her ear, off key as usual but well meant, to Michael Bolton's new release 'How Am I Supposed to Live Without You?', except that he sang "Live Without Moo". At least she had been able to hold her head up with the best looking, most grown-up bloke in the room. James, with his broad shoulders, weathered, rugged face and short, neatly cut curls, showed up the other boys as skinny youths with their ridiculous floppy curtains of hair. James was a good, kind husband. She was a lucky girl.

**Heaving herself from the bath, she towelled herself dry and scooted along to their bedroom, where her dress hung glowering on the wardrobe waiting.**

# Lilli 9

**Giving birth to Francesca was a far better experience than when she had had William.**

She was dreading it but, funnily enough, it just seemed all so much less dramatic. The midwives gave her gas and air when she asked for it politely and were happy to dispense pethidine when she got going. It all seemed so much calmer. She didn't swear at all, she didn't yell, not much anyway, not even at James when he repeated all his best calving horror stories to a new audience.

When she felt the urge to push, it seemed as if she had done this as many times as the farm's cows and she behaved serenely, panting and holding back when quietly requested and pushing sturdily when instructed to do so.

Francesca slopped out without a cry, which worried her for a horrible jittery moment. When Francesca was placed in her arms, her new daughter stared at her, directly into her eyes. Lilli was enchanted. James was instantly besotted as he took her tiny fingers in his big rough hand.

Lilli was so happy as James enfolded them both in a huge bear hug and kissed her on her sweaty head. "You clever, clever Moo. We will make a prize-winning cow of you yet!"

**Not many people get a baby as their twenty-first birthday present.**

# Lilli 10

**Lilli heard on the grapevine that Nikki was getting married so was very excited to receive what was clearly an invitation.**

Lilli heard that she was marrying Graham, a very clever fellow mathematician that she had met at Edinburgh University. He wasn't particularly much to look at, apparently, was at least an inch shorter than Nikki, even before the added height of her mad hair, but was supremely intelligent and had been offered a host of jobs on the milk round, before choosing Reuters.

He was already doing extremely well, winning several promotions, and they were buying their first home in London with an enormous mortgage that they could easily afford. Nikki was working as an accountant, which suited her meticulous and quiet nature. It sounded as if they were very happy – and Nikki wasn't up the duff, as far as she knew, so they must have had the whole proposal and saying yes thing.

Lilli was delighted for her friend and laughingly harked back to their childish conversation at school about being "extremely careful who you married". Nikki had chosen very well indeed. A long way from her loathed council house.

Lolling at the battered pine kitchen table, she ripped open the fancy envelope chaotically.

She pulled out the card. Her face dropped. She and James had only been invited for the evening do. She knew that she and Nikki had drifted apart a bit as their lives had taken such different directions and that Nikki, of course, had naturally gathered a whole new set of friends along the way.

She knew she should be grateful to have been asked at all, but it still hurt.

Lilli was twenty-five. Exactly halfway to that milestone of fifty that they speculated on all those years ago at school. "Be careful who you marry" echoed in her head. James was a real sweetie. He would never set the world on fire and his conversation did revolve around his incredible herd of Sussex cows, rugby, cricket, more about cows, but not much else. He was kind and loyal, had a quirky sense of the ridiculous, teased her endlessly and had never once made a thing about having to get married. He was also very sexy, and she thoroughly enjoyed their love making, but she wasn't sure that you were meant to think that about your own husband.

She was very content, and it showed in her ever-burgeoning belly. She loved her kids and it was okay being a mum but, to be honest, it was very much more boring than she had anticipated.

Sporadic news from her old friends from school made her feel inadequate, uneducated, parochial and dull. She heard via Nikki, passing news on from a Christmas letter, that Tina had moved to California with her new husband, Pete, to work together in Silicon Valley.

*They were clearly both as clever as each other. A good match.*

Nikki, having moved to London after graduating, could be just as many miles away as the States.

She heard that Liz had already married Jim, a very fine specimen of a man with his chiselled jaw and good prospects. He was in the Army. Lilli had lost touch with Liz but was still slightly hurt that she hadn't been invited to their wedding. She knew that Nikki and other old school mates had been bridesmaids. She supposed that you couldn't keep in touch with everyone, particularly as so many school friends had gone to university at all corners of the country and subsequently moved away from here.

*It is so easy to lose touch. Even with your own mum and dad.*

Lilli shook her head sadly. There was little point sending out a round robin Christmas letter herself, she had nothing to boast about. No holidays abroad, no parties, except for cosy farmer get togethers. Just the usual round of going to the pub, meeting up with close mates, like Daniel and his wife, Sarah, chatting to local people about farming and their wives, gossiping about children and schools.

Was it rude to even think that the friends that she now had, even the ones she had met at the school gates, were just a bit – *well, how can I put this?* – not very interesting? Perhaps she was just as boring herself. But honestly? She yearned for intellectual stimulation.

She had thrown all her energy and intellect into being a mum. She had studied every manual on the subject as if studying for a degree and made it her mission to be the best mum she could be. She tried to be up with the very latest trends in child rearing, pontificating widely on how she treated both her children, as if they were neither boys nor girls but letting them be whatever they wanted to be.

Little Willy was "always a handful", which was a kind way of describing their constant battles. Outrageously precocious, doted on by Nanny Bap and, despite her trying over and over again, William just would not conform to any of the rules and pronouncements in any of her library of books. He was a total hooligan with his back chat, over enthusiastic hugs and kisses that were designed to bowl her over, his total disobedience and always doing the opposite of whatever she asked.

Nanny Bap spent her whole time dousing Willy in TCP, in her overwhelming fear of sepsis, as he seemed to be constantly grazed or cut. When he wasn't, he was just covered in bruises.

He was definitely happiest on the farm in dirty jeans and wellies, smelling of cow poo like his dad, and magnetically attracted to any piece of dangerous farming machinery he could get his grubby, chubby hands on. She wasn't sure that she liked him very much, but she did love him.

She had breathed a sigh of relief when she was able to pack him off to playgroup and then nursery school and then primary school. He toddled off joyfully to discover blood brothers to fight with, shooting everyone in sight (kapow-kapow), scribble frantically in his books (and other children's), and be reprimanded again and again. It made Little Willy chortle with glee, and James cackle "a chip off the old block". It made Lilli despair and feel not awfully sure where she fitted in. Not only was he the spitting image of his dad, he seemed to have his laid back, happy-go-lucky nature too. Despite all her best efforts, he was stereotypically a boy – a daddy's boy.

Francesca on the other hand was a constant joy. She was a delightful little girl, everything you could possibly want a daughter to be. Pretty, lively, clever and she played her imaginary games with her dolls and her farm animals quietly and with great sense of purpose. She loved to learn nursery rhymes, clapping and smiling, reading books, meticulously studying every picture, and her motor skills were incredible, inscribing real letters, remarkable for such a tiny little thing. She skipped about, delicately avoiding anything dirty, and insisted on wearing pretty pink dresses.

*Bang goes my feminist theories.*

Just as William was a mini-James to look at, Francesca was a mini-Lilli – except that Francesca was skinny as a stick insect next to the mushrooming mass that Lilli seemed to have become. A classic, picture-book family.

Francesca was starting reception in September and Lilli would miss her. What would she do all day?

She sighed, feeling sorry for herself.

**She would just have to put a brave face on it and make sure she looked good and held her head high at Nikki's evening wedding reception.**

# Lilli 11

**Lilli tried to lose some weight in time for the wedding, but it was just so difficult.**

With the kids at school all day and nothing to occupy herself, she would find herself absent-mindedly working her way through a packet of the children's biscuits while thumbing through a magazine.

She thought that she would wear the same outfit she had worn to the Young Farmers' New Year's Eve party, but somehow she had managed to put on even more weight. She tried it on and paraded in front of Barbara who had said, as gently as she could, "I'm not sure, dear. It looks quite uncomfortable." It did feel uncomfortable. She couldn't breathe and there was no way she would be able to sit down in it. She burst into tears.

Lovely Barbara scooped her up and they nipped into Tunbridge Wells and found something more suitable, and a size or two larger, in Peter Robinson's. Barbara also treated her to a trim at the hairdressers, much needed as her hair had grown so much, and she was sure it was going grey – she could swear that the hairdresser surreptitiously plucked out a white hair.

*For God's sake, I am only twenty-five years old!*

As they walked into the Elizabethan barn for the evening reception, they handed in their coats, hearing the cacophony of a good party in the near distance. James fondled her bum, took her by the hand, she was a bit sweaty from nerves, and gave her a massive squeeze of encouragement. "Come on, gorgeous. These are your friends! Chin up, boobs out… and very nice boobs they are too." He stared at her cleavage, which did rather seem to be on show.

*What a kind, understanding husband.*

She gave him a wobbly smile. Damp hand in strong, leathery hand, Lilli tentatively advanced into a chaotic scene of messy tables, riotous flowers, jacketless men and tottering women with their hair gone madly awry and their make-up wandering down their faces. She couldn't see anyone that she recognised.

Nikki swooped down on her, dragging along her new husband, enfolded her in a great big hug and started introducing Graham to them when they were promptly whisked away by the master of ceremonies to do something important and bridal. Lilli didn't see her again to speak to but watched her cutting the cake, dancing joyfully, so happy. When she came to throw her bouquet, she watched from a distance.

*I am a married woman of seven years… and do you know? There isn't an itch in sight. I am happy with my James. I hope that Nikki will be as lucky.*

Tina and Liz were busy being bridesmaids, dressed in identical slinky, blue satin dresses, and clearly already very pissed, having started drinking early in the afternoon. They didn't acknowledge her. She didn't try and talk to them; she felt too embarrassed.

*Do they actually recognise me? Am I so fat and hideous and different? Have they even realised that I am here?*

Lilli was mortified. After standing around awkwardly and knocking back a couple of glasses of bubbly, she felt better and decided that they might as well try and enjoy themselves. They should hit the dance floor, as the band were brilliant. They started up 'Girls Just Want to Have Fun'.

*Yes, I do!*

"Come on, James…" He hated dancing but he did anyway to please her. She loved the way he danced, just slightly out of time with the music.

Barbara was staying overnight with William and Francesca so that she and James "could let their hair down", so Lilli proceeded to get supremely and uproariously pissed. She couldn't remember the taxi ride home or getting into bed, but vaguely remembered some boisterous, giggly sex.

Thank God that Barbara was there to hold the fort in the morning. She greeted Lilli far too cheerfully as she eventually staggered into the kitchen, feeling appalling; her eyeballs appeared to have swollen to three times their normal size and her mouth was like the floor of the milking parlour.

William and Francesca had clearly breakfasted hours ago and were happily playing under Nanny Bap's benevolent eye. Lilli gingerly bent over to give them a motherly morning hug, but William recoiled from her protesting, "Yuck, dog poo breath."

She shuffled to the table, sat down heavily. Awaiting her was the best hangover cure of them all: aromatic bacon butties and a huge mug of strong coffee. "Barbara, you are the top of the pops!"

Opening her mouth as wide as she could, she chomped into the oozing toast, with a trickle of bacon fat dribbling down her arm. Wellington the dog was stationed hopefully at her feet, licking his lips flaccidly. Her tummy felt nauseous and kept doing that flipping thing, not just from the booze but as a hangover from the feeling of having been so disregarded by her peers.

Lilli felt low for a few days, was a bit snappy with the children and chuntered away to a sympathetic Barbara about how inadequate she felt, how bored, and boring, she had become. James continued to go about his usual daily routine, seemingly not listening. She was even boring him.

By Wednesday, it seemed that James had had enough. In his socks, cradling a cup of tea, bum warming on the Aga, he suddenly interrupted Barbara's supportive murmuring.

"Hey, moaning Moo, what do you want to do about it? Just get off your considerably lovely arse and do whatever needs to be done to change things! We can make anything happen to put a smile back on your chubby chops."

He planted a kiss on the top of her head, squeezed her shoulders, patted her bum *(I wish he wouldn't do that!)*, and swished out to do the afternoon milking. He was followed by the dog clattering unsteadily over the limestone tiles (he was becoming very creaky in old age), and left Lilli, with her mouth hanging open, looking at an equally astonished Barbara.

*As simple as that? He is right I can do anything I want – but what?*

She contemplated dreamily for the rest of the day, ruminated as she shovelled biscuits into her face, pondered some more as she laconically pretended to turn the pages of her book in bed, and she was admonished as she cuddled with James, "Hello, Major James to ground control…"

By the time the kids were safely delivered to school, she had sort of made up her mind. Lilli had always wanted to go into computing like many of her peers. It was the trendy thing to do, with great prospects for making a good living. She had deliberately done the right A Levels and had had the offer of a place to read Maths and Computing at East Anglia. Perhaps she could still do a degree but through the Open University.

She dug out her Chemistry, Physics and Maths text books. A quick flick through left her amazed at the convoluted gobbledygook that now stared her in the face. Could she put one brain cell in front of another anymore?

*Can I?*

If she kept it to herself and James, and Nanny Bap, she wouldn't look foolish – and her mum would never know so she couldn't say 'told you so' with her disdainful glare. She felt sad when Mum popped into her head. She missed the mum she remembered before the big fall out and the cold war.

She went to the library, determined to find out all about it and, within days, sent off for the forms. She was actually very excited. As he handed over a cheque to go in with her application, James gave her a great big wet kiss, worthy of Wellington, and slapped her bum.

**"That's my girl. Go get it, Moo."**

# Lilli 12

**"Happy birthday to you, happy birthday to you, happy birthday dear Mummy, happy birthday to you."**

William sang lustily, waving a dripping cereal spoon in his hand, as out of tune as his father always was. His other arm was in a plaster cast after falling off a cow and breaking his wrist. It had been hard to explain to the people in casualty at the time.

Francesca coyly joining in was absolutely in tune.

*She takes after my mum.*

That thought made her feel a bit sad, so Lilli boomed out, overcompensating. "Thirty. Bloody hell, I am getting old!"

Lilli sat at the head of the head of the kitchen table, an honour bestowed on anyone with a birthday in the Arbuthnott household, surrounded by a mound of cards, torn envelopes and crumpled wrapping paper. James, looking completely out of place, usurped from the head of the family's seat, retorted, "Time flies when you are enjoying yourself, Moo!"

Barbara shovelled everything out of the way, efficiently sorting the rubbish from the important bits, and placed a plate piled high with every breakfast thing imaginable in front of Lilli. "Happy birthday, ducks! Tuck in."

Barbara seemed to have taken up the position of honorary housekeeper – and chief feeder. For the past five years, Lilli had fallen into a good routine. Breakfast, served by Barbara, take the kids to school in Lamberhurst, return to a mug of coffee handed to her by Barbara and then, with no other choice, into the dining room, which became her very own workplace.

Break for lunch, made by Barbara, more studying, mid-afternoon cup of tea served by Barbara, leave her books and collect the kids from school and then play with them – well, Francesca, as Little Willy still wasn't keen to engage with her – until their bedtime. She loved it, every stimulating, satisfying, mind-exercising minute of it. Suddenly, she felt like herself again after all these years.

Not for much longer though. She just had to finish off her final credit, hand her coursework in and then, hopefully, fingers crossed, she would be the proud possessor of an Honours Degree in Computer Studies.

*What next?*

It was exciting, not daunting. The possibilities seemed endless. Should she try and get some term time work in Tunbridge Wells to build on her studies? Perhaps she could get some freelance programming work?

She would have more time for riding. Francesca was very keen and James somehow managed to conjure up the sweetest little pony: a black, twelve-hand, Welsh Section A – whatever that means – who most originally was called Jet. At the same time, he acquired a huge old placid cob named George, who seemed quite happy to take Lilli's weight without a murmur. She'd been very worried the first time she had tentatively climbed aboard, but George continued to fill his face with grass. "You two should get on like a house on fire," laughed James. They did. She loved George to bits.

Francesca was a neat and tidy rider and very keen to sign up with the Pony Club, like all her classmates. James seemed to know all about it, but Lilli was completely ignorant.

Lilli found herself reading The Pony Club Manual of Horsemanship surreptitiously when she didn't think that James or Francesca were looking. She could learn. If she could crack computers, she could cope with four-legged beasts.

William still disappeared at every free moment to be with James – it wouldn't be long before his legs were long enough to be driving the tractors, not just the quad bike. He didn't notice whether she was there or not. Every morning, as soon as breakfast was finished, James would pronounce, "Right you lot. Some of us have work to do. Are you coming, Welly? And you, Little Willy!"

*I wish you wouldn't still call him that. He will get a complex.*

Complex or not, William leapt out of his chair, and Wellington staggered out of his bed, he was too old to leap anymore, and they all scuttled off to wherever boys went on the farm, James kissing her on the top of her head as he went. He couldn't get at her bum, she was sitting on it.

**She smiled contentedly; all was well with her world.**

# Lilli 13

**The Millennium was an extraordinary time for everyone.**

It heralded not just a new century and a new thousand years but a whole new epoch. From where she was standing, she could see such change around the corner in computing, with the whole dot.com thing. The bubble may have burst but she was sure there was a lot more to come.

It was humbling to be the generation that was going to celebrate a millennium. So many people must have been excited by the new centuries through the ages, let alone this. Lilli wondered what it would have been like as 1900 came in, before computers and TV, before cars and mobile phones, when farmers still milked by hand. And what about 1800? She was a little vague on history and wasn't sure what was going on then but thought it was around the time that King George went mad. Amazing. And 1700? And back to the last millennium, 1000, when Ethelred the Unready was in charge.

*A whole different world then. Wow.*

It was funny how everyone was going on and on about the 'Millennium Bug' with voices of doom. She was quite certain that, after all the work she and her colleagues had done over the last year or two, there would not be a problem.

*Fingers crossed.*

It was the best thing that could have happened to her. With the whole furore, everyone wanted any programmer they could find, however little their experience, so it had given her new career an enormous boost. Perhaps it would turn out to be a damp squib – or "damp squid" as James always said.

*He is so funny.*

Lilli turned to James and grinned up at him. His face was lit up by the light of the enormous bonfire that all the villagers had amassed on Lamberhurst Down to celebrate the new millennium. The whole place was packed and alive with happy chatter. Kids were running around everywhere, chasing each other, shouting total rubbish, delighted to be allowed to stay up so late. There was just under fifty minutes to go before the witching hour.

Lilli and James were with Daniel and Sarah. Other farmer friends drifted to join them and the conversation wandered happily around cows, yields and calving rates and, indignantly, about the reforms of the Common Agricultural Policy that was having such an enormous impact. She wasn't listening but was content to snuggle up to James, his arm casually resting across her shoulders.

"Diversification? Diversification? Why the hell should we have to start diversifying when our objective is to simply produce milk at a dirt-cheap price for the whole bloody, ungrateful country?" Daniel was getting over excited. He always did when he was on his favourite subject.

"I'm thinking of turning the oast house into a holiday cottage. It isn't much use for anything else since we gave up hop picking. That's diversification for you."

Lilli gazed languidly around at the crowds, spotting people she knew.

*I am sure that's Liz from school. I ought to go and say hello but what would we talk about after all this time?*

"It has all changed since I was a lad. It was all mixed farms when I was growing up." It was a story that everyone had heard Wally Watkins tell many a time. "We all had some sheep, some cows or bullocks and the hops... Proper mixed farming, but now... it is sad to see that old way of life go. Even Paul Tompsett and Percy Henley, over towards Goudhurst, are threatening to scrub all their hop gardens. The end of an era."

Wally Watkins' reminiscences were brought to a halt by the curious sight of a posh-looking chap in a Barbour and green wellies staggering past with two plastic glasses in his hands. He was clearly pissed. His feet struggled to keep up with his head and shoulders and he was scrabbling along faster and faster.

James and Daniel, as one, started up a long "Whoa", altering the pitch with the jerky erring. Suddenly he leant too far and fell flat on his face. It was hilarious. What could they all do except roar with laughter?

The posh bloke lay still for a full minute, his hands still clutching the glasses. Eventually, James stopped laughing for long enough to give him a hand. "Up you come, mate. A very merry New Millennium to you."

James hauled the man to his feet. They couldn't stop laughing even more at the sight of his face, covered in mud. "Thank you so much, my man, so much… must have tripped… the uneven ground…" He scuttled off, still clutching the glasses firmly in each hand, at which point the group of friends descended into uncontrollable, hysterical mirth.

*I'm sure that was Patrick Shepley-Botham. We all fancied him like mad at school. Certainly don't fancy him much now – look at the state of him. Give me my James any day.*

James brought himself under control long enough to say, "That makes me think… would anyone like another pint? At least they are still brewing Shepherd's Neame locally, hops or no hops, and bloody excellent it is too!

"And while I'm on the way to the bar, I'll check to see if our children are still alive, Moo. I last saw Little Willy trying to blag a pint about an hour ago. Fortunately, I think everyone knows he is only thirteen. And I'd better get a hog roast for Francesca and Mum; they must be starving – wherever they've got to."

Lilli felt a chill as James unwrapped himself but was completely warm inside.

**She couldn't help giggling intermittently at the hilarious performance by the posh Patrick Shepley-Botham.**

# Lilli 14

**Little Willy wandered in through the kitchen door.**

"Hello, Mum, I could murder some lunch."

"Willy, what on earth are you doing at home? You are meant to be at school."

"Ah well, slight problem, Mum. I've been suspended."

"Again! What for this time?"

"Smoking."

"But you promised you weren't smoking…"

"Indeed. I fully understand that a promise is a promise. I haven't been smoking."

"For heaven's sake, Willy, stop talking in riddles."

"It's very simple, Mum. If they think I am smoking they suspend me, I get to come home. I like being at home loads more than I like being at school, so I let them think I'm smoking. Job done, QED. Boom."

"Oh, for heaven's sake. Wait until I tell your father."

"No worries, Mum, I'll go and tell him myself. I'm sure he'd like a hand with the calving, but I would kill for a sandwich or something first."

*One, two, three, four, five… This child will be the death of me. Thank God for Francesca.*

# Lilli 15

***Thirty-five next month. Good grief!*** **She wasn't feeling too bad for thirty-five.**

Lilli was thoroughly enjoying her job at Kent and Sussex Computing. It turned out that she was rather good at it and had gathered a team of three programmers under her wing. It took only ten minutes to drive into Tunbridge Wells and drop Francesca off at school and she loved the girly chats on the way. She knew everything that there was to know about her beloved little girl.

It was great that her clever, clever daughter had won a place at the grammar school. She was definitely on track to get good GCSEs, her A Level grades and go to uni.

*She'd better not screw it up and get pregnant like I did.*

Lilli watched her like a hawk.

Little Willy (for God's sake, why did she keep calling him that too? He was far too old at seventeen – and had made it quite clear that the name was clearly contradictory) had never made it academically but was like a sheep in clover, or a pig in shit, or a cow in… whatever… having a ball at Wye College and soon becoming a double act with his dad on the farm. Willy was desperate to introduce modern systems like robotic milking but bided his time. It worked well.

During the holidays they shared the milking and she and James actually had a social life and went out and about with Daniel and Sarah. James still smelt of cow poo however many showers he took, but so did Daniel. Lilli and Sarah were quite accustomed to it after all these years.

James was such a party animal – very amusing – although he still seemed to mostly talk about cows, cricket and rugby. She was so lucky to have him.

*"Be careful who you marry, girls" – I've done okay as it happens.*

She was also very proud of herself because she'd lost a whole stone. She and Barbara joined Slimming World, becoming devotees of the Lamberhurst sect. Barbara had gone completely over the top and reinvented her cuisine to be no fat, no carbs, no anything at all, but still supremely delicious.

She still did potatoes for James and William, the bread maker churned out its daily loaf, which James and Little Willy smothered with half a packet of butter on each slice.

"Someone's got to support the dairy industry, Moo!"

She and Barbara were very saintly and helped each other resist temptation, and Francesca was quite content to eat anything that was put in front of her. Such an easy child. To be honest, Lilli didn't think any of the family noticed the difference – in the food or her weight.

She regularly went riding on old George. He was getting on in years, and very hairy, but they enjoyed each other's company. She kept to the multitude of back lanes so no-one could see her bobbling along; she would never be a stylish rider. It was rather nice to be out in the fresh air, plodding along at a gentle pace, between the high banks and hedges and the hazel woodland. Up Sweetings Lane, round the top and back past Yew Tree Farm and Maitlands Farm.

She often saw deer crashing through the undergrowth, squirrels busy carting around beech nuts and flashes of magpies yacking at her from the branches. For fun, she would yack back, or sing.

*Yup, life is good.*

# Lilli 16

***What is going on?***

It may have been a chance remark but the hairs on the back of Lilli's neck were on full alert, standing to attention. She'd been in the new delicatessen that had recently opened in Lamberhurst, taking over from the old general store, when she bumped into Louise Middleton.

"Francesca seems to be getting on very well with Doctor MacLellan, I hear, and he doesn't actually teach her. I am sure that my Pippa is making something out of nothing, but you never know, do you? Silly teenage crushes!"

*Silly tinkling bloody laugh. What am I meant to say?*

Lilli didn't say anything, she just gawped.

"Oh well, I'm sure there is a perfectly innocent explanation. These girls do like to make something out of nothing, don't they? Are you coming to the PTA Quiz Night? It is only five pounds and you get a glass of wine."

That was the first time.

Now here she was in the National Westminster Bank at Wadhurst.

"We have to keep our eyes wide open with our girls, don't we? They get up to all sorts of mischief at this age."

*Thanks, Penny Featherstone, mother of Sabrina in the same class as Francesca. What do you really mean?*

"That is the trouble with employing male teachers, I suppose, at an all-girls grammar. I can't think why they would allow them to travel on the bus with our girls. It seems extraordinary to sit with the same girl every day chatting conspiratorially. So openly. I would have thought that the school would have put a stop to it before it went… well, too far."

Penny looked at Lilli as if expecting her to join in at some point.

"You do know what is going on with Francesca and this Doctor MacLellan, don't you?"

Lilli didn't know what to say and looked gormlessly at Penny.

"Oh dear. I'm so sorry, Elizabeth. I am sure I am talking out of turn. Just meaningless schoolgirl gossip, reading things into something that is completely innocent."

*Shit, shit, shit. This is the second "rumour" that's been casually put my way… This one is hardly subtle but it's perfectly clear what Penny is getting at. Francesca must NOT throw it all away like I did.*

**Oh God, I sound like Mother.**

# Lilli 17

**"Francesca, my darling. We need to talk."**

"Mm?"

"I might have quite the wrong end of the stick – you know your old mum – but... but... Doctor MacLellan... How.... what... do you....?"

"What on earth are you going on about, Mum?"

Francesca looked perfectly innocent. Lilli was a bit unsure how to proceed.

*Stupid school rumours?*

"People have been saying..."

"Saying what?"

"Well, they are suggesting that... you and Doctor MacLellan..."

"Oh, for heaven's sake, Mum, what do you take me for? He is a brilliant teacher. If it wasn't for him, I wouldn't understand a thing about Physics."

"But I did Physics... I could help..."

"You Mum, I think not! He's so clever and helps me understand things. He's old enough to be my father, for God's sake. You don't want to listen to gossip!"

*Ouch, I used to be clever too. Anyway, shall I leave it there? Does she protest too much?*

Lilli hesitated.

"So, is that it? Is that what you wanted to talk about, Mum? For heaven's sake. I must go and get stuck into my Maths prep – it is due in on Monday and I have several shifts at the pub over the weekend so won't have time."

"That sounds very important, the Maths I mean..."

*Yay, chip off the old block in the science department – mine, of course, not James's – but am I missing something important? Should I be worried?*

Taking the pause as an opportunity to escape, Francesca scooted out of the kitchen, turning back briefly, "Oh and can you dig out my passport, please? I need it for the school trip…"

Before Lilli could gather her thoughts about this extra piece of information the phone rang, interrupting. It made Lilli jump. She seemed to be more het up than she realised. Francesca scampered off to the dining room – her adopted place of study. Just like her mum.

"Hello, Hoathly Farm. Oh hi, Wally! No, he isn't in yet… still milking. Yeah, I know! Try later. Bye."

*Was it worth raising with James? He would probably just say, "are you sure you are not overreacting again? You know how you do, silly Moo! Francesca is a good girl – not like her wicked schoolgirl mother!" Hmm.*

**It wouldn't do any harm to have a quiet word with the Headmistress, though… especially about him travelling on the bus.**

# Lilli 18

**Lilli was terrified.**

Standing at the front door were two burly policemen, they looked like giant magpies in their black uniforms, bristling with shiny things, and a smaller man in a jacket and tie.

*What the hell can they want?*

She opened the front door, unused for years, not since that ill-fated visit from her mum all those years ago, and very stiff, so it was quite a struggle. She wrestled it open eventually. Barbara appeared behind her, looking as worried as Lilli felt. In unison they peered up at the two officers, anxiously.

"Mrs Arbuthnott?"

"Yes," she and Barbara replied in echo.

"Good afternoon. I am Detective Inspector Fuggle." The plain clothed man stated, thrusting a warrant card at them, although it was rather obvious what they were. "This is PC Thompson and this is PC Stemp. I wonder if we could come in for a moment."

"Yes, of course, but…" Lilli was flustered, her head and stomach fluttering.

*Where shall I take them? Why are they here? Francesca is in the dining room studying, the sitting room isn't set up for visitors, I haven't lit the fire for the evening yet. What do they want? Oh my God, has somebody died? Is James okay…? Little Willy? Oh God, what has bloody Willy been up to now?*

She led them to the kitchen and vaguely waved her arms at the chairs around the scrubbed pine table. She felt ridiculously peeved that the Inspector bloke immediately took James's chair at the head of the table. She couldn't speak – she was too petrified. She thought she might cry.

Ever practical, Barbara hovered around and offered them tea, but they were obviously intent on the reason for their visit. So was Lilli. Barbara made some feeble meaningless mumbles, flapped a hand at Lilli, mouthed, "I'll see you later" and slunk out via the back door, leaving Lilli sitting like a deer in the headlights. The policemen looked so unreal.

"We are investigating reports of a missing person who has not been seen since Wednesday afternoon when they left work."

Lilli nodded.

"You are known to horse ride in the vicinity of where the missing person cycles from work so you might have seen something."

Lilli nodded but then thought she should shake her head. She was a bit confused as to what she was meant to be doing. She thought back to Wednesday. Slimming World evening. With Barbara.

*I didn't go for a ride on Wednesday. Or Thursday. Or Friday.*

"I'm getting a bit lazy."

They stared at her expectantly. Did she say that out loud?

She said more firmly, "I didn't go for a ride on Wednesday... or Thursday."

"So you haven't seen anything unusual, or different?"

She racked her brains for something sensible to comment on. She genuinely wanted to help.

"No. I'm sorry I can't think of anything at all."

"It isn't just you that we need to talk to, Mrs Arbuthnott. If I could explain?"

Lilli nodded, still rigidly uptight.

"I wonder if we might talk to your daughter."

Lilli was shocked.

"What on earth has Francesca got to do with any of this?"

"We believe that your daughter knows the missing person. He teaches at her school – a Doctor MacLellan."

Lilli thought that her head might explode. She could feel everything, whatever everything was, rushing into her head. A strange, cold feeling trickled down her scalp. She couldn't move.

*Wednesday. Wednesday. When Barbara and I returned from Slimming World, Francesca wasn't there. She came in late. She was upset about something.*

"Mrs Arbuthnott?"

The plain clothes policeman, she'd forgotten his name as soon as he'd said it, was looking at her. She jumped. Remembered his request.

"I'll get her."

*What had Francesca said? She had said something odd...*

She stumbled to the dining room, her legs like jelly.

"Francesca, darling... it is the police... they would like a word..."

"About what? What have I done? Why?" She looked baffled and, at the same time, afraid. Who wouldn't?

"I'll let them explain, darling. I'm sure it won't take long."

Francesca sat for a while, on the verge of easing herself from the chair, staring intently at the carpet.

"It's about Doctor MacLellan, isn't it, Mum?"

"Yes." A pause. "Why do you say that, darling? What do you know?"

"He has disappeared, apparently. Just vanished. The plod have been all over school asking questions. No-one can talk about anything else."

"You haven't said anything..."

"Well, Mum, that's hardly surprising, is it? The way you accused me of... well implied... whatever..."

"Well, my darling, let's get this sorted out."

*Oh God, it was "I went to meet someone but it was a no show." I'm sure it was. How is Francesca involved in this?*

Francesca shuffled behind Lilli into the kitchen. Lilli felt the imposition of the bulky figures all over again. She and Francesca took seats as far away as possible but then seemed like prisoners in the dock. She thought it best not to move again, it would look stupid.

"Now, let us take this one step at a time, Francesca. Do you know where Doctor MacLellan is?"

"No, I don't." Francesca was staring at him. Her eyes wide in fear, like Bambi.

"When did you last see Doctor MacLellan?"

"Um... on Wednesday. At school."

"Did you talk?"

Hesitation. "No."

"You were seen giving a double thumbs up sign to Doctor MacLellan in the canteen. He did the same back to you. Is that right?"

"Yes, but..."

"What was that for exactly, Francesca?"

Silence. She seemed to be examining the kitchen clock.

"Had you arranged to meet on Wednesday?"

"Yes, but... you don't understand." Sigh.

*She had arranged to meet the bloody man. The bloody pervert.*

"What don't we understand, Francesca? Where had you arranged to meet? Why had you arranged to meet?"

"He didn't turn up. I waited for ages. Honestly… he didn't turn up and when he wasn't at school I wondered if something had happened… and then it had… but I don't know what."

*She had said it was a no show.*

Francesca sobbed and let rip with a torrent of jumbled sentences.

"He was helping me… that is all. And he said that he could get Mum's birthday present so that it would be a surprise. Dad tells Mum everything, he is hopeless. He's a nice man… I do like him… he isn't like a teacher… but not in that way. And the Physics. I couldn't do it without him. Honest truth, that is all there is to it. I know everyone gossips but I don't care. He is sad. He is so sad because he couldn't have kids… he always said that I was exactly how he imagined his daughter would have been… The others say he is a paedo, but he isn't…"

"Would you be willing for us to examine your mobile telephone, Francesca?"

Francesca looked alarmed, took a sharp intake of breath and pursed her lips. All eyes were watching her every gesture.

"I left it at school."

Lilli knew damned well that it was sitting on the dining room table. If Francesca was as innocent as she was making out then why on earth would she not want them to have the phone?

"Perhaps we could collect it from you there, Francesca, tomorrow?"

Francesca started crying and, through the tears and the snot, squeaked, "Yes, okay, yes." But she didn't look very happy about it. "If I can find it."

*Perhaps, if I give it to them, they'll find out that Francesca has nothing to do with this stupid man and then go away. I can then get to the bottom of all this with Francesca.*

"Darling, I've seen your phone. You must have forgotten. Let me just get it and be done with all this nonsense." Francesca looked horrified.

Oh God. What have I done? Can I go back on this, pretend it was mine that I had seen. No, that would be so obvious.

Lilli leapt up, ran to the dining room, grabbed the phone from the table where Francesca had left it, snatched it up and ran as fast as she could back to the kitchen where Francesca was slumped sobbing her heart out.

Lilli was trembling at Francesca's distress, but she was also deeply concerned about her involvement with this bloody man. What was the truth anyway? What the hell had Francesca been up to? She heard herself shouting, "No, no, no... enough, enough. Stop, stop. I think we need legal advice before this horrible interrogation, these insinuations, go any further. Take the bloody phone. Leave. Leave right now. I need to talk to James. My husband. Just go, please."

She showed them to the back door, shooing them out like sheep, flapping her hands at them, "Go, go..."

They were confused, they'd parked at the front and clearly didn't know where they were.

Leaving them peering about themselves, she slammed the door. Returning, she slumped into James's chair, holding on like grim death to the arms, waiting for the policemen to go. Francesca was hunched across the table, her shoulders heaving. For some reason, it reminded her of that awful row with her mum. She had sobbed like that too.

*Oh God, what have I done, giving them her phone? What was going on with this depraved Doctor MacLellan? Something was – but what? Was there more to this… Had he been grooming her? Had she reciprocated… dear God, please not… she had better not be pregnant… and now he'd disappeared.*

Lilli heard the police car leave. She pulled herself together, tried to stop her heart racing out of control, knew she must be calm. "Now darling. Just sit there. Calm down. Don't move a muscle. I am going to get Dad."

**She patted Francesca on the shoulder, flung on a cagoule and headed for the milking parlour, forgetting she was still in her slippers.**

# Lilli 19

**Francesca sat there, tears rolling down her cheeks, as the police read out her text messages inexorably – one by one.**

Lilli, bolt upright, hung on their every word.

*Oh God, I wish James were here. Are they allowed to do this?*

The Inspector – whatever was his name? Something meaningless – intoned…

> *Okay. I give in. It will have to be secret. I don't think others would approve.*
> *Yay. Thank you thank you. I promise I won't breathe a word to a soul. Meet Café Nero?*
> *OK*
> *Meet on bus?*
> *No. Banned from bus. Cycling now.*
> *Tomorrow. At school.*
> *No. Too much trouble.*
> *Please.*
> *No.*

"So your meetings with Doctor MacLellan were secret, Francesca?"

"Yes, because everyone would get the wrong idea…"

The Inspector cocked his head and looked at Francesca. It could only be described as askance. Francesca blushed.

"And why was Doctor MacLellan banned from travelling on the bus with you, Francesca?"

"It was me," interjected Lilli. "I stopped him going on the bus. I had a word with Mrs Wellbourne when all the rumours were flying around."

"Oh God, Mum! Why? Why didn't you tell me and talk to me?"

"I did, darling, I did but..."

The Inspector looked irritated at the interruption.

"May I go on?" He sniffed and continued to read out loud.

*How did test go?*
*It is too early to say. Fingers crossed.*
*Whatever the outcome I am here. Tell me as soon as you get the result?*
*OK.*
*Sleep well don't worry.*
*Fantastic. Wonderful result. Phew.*

"The test, Francesca, what test would that have been?"

"Physics mock, A Level."

"Are you quite sure about that, Francesca. Not a pregnancy test? It sounds rather like it."

Francesca shrieked in hysterics. Lilli went to leap up and go to her. One of the black heavies put out a restraining arm.

*Passport?*
*Oops nearly forgot again.*

"And the passport, Francesca? What did you need that for?"

"It was the school trip. I'd been upset because I got told off for missing the deadline to hand them in... I was upset... he was just being kind."

The Inspector looked back at the phone.

*I have got the cash together. Tomorrow?*
*Do you want to go ahead? Are you absolutely sure?*
*Yes.*
*OK.*
*Meet you at the secret place. LOL*

"What was the money for, Francesca? Were you planning on going somewhere? Together? Why didn't Doctor MacLellan follow through? Where is he now?"

"We'd arranged to meet... it was a secret. Look for God's sake, I just asked him to get me an iPad for Mum... her special birthday... her fortieth. What is wrong with you pervs that you are making this out... oh Jesus. He's a nice guy. He's just a sad old man... I have no idea where he is..." Francesca moaned.

The Inspector carried on, slightly louder.

*Where are you?*
*What went wrong?*
*Where are you?"*

"And there follows a list of calls to the same number." The Inspector counted them, dabbing at the screen and mouthing the numbers like a child. "Thirteen. And then a last text."

*What is going on?*

"From this, Francesca, we can surmise that, as you said, he didn't turn up. Who else knew about where he would be, Francesca? Did you tell your dad, if not your mum?"

**"No, no…" Francesca's voice gave out as she wailed in agony.**

# Lilli 20

**By the time her fortieth birthday arrived, Lilli was feeling subdued.**

The whole ghastly business with Francesca and Doctor MacLellan soured everything. The man had simply vanished. All sorts of rumours were circulating, a difficult childless marriage, a nervous breakdown, culpability for the loss of a space shuttle no less (*seems a bit far-fetched*). His rumoured relationship with Francesca.

*I wish they would just bloody stop about Francesca.*

His poor wife. Lilli wondered what she was thinking about it. There had been no note. No-one had seen him since he cycled out of the school gates that fateful Wednesday. Apparently, he left behind everything except what he was standing up in that day. A navy cagoule and a dark bobble hat and his laptop and phone, they thought. No-one knew where he had gone.

*Except for a mission to meet Francesca. Where has he gone? Clearly a disturbed man. A mystery.*

The police just seemed to have let the whole thing string out, left hanging in the air. Many thought it must be suicide but didn't like to say so. Francesca stuck to her story – word for word. The police looked very sceptical.

*Was there anything in it? I must believe Francesca. I must.*

Even James had been interviewed. It was totally clear that he had been milking that evening, all his recordings of data showed that.

*At least Barbara and I could vouch for each other, as could all the other fat ladies at Slimming World.*

James was frosty with her for not being more supportive of Francesca and not instantly believing her side of the story. Francesca was livid with her for having the temerity to hand her phone over to the police without even asking her. She ranted at Lilli just as Lilli had raved at her own mother so many years ago. The tension was palpable and, since the most appalling shouting match, Francesca seemed to be avoiding her like the plague. Was this an irreparable rift?

*Like with Mum?*

She'd never been able to patch things up with her own mother. Could she ever retrieve Francesca's trust? Thank God for Barbara, it made the clock turn back to happy days to deliberately call her Nanny Bap, always cheerful, always pretending that there was nothing wrong.

She felt a bit awkward to be taking the birthday seat at the head of the table that morning, a small pile of cards and presents at her place. Barbara laid before her the customary full English breakfast, Slimming World style, so no fried bread or hash browns. James grinned at her from the other end of the table. Little Willy was stuffing cereal into his mouth with great gusto, quite unusually all in one piece and with no visible injuries. Francesca sat primly, looking mostly at her plate.

Lilli tried hard to be super cheerful and act as if nothing was amiss. She opened her present from James – an exquisite pair of earrings. "Oh, James!" she exhaled, absolutely amazed and instantly thinking Francesca must have helped to select such a beautiful gift. That was at least progress. "Well, forty is a big milestone, Moo. I even went into a shop in Monson Road and chose them all by myself. Seriously. I must like you a lot to have done that!"

"Thank you, thank you. I shall treasure them forever and ever." She blew him a kiss but, at the same time, she was a bit sad that Francesca hadn't helped him.

Little Willy looked up and, with his mouth still full, spluttered, "I was going to get you a card, Mum, but I was so busy and I knew that Dad would come up trumps, but happy birthday anyway, you ancient being."

She then opened the card from Francesca. It was rather a plain one, not one of her usual clever, funny ones. Francesca was looking out of the window.

*Dear Mum, I really was going to get you an iPad. I promise. Love Francesca x*

Lilli's heart sank. It was Francesca's consistent story to explain away the whole Doctor MacLellan business. She claimed that, as well as having secret Physics coaching, she'd given a whole wad of cash to him to buy Lilli a fantastic fortieth birthday present. The cash and the iPad, if there had ever been one, apparently disappeared with him.

*Apparently.*

Lilli burst into tears, she just couldn't help it. Francesca burst into tears and rushed from the room.

**James went after her, saying crossly over his shoulder as he left the kitchen, "For heaven's sake, Moo, what have you done now!"**

# Lilli 21

**Francesca went into school to get her A Level results.**

They didn't post them anymore, you had to go and face your peers. She stated categorically that she didn't want Lilli to come with her so Lilli sat in the kitchen with Barbara, nursing a coffee and mentally tapping her feet. Francesca took forever. Deliberately, Lilli was sure.

Ages later, she slipped through the back door. Barbara managed to get in first. "Well, my little duck. How did you get on?"

"An A and two Bs. I can go to Edinburgh because the A was in Physics – thanks to Doctor MacLellan."

"Well done, darling, well done!" Lilli shouted, a little too heartily. Francesca didn't even acknowledge her.

*All because of bloody Doctor MacLellan. The elephant in the room. Well, not in the room – wherever he is. Had he had the cheek to take five hundred quid off a teenager and leg it.*

***Surely he must be dead but by whose hand? His – or was there someone else?***

# Lilli 22

**It was exceedingly exciting going to Edinburgh for Francesca's graduation and Lilli was popping with pride.**

Somehow Francesca managed to fend off all requests to go and visit her throughout her degree. She and James made the trek up to Edinburgh for Francesca's very first term to deposit Francesca at Pollock Halls (which made Lilli giggle when James pronounced the P very carefully) and that had been their only foray.

She hugged Francesca as tightly as she could. She didn't want to let her go. There were so many things she wanted to say, but they were stuck in her throat with her sob. Francesca at least relented and relaxed into her hug, squeezed her back. At least that was something. Lilli treasured it.

Lilli bought a rather fancy suit for the occasion. Barbara wanted her to get a hat too, but Francesca looked horrified at the thought.

James said rather sarcastically, "She isn't getting married, Moo!"

Lilli was frankly amazed when they descended on the McEwan Hall to see what seemed like hundreds and thousands of graduates in gowns and hats milling around with parents and friends. It was like a parliament of rooks, bobbing about, black wings fluttering in the wind.

She had no idea that there were so many clever young people at the one university, let alone in the country. It was funny to think that one of these bright young things would have been Nikki twenty odd years ago. And Doctor MacLellan.

*Bugger. Don't want to think of him today, even though Francesca still goes on about how it was him who "set her on the path to success in Physics". He has never been seen again. Ever. Weird.*

"Look, there she is." James was so excited and patted Lilli absent-mindedly on her bum. And there she was. Francesca. So very like her when she was twenty-one, except she was slim and well-groomed and looked so grown up in towering heels and floating gown.

She opened her arms and Francesca stepped in – after a slight hesitation.

From what felt like a dress circle, the procession of graduates was like a black snake, but Lilli somehow found Francesca immediately and watched her every step of the way as she queued for her turn, strode confidently across the stage, received her degree and was hit on the head with it by the Chancellor before she took it. What a strange tradition. It looked as if she was avoiding the blow and James laughed out loud and squeezed her thigh. Tears of delight filled her own eyes, of pride too and something else. Regret?

She was looking forward to reclaiming Francesca after the ceremony. They were going to lunch at a very posh restaurant along the Royal Mile. James was determined to have haggis. She pasted on her very best smile.

**"James, we must take lots of pics for Little Willy."**

# Lilli 23

**"It's my birthday and I'll sing if I want to!" and she did.**
Lilli and George plodded along the lane. George snatched at the branches of hazel that trailed over the hedges and invaded the lane. They went through the narrow, high-banked bend between Hoghole Lane Cottage and Magpies, Lilli on high alert for cars. There wasn't much room for George and a car. She tried to kick George into a trot, but he couldn't be bothered. He only trotted on the way home these days, the ancient old beast.

"Not as old as me yet, Georgie boy. Forty-five."

At the top they turned left and lumbered along Sweetings Lane. She happily recalled the ritual breakfast.

Dear Barbara, seventy but still as sprightly as ever, had served up the full English and Lilli had, as usual, taken James's seat at the head of the table. She had surveyed James, William and Barbara like a queen.

She was sad that Francesca wasn't there, and not even a card, but at the same time pleased for her that she was starting her PhD at Edinburgh. What else could she have done after earning a First in her Master of Physics? Clever, clever girl.

"You see, Moo, she does take after her old dad, after all."

*Ha-ha, James.*

James had given her a very smart handbag. He must have chosen it himself with Francesca away. What a darling. She had leapt up to give him a grateful hug and warm kiss. He'd said in his inimitable fashion, "Don't be daft. Get off me, Moo, I am eating my breakfast." Before slapping her on the bum. She had giggled happily, sounding more like a teenager than a middle-aged old bag, and he had flung his arm around her waist, pulling her towards him.

William had protested, "Mu-um. Da-ad. Stop it – not in front of the children please!"

Lilli laughed again at the thought of it.

Her happy thoughts were interrupted by the sound of a car in the near distance. It was revving very hard.

"I think someone needs to change gear, don't you, George?"

It was the last coherent thought that she had before the noisy car flew around the bend and struck. Slamming into his broad chest, George was catapulted into the air, falling heavily on the roof and bouncing over. Lilli was underneath and then on top of George. Lilli landed first on the solid tarmac. The full weight of George pulverised her.

**It was over in a second, but Lilli was beyond being aware of what was happening.**

# Lilli 24

**Lilli came to.**

She was in agony. She tried to cry out but whimpered pitifully. She couldn't move. She tried but horrendous searing pains shot through her body and sparked through her head.

She was cold and her teeth were involuntarily biting her tongue. She couldn't get her tongue to retract. She could smell something rank. She felt sick. Something was poking her hard in her back. She couldn't open her eyes; it was too difficult.

*Help me, please.*

She could only say it inside her head.

**She drifted away from the pain.**

# Lilli 25

**"Elizabeth, can you hear me?"**

*Kind voice. Help me, please help me.*

"I can't get a response. She is breathing but she is very cold. Elizabeth, can you hear me?" A pause. "For God's sake, let's get her out of this dump."

*Don't touch me please. Don't move me. It hurts so much…*

"What the hell is that underneath her? It's an old bike… and, bloody hell, that looks like bones…"

**I feel sick.**

# Lilli 26

**Lilli thought she might be awake.**

She could smell a clean aroma. She was warm.
Something was beeping regularly behind her head. She
didn't want to move. She couldn't open her eyes. A spasm
of pain pierced her chest as bad as any labour pain. She
couldn't breathe, something was rammed in her throat. She
heard someone whimper.

*Too tired.*

# Lilli 27

**Lilli woke to hear William.**

He sounded as if he was crying. He hadn't cried since he was a baby, when he never seemed to stop.

"Mum, I love you so much." A hesitation. "I always have. I was such a little shit, but I have no idea why now. Can you forgive me?" A pause, a sniff and a hiccup. "Do you think she can hear me, Dad?"

Lilli tried to reply but nothing seemed to be working. She couldn't swallow.

*Little Willy. My precious boy.*

Dear, darling James answered for her instead. "I am sure she can. Can't you, Moo? And you know that she has always loved you, even though you were a complete pain in the arse. She has done nothing all her life other than love us all unconditionally. She is a diamond. Aren't you, Moo? The best wife and mum we could ever have asked for."

Her hand was covered by his. She knew his touch, the rough skin. She attempted to smell him and his comforting aroma, but she couldn't catch the cow poo above the overpowering sanitised odour.

*I must be in hospital.*

**She drifted.**

# Lilli 28

**She surfaced again.**

James was burbling away, talking nonsense, probably about cows and cricket and rugger. She couldn't make out much of what he was saying. He was holding her hand, rubbing her palm rhythmically with his thumb. It was soothing.

"We realised something was wrong when George came trotting back into the yard. We assumed that she'd taken a tumble. We looked everywhere."

*I don't feel well.*

He stopped suddenly.

"She definitely moved then... Are you all right there, Moo? I am here... Come on, old girl. Get yourself better soon, my love. Keep fighting."

She tried to speak but it just didn't seem to be happening.

"But how did you find her?"

*It is Mum. Mum, I haven't seen you forever.*

"Thank God she had her phone with her otherwise we would never have found her. It was the find-your-phone app..."

"But what's all this about the other things that they found. It all sounds very cryptic?"

*Dad? Oh, hello Dad. Hello.*

They ignored her and James continued, "It was odd that they found the bike and bag there, right underneath her. They have more than a strong suspicion about the bike and the bag... It was a brand new iPad in its packaging... and there was a note. At first, they thought that the bones were his, but they quickly realised that it was a deer. Most odd. Of course, it has brought it all back into the public eye, opened it all up again like a gaping wound. Poor Mrs MacLellan. But I can't think of her at the moment, I can only think of my Moo. They'd better catch the bastard who did this to her…"

"Oh, James, I feel so awful. All this time wasted. I have always loved her, you must know. I am so sorry… Lillibet, I am so sorry." Mum sobbed.

Dad soothed her, "Hush, dear. We're all to blame for this ridiculous mess. We're here now."

"Here comes Francesca and Mum. I'm sorry but we can only have a few of us with her at one time so I'm going to have to hurry you out." Mum started weeping and James remonstrated, "Please hold yourself together. Francesca can't know that it is so bad. She also knows all about the other discovery – she is naturally very upset. It has brought back the whole Doctor MacLellan thing…"

James let go of her hand. It felt naked and exposed. She tried to reach out and take it back. She heard clothing swoosh, the squeak of a door, Mum's crying fading into the distance.

She heard Francesca's voice and the sound of rustling embraces, murmured greetings. And Barbara too. She tried to speak, but it was too difficult.

"How is she today, James, love?"

"Not so bad, considering… much perkier, breathing on her own. I hope you brought along the TCP, Mum."

Barbara chuckled but it turned into a strangled sob.

She felt a light touch on her hand.

"Hi, Mum."

*Francesca is here! How lovely. She so wanted to say hello, but it wouldn't come out.*

Francesca took her hand gently, lovingly. "Mum, I'm so sorry. Please forgive me for all that stuff. I love you so much. I was just a puerile teenager…" she whispered. "I love you, Mum… I do…"

*My little girl, of course I forgive you. I love you.*

As Francesca wept, she could feel the tears on her hand.

*I wish I could wrap you in my arms, my little darling, like I did when you were small, when we were so close.*

**James covered her other hand in his and she could drift away, feeling safe.**

# Lilli 29

**She woke with a start.**

Her eyes opened briefly, but it was very dim and her eyelids felt so heavy. She could hear an erratic beep. A crushing pain in her chest. She couldn't get her breath.

"It's all okay, my darling. I am here. Hold on, my precious. I am not going anywhere."

*That's nice. I want to tell you something, James. I have never said this before, but I love you. I am so happy that I married you. I love you so much.*

All James could hear was a sighing, lingering breath. He stopped, looked, waited. Someone came rustling in.

**"I think she has gone."**

# Mouse 1

**She could hear steps on the landing.**

Here was her chance. She was terrified but she had to do it, sooner rather than later.

"Mum. Could you come in here for a minute, please?"

"Mouse, it isn't Mum, it's Dad. Anything I can help you with? You don't sound very happy."

*Mouse. He always calls me that. I am a little mouse, afraid and quivering.*

"Oh, nothing important, Dad. Just need to ask Mum about something."

*Nothing important. I have to be kidding.*

"I'm on my way down. I will send her up."

She waited.

*Hold your nerve, silly little mouse. You have to tell her.*

"Hello, love. Dad said you needed me. What is it? Are you okay?"

"I need to tell you something."

"This sounds serious."

Mouse firmly closed the door behind her and half whispered, a bit shakily, "Do you swear that, whatever I tell you, you won't tell a soul, not even Dad or Susie?"

"Of course."

"Do you promise?" Promises were sacrosanct in their family.

"I promise, if that is what you want." She looked very worried.

*And so you should be. I'd better just get on with it. Here goes.*

"Mum, I think I'm probably, well, a bit pregnant."

Mum appeared to be winded. It was absolutely the sort of the reaction Mouse had been expecting, but it didn't make it any easier. Having been brave enough to start this conversation, Mouse now trembled, clenched her fists, dug her fingernails into her palm and tried very hard not to cry. She had half-hoped for a comforting hug following her pronouncement but had accepted, in her six million rehearsals of the conversation, that her news would not be greeted with pleasure.

Mum stood there, holding her breath. She seemed to be thinking.

*At least she doesn't appear to be completely furious. What is she thinking?*

Mouse didn't like to interrupt. She was holding her breath too. The tears started rolling down her cheeks. After forever, Mum turned and looked at her and then looked away immediately, as if ashamed of her.

"How far on are you?"

Mouse decided to mirror her mum's attitude and tell her straight. "About two months and a bit. I have missed a couple of periods and I know exactly when it happened. I didn't think… and we were… I didn't mean… I never thought…"

Her mother closed her eyes and let out a strange huff. "I don't want to know about any of that, not even who. I just can't…" she paused. "Does the father know?"

"Yes." Muttered.

"What does he think?"

"Well, he rather assumed that I would get rid of it. I have avoided him since then. Actually, I don't know him that well…"

"For heaven's sake…" More silence. Mouse thought she heard her mother hiss "slut", but she couldn't be absolutely certain.

Staring fixedly at Mouse's collage of photos of her school friends, Mum started talking in a measured, detached way. "I think that the best thing that we can do is go to Marie Stopes and get this stupid mistake sorted out. Straight away. Discreetly. Before you show."

Mouse stayed silent, the tears splashing freely down her front. She felt guilty and stupid and mortified, and she hadn't thought through any 'what next?' scenarios. She had half hoped that she would just have the baby and her mum would help her look after it. She hadn't expected this.

She didn't like the idea of getting rid of it… getting rid of her or him… but she could see that her mum had a point. It had been a stupid mistake. She tried to tell her mum, "But couldn't I…?", but her mum continued talking over her.

"I have inadvisably promised not to tell Dad or Susie, but no-one other than us needs to know. Not even our GP needs to know. I would rather she didn't, it would be awkward when she comes to dinner."

A miserable little, "Yes, Mum." And a sniff to try and hold back the drip in her nose from the tears.

"Do you think that you can refrain from blabbing about this to your friends? If you tell any of them then everyone will realise."

"I will try." It came out strangulated and half hiccupped.

"Try isn't good enough. You got yourself into this situation so you must get yourself out of it. No-one other than you and I must ever know. Ever. Do you promise?"

She couldn't do anything else. "I promise, Mum," Mouse murmured. An inviolable pact.

"I mean it… never. No good could ever come of it. I need to go now or Dad and Susie will wonder what is going on. Leave it to me and I will work out the arrangements." She went silent, obviously thinking again. She was proving to be so efficient, so decisive in a crisis.

"We will tell everyone that you are going to the dentist. We can say that you are having a wisdom tooth out, then, if you need a day or two to recover, I have no idea how these things actually work, but you can have the extra time off school if it is needed. It will explain away a lot. A lot of things…"

Mouse gurgled on a sob.

"Now, for God's sake, go and wipe your eyes, pull yourself together, stop snivelling. It isn't the end of the world. We don't want Dad and Susie seeing you in a state. They will start asking questions."

Mouse took a step towards her, hoping that she might get at least a reassuring hug. It wasn't going to happen. Her mother whisked out of her room.

"Thanks, Mum." Mum hadn't heard.

*What have I agreed to?*

# Mouse 2

**Her A Level results had arrived in the bundle of post.**

It was unusual for her to get something.

Mouse had worked her socks off revising for her A Levels, every moment of every day of study leave, in her room swotting; it had been cathartic and atoned for her schoolgirl foolishness. She didn't even want to think about it, the whole horrible, messy business. It had been horrible, appalling and like a slow-motion horror movie. It was clinical. It had been relatively pain-free, except for the cramps for days afterwards. She felt as if not just the baby had been dragged from deep within her body but something else too, something intangible that she would never get back. It kept popping into her head like a nightmare.

*Don't think about it. Don't think about it. Pull yourself together.*

She opened the envelope eagerly and was thrilled to get As in both Physics and Maths, it made up for it all, sort of. It was disappointing to only get a B in Chemistry.

*I must have just missed that Chemistry A grade by a whisker. Damn. That is so irritating, I could kick myself very, very hard. At least my grades are good enough for Imperial College – just.*

"Wahoo. Imperial College here I come!" She tried to sound extra enthusiastic for her parents, who were clearly delighted for her, and hugged her and kissed her. Her mother said, "There you are, you see, off to university, clever girl", which could have meant nothing, but it stung all the same.

Susie looked a bit bored by the whole thing and didn't comment.

"Please can I go and ring the others and see how they got on? I bet Tina has got in to Imperial as well. I hope so. I don't want to go on my own." Mouse dashed off to find the telephone in the hall.

*I bet Tina got straight As – she is so clever. How annoying about that bloody B.*

# Mouse 3

**Thank heavens for Tina.**

Mouse found the whole university thing much more daunting than she was expecting.

They had deliberately chosen to be in the same hall of residence, Hulme Hall, but their rooms were miles away from each other, along narrow corridors and up spiral staircases. It was like a giant-sized game of snakes and ladders.

The rooms were like prison cells, cleverly equipped with a bed, armchair, desk with cork pinboard above and a cupboard that hid a wash basin. It was very functional and anonymous. At least there was a window that looked over some park, like gardens with giant trees. She hadn't expected to miss the countryside, which she had always taken for granted, quite so much.

Once inside her room, the door closed and she was completely hidden away from the hundreds of other students that were slotted in to the building. She knew there were others there because she could hear footsteps and doors opening and closing and the very occasional bit of chatter. It felt very secretive and a little bit sinister.

She put up her collages of friends' photos on the pinboard, put all her stuff in the cupboard, and arranged all her brand-new stationery on the desk. It felt a little bit more homely and as if it could be distinguished from all the other identical rooms as hers.

**She went to find Tina as soon as she could and they went in search of the canteen.**

# Mouse 4

**Tina towed Mouse around the vast Freshers' Fair, ducking and diving between hordes of people.**

Unlike real life, everyone here in this strange inner world was the same age. Each person was so different and individual, some tall, others short, some ugly, some pretty, which was an obvious difference, but it was all the different haircuts and clothes and attitudes. She knew that she was just a middle of the road ordinary person, medium height, medium build, medium brown hair, medium length, okay looking but not particularly pretty, conventional clothes.

It was fascinating to discover a whole new realm of distinct personalities that Mouse had never come across before in the limited preserve of the Home Counties. She heard so many different accents, many she had only ever heard on TV, and even foreign languages. The Tower of Babel came to mind. So many people who had lived their lives in completely different ways before ending up here.

*I wonder if anyone else has had a termination. Stop it, you idiot. Move on.*

There seemed to be a club for everything to satisfy the eclectic mix of students: Beekeeping, Real Ale, Jailbreak, Christian Society, Jewish Society, Cavalier Appreciation (the blokes in beards that supported King Charles, not the dogs). Some were extremely bizarre. She was tempted to join one of the weird ones just to see who else turned up. She and Tina joined the down to earth hockey club and tennis club.

Tina seemed to sail through Freshers' Week, chatting away to strangers who quickly became friends. She had a radar for finding where all the best parties were – and avoiding the worst of the bores and the geeks and the frankly weird. Mouse happily trailed along, wondering how such a heterogeneous bunch of people had managed to get into such a high-powered university.

Only one or two from any school would have applied and been accepted and yet here there were just thousands of students. She had felt very special to have been offered a place, but her pride in that achievement had been completely diluted. All of these hordes of people would have the same sort of A Level grades and filled out their UCAS forms to show what exciting and thrusting people they were. She had deliberately done interesting things to make herself stand out from the crowd to join this seemingly exclusive institution. Such a lot of the young people that milled around looked anything but exciting. In fact, many were just plain bizarre.

*I wonder if anyone else has had an abortion. For God's sake, stop thinking about it.*

The first real lecture was an eye opener. There was no classroom to gather in to meet fellow students, no class teacher to tell you what was going on. No rules. Together they tracked down the Huxley Building that they had been told to go to and eventually found Lecture Theatre 1 on Level 3, which was actually on the first floor. Very confusing. An intelligence test?

Mouse was amazed as they pushed open the swing doors. It was the same size as the Odeon cinema in Tunbridge Wells. It looked nothing like a classroom. Tiers of seats rose, already populated with hundreds of faces randomly dotted about with spaces self-consciously between them. Mouse gawped.

"Where shall we sit? Front or back?" Tina was already bounding up the nearest gangway, with Mouse following in trepidation.

"These seats taken?" Tina boldly asked an attractive Asian boy before manoeuvring into the row. She rustled about, digging things out of her bag, piling them on the shelf, removing her sweater, draping it over the back of her chair before wriggling her bottom into the seat and settling like a hen on her nest.

Mouse tentatively followed and perched cautiously.

*This is so nothing like school.*

# Mouse 5

**Both Mouse and Tina sailed through their first-year exams.**

It helped being in a team with Tina and their old familiar ways of working diligently at school continued.

For their second year, Tina found a great place: a typically London terraced house with three bedrooms in a cheap, run down, slightly dodgy area behind Holland Park. It was to be their home for the remaining two years at university. Sharing the second big bedroom with Annie, a girl they had met through hockey, made it even cheaper. Tina took the second of the two large double rooms and moved in her boyfriend, Pete.

A friend of Pete's moved into the tiny back bedroom, but they hardly saw him because he seemed to spend most of his time at his girlfriend's place. They often wondered why he bothered to pay the rent for a room so irregularly used.

She wasn't sure whether it was an entirely conscious decision to share a room when they all moved out of the student halls and into flats, but it did mean that she had the perfect excuse not to invite boys over.

Mouse carefully evaded any relationships and definitely avoided sex. She was scared of committing herself to anyone because there seemed to be an immediate expectation that she would sleep with a boy, as seemed to be the case with everyone else, and she was terrified that she might get pregnant again.

The simple operation to excise the tiny, perfectly formed little person from her body had scarred her deeply, far more than she thought it would. She had promised her mother that she wouldn't tell anyone, so she couldn't talk about the feelings that haunted her. Not even with Tina.

She tried so hard but couldn't help dwelling on it and found herself in the library looking up the details of what the foetus would have looked like when she had terminated its little life. She yearned to talk about it and lay to rest the thoughts of a small child that could now be toddling around. She had considered going to the Student Listening Service... but would that break the pact made with her mother? She found herself staring at children on the tube and on buses and had to force herself to look away before their parents started shifting uncomfortably.

She joined Universal Aunts and was assigned regular jobs babysitting, which fitted in well with her degree. It also fed her obsession with babies and toddlers. She was paid to freely cuddle and play with other people's babies, sit in other people's warm flats in upmarket places and eat their fancy food while studying in great comfort. She always asked for the taxi fare home, willingly given, and then leapt on the night bus. As a result of her solid experience, it was easy to find holiday jobs nannying, especially over the long summer break. *The Lady* magazine was full of them. It wasn't just for the money.

Mouse was very circumspect with her money and didn't like to waste it on glamorous, superfluous things. It gave her a comforting sense of control. She bought an endless supply of jeans from Portobello Market and loads of cheap tops from Primark, merely to keep her warm. She never bothered with make-up. Why should she dress up to attract men?

**Her atonement for having so readily rid herself of her child.**

# Mouse 6

**Meeting David was a breath of fresh air.**

He seemed to enjoy her company and told her she was pretty. He liked the fact that she didn't wear make-up. They had a good laugh; played tennis (he wasn't very good, but it didn't matter); did loads of interesting things, visiting all the free museums and exhibitions that they could and sightseeing like tourists. They appeared to share the same values. He didn't set the world on fire in the looks department, with his too-large nose and receding hairline, but he seemed to be a genuinely kind man. His manners were impeccable.

David had been brought up to be a staunch Catholic. He didn't believe in contraception and so he didn't believe in sex before marriage. It seemed anomalous to Mouse that he did allow oral sex, which at least stopped it from all becoming horribly frustrating, and meant that there was no risk of pregnancy.

David was a scholastic sort of chap, and was fascinated with art and culture, which was new, and refreshing, for a scientist. Mouse suddenly discovered a use for her squirreled away cash from all that babysitting and holiday jobs – city breaks. She was thrilled to discover Paris, travelling under the channel on the train, walking miles and miles hand in hand with David to view all the sights, spending hours in the Louvre.

She was fascinated by the idiosyncrasies of Berlin, standing in awe at the Brandenburg Gate and seeing the communist soldiers at their posts, clearly armed and dangerous. She loved Venice and exploring along the endless canals, tiny hideaway back lanes and sudden open squares, and the majestic Catholic cathedrals. They sat in St Mark's Square but took one look at the price of a coffee and moved well away from the cafes, heading back to the cheaper places near their hostel.

She was in her ultimate year at Imperial, working up to her finals. Her parents were making a big fuss over her twenty-first and were talking about a big family get together. Mum had her eye on the George and Dragon in Lamberhurst, where you could hire a large room for the evening. It would all be very circumspect if her mother was organising it. Mouse preferred the idea of a fun party in London with friends.

"Do both!" pronounced Tina, so they put their heads together and decided to put on a joint shindig at their house. If they shifted the furniture from the living room into the always vacant back bedroom, they could fit loads of people in… all their friends from Maths, hockey and tennis. They decided to have a Bad Taste party for a laugh.

Mouse and David, Tina and Pete, and Annie and her boyfriend, Charlie, sat round the table with two bottles of cheap red wine, an odd assortment of glassware, a family-sized packet of crisps and a box of Maltesers and had fun coming up with all sorts of ideas. David didn't join in, but Tina and Pete made up for it with their crazy suggestions.

"What are we all going to dress up as?" Tina opened the discussion.

"Hitler… a Nazi?"

"Boring… too predictable."

"Charles and Diana with Camilla…"

"And James Hewitt by the sound of things…"

"Ceausescu… being executed?"

"How was he executed?"

"Don't know…"

"Back-street abortionist?"

"Too bad taste – not funny…"

Mouse froze and tried to keep a smile on her face, but it was very difficult. It leached the fun out of the whole idea.

"Herald of Free Enterprise passenger… or what about Hillsborough?"

"Eugghhh… not good."

By the time they had done every disaster to death, and drunk their way through the first bottle, Mouse, who had knocked back the wine from a chipped brandy glass like an anaesthetic, had tried to put behind her the unfortunate suggested proposition with its heart-stopping revulsion and despair. She decided to dress as Lorena Bobbitt with a knife and a sausage smeared in ketchup. David refused to be Mr Bobbitt.

"We need to open that other bottle of wine… and what are we going to eat and drink?" Mouse was trying very hard to enjoy herself again.

"Puke soup…" called out Tina.

"What?"

"Veggie soup with diced carrots – there is always diced carrots in sick."

"Guacamole always looks like vomit to me…" added Pete.

"Dog vomit chilli…"

"Enough with the vomit!" David protested.

"Dog poo sausages…"

"Bloody Marys of course, and a cocktail in a washing up bowl… with pretend flies floating in it…"

"Hey, this is going to be such a great party – much better than anything at the George and Dragon, my old friend!" Tina raised a tooth mug of wine in Mouse's direction.

Throwing an arm around David's shoulders and giving him a loving squeeze, and receiving a quick sloppy kiss in return, she slurped down another glass of wine.

David interjected, "I want to take you out for dinner to celebrate as well. Somewhere smart. Perhaps you might even be persuaded into wearing a dress. Now that would be a first. Make sure it is super-glamorous for a very posh night out."

"That sounds very exciting! Where, where?" This was a first for David, and for her, and not one of their usual student-priced outings at all. It was clearly an antidote to the Bad Taste party, which wasn't his scene.

**"I want it to be a very special surprise."**

# Mouse 7

**David was so sweet.**

It was her actual twenty-first birthday and he made sure she had a lovely soak in the bath and then greeted her with red roses and a bottle of champagne. Tina and Pete had been chased out of the house for the evening with strict instructions to leave the field clear for the newly romantic David's carefully orchestrated special evening.

They took the tube to South Kensington, home of Imperial College, which was a bit confusing for Mouse. Surely after all the effort to find a dress and shoes with heels, just small ones, she wasn't going to end up at a student place.

*Where are we going?*

He then led her down Pelham Street, a residential area, it seemed. She was very confused and also tottering rather a lot from the effects of the champagne and her unfamiliar heels. Her unaccustomed skirt felt draughty round her bottom.

Mouse simply couldn't believe it when they arrived outside Bibendum. Its iconic façade looked amazing, the old building with its very odd Michelin Man smoking a cigar, transformed into a restaurant with much fanfare by Terence Conran. Everyone had heard about it. She was gobsmacked but that was where dear David had booked for dinner.

"Wow. Fabulous." She hoped that she was dressed appropriately and wouldn't make a fool of herself.

*David seems a bit nervous. No wonder, this is all pretty scary. It's going to cost him an arm and a leg. I hope he isn't worried that I won't come up to scratch.*

Mouse smiled at him encouragingly and tried to look as if she was more comfortable than she actually felt. She felt like a small child dressed as a grown-up and playing at going out to dinner.

Dinner was delicious. She played it safe and chose what the waiter recommended, the signature dishes, oysters and steak au poivre. She was concerned to find that her menu didn't have any prices on it, so she couldn't choose the cheaper options. She watched David's face carefully as she made her choices, looking for clues.

*Just how much is David splashing out on me?*

It was difficult to act normally in such grand surroundings and she found herself a bit tongue-tied. David wasn't his usual chatty self either. He was also overawed by such unaccustomed luxury. She was pleased when they agreed to share an incredible confection of orange and champagne jelly, partly because David was looking more and more anxious and she dreaded to think how much two would cost.

She was surprised when David ordered coffee declaring, "We need coffee to give it time for it all to go down." True, she was stuffed but, even so, coffee would be free at home. When coffee arrived, David rose.

*Is he going to the toilet?*

He came round to her side of the table as if to hug her or kiss her or something, but suddenly he went down on one knee and produced a red velvet box from his pocket. She couldn't believe it.

*Oh my God, is this what I think it is?*

An extraordinary tremor went through her, rather prickly and brought a flush of heat to her face. It had caught her completely on the hop. He opened the box with a flourish to reveal a diamond solitaire. He must have spent a fortune.

"I love you, my darling. Will you marry me? Please?"

Mouse didn't hesitate.

"Of course, of course! Oh, thank you, David."

*He wants to marry me! We are going to get married and have lots of little David babies. Oh, thank you, God for this absolution.*

He leant down to kiss her but slipped slightly and ended up kissing her chin. She grinned, thrilled, absolutely delighted. A funny thought popped up out of nowhere:

***So this is who I am going to marry!***

# Mouse 8

**Mum went into overdrive.**

She loved David and his impeccable manners and couldn't talk about anything other than their forthcoming nuptials. She waved away the difficulties of an interdenominational marriage and priest and Catholic training for Mouse. She enthusiastically agreed that Mouse should sign a pact that the children would be brought up as Catholics. Mouse decided it would be easiest just to go along with it. Dad couldn't get a word in edgeways.

"When are you two lovebirds thinking of? June would be perfect, more reliable weather than May and lots of lovely flowers in season."

"Who are going to be your bridesmaids? Susie, of course, but who else?"

"Tina… Annie…"

"What had you in mind for bridesmaid dresses?"

"Um…"

"What about colours?"

"I like turquoise… I think…do you, David?"

"And flowers?"

"I don't know very much about flowers…"

"And… blah, blah… and…"

*Who knew that there were so many bloody questions? Mum is driving me mad.*

David seemed to want lots of decisions too and seemed to have made rather a lot on his own. They sat together snuggled up on the sofa.

"Should we wait until we have graduated? I'd like to get married as soon as possible."

*Ah, how sweet. In such a hurry. He loves me so much.*

"Are you going to work after we get married? We will have to rent for a while anyway. We might as well stay here in the short term; it is so cheap, and we can save up like mad for our first home. There is no way we can afford to buy in London, so I suppose we should buy in Essex."

*Essex? Why Essex? Just because your family come from there? Why not Kent?*

"I am guessing that we will see what God brings in the way of children. You clearly adore children! Perhaps we should get a house now, just in case, and I must get established in a career."

Mouse was overcome by the endless questions, the pressure of getting the answers right to make everyone happy, the emotion of planning for the future, planning babies that would be allowed to come into this world. A sudden horrible feeling of total loss for her baby that never was overwhelmed her. She burst into tears.

*I must tell David.*

"What is it, sweetheart?"

She couldn't stop the engulfing feeling of loss and guilt. The misery was suffocating. Suddenly it all seemed vital to tell David what had happened about the whole horrible business. Marriage was about total honesty and trust. Surely a promise didn't count when it was your husband to be? She could go forward absolved, forgiven and free. It would be like wiping all the heartache away and she could move on at last and put it truly behind her.

"David. If we are getting married, then I have to be totally honest with you. There is something I must tell you."

"Of course, my love."

She whispered it. "When I was at school, I had to have a termination."

"A termination?"

"Yes." She didn't like to use the other word for it.

"Do you mean an abortion?"

"Yes." It came out as a miserable little murmur.

David was absolutely silent. Completely still. He appeared winded. He wasn't looking at her.

*Like Mum that hideous day.*

David stood there, holding his breath. He was staring at the wall. He seemed to be thinking.

*At least he doesn't appear to be completely furious. What is he thinking?*

Mouse didn't like to interrupt his thoughts. She was holding her breath too. More tears rolled down her cheeks. After forever, David turned and looked at her and then looked away immediately as if she was a stranger.

"How far on were you?"

Mouse decided to tell him the whole truth. "About two months and a bit. I missed a couple of periods and I know exactly when it happened. I didn't think… and I was so young… I didn't mean… I have been sad and regretted it for every single day ever since…"

David closed his eyes and let out a strange huff. "I don't want to know about any of that, not even who. I just can't…"

Mouse reached over to him and tried to snuggle into his chest.

Staring fixedly at her collage of friends' photos on the wall, he started talking in a measured, detached way. "I think that the best thing that I can do is walk out of here. Now. I just can't…"

He took a deep breath, exhaled slowly, and still wouldn't look at her. "I am going."

He stood up, throwing her off like removing a coat and hovered over her. "Do you know what? I feel sick to the stomach. I can't believe that you would... You know, of course, that I can't marry you. You know that I am a Catholic. You know how I feel about... that. I can't believe that you could have done such a heinous thing. I can't believe that you have waited until now to tell me. It is just... impossible." He shook his head.

"You will have to sort out things with your mum and dad about the wedding plans. Straight away."

Mouse stayed silent, the tears splashing freely down her front. She felt guilty and stupid and mortified.

*Why did I say anything?*

He read her mind. "Well, at least you have told me now before we actually got married, but you got yourself into this situation so you must get yourself out of it. No-one must ever know the real reason that we are breaking off our engagement. Ever. Do you promise? I couldn't bear to be even associated with this... this wicked act..."

She couldn't really do or say anything else. "I promise," Mouse murmured. Another pact. She had broken the promise to her mum and look what had happened. It was entirely her own fault.

"We can tell everyone that you have decided that you are too young to get married yet and have changed your mind. I'm afraid that you must take the rap on this, say it is your decision. It is only fair. They will believe it if we both say the same thing."

"Yes, David." Cut short by the surge of an asphyxiating sob.

"You do realise, don't you, that that is just so totally unforgivable. Not just because I'm a Catholic but because it is totally immoral. A sin. It is murder. You must see that."

"I do, I was too young… I am so sorry, I am so sorry." She found herself mouthing to his departing back.

She collapsed on the sofa and heaved and sobbed and hysterically moaned in agony. She heard him leave the room, almost running to get away.

She was hysterical. She felt sick. Her chest hurt. She was suffocating. She was sobbing desperately when she heard the slam of the front door. David had gone.

*He has gone.*

# Mouse 9

**Tina couldn't understand what was going on, but she just took it at face value, a good friend.**

She dangled any spare men that she could think of in front of Mouse and Mouse would go for a few dates just to keep Tina happy. It was so obvious to the men as well as to Mouse what Tina was trying to do. It was off-putting for them both.

Mouse drowned her grief in work.

*It is ironic that once again I am trying to lose myself in studying.*

The extra hours of slog paid off and she walked away with a first, which gave her pick of the jobs. Mouse chose the graduate entry scheme place with IBM. It was fantastic. She loved the structure of the programme and getting her hands onto computers in a thoroughly practical, predictable way. Programming was fun, it was easy, but she wanted to do more than just that.

She had been very surprised to find that once you joined a real company there were so many different jobs that people did, there weren't just the obvious ones that she associated with IT: programmer and technician. She discovered a whole world of sales, sales support, marketing, management, personnel, and opted to go down the sales support route, with the view to eventually having the courage to move into sales.

She was diligent, did a thorough job, and her written proposals and attention to detail were renowned. She loved being part of a team that won lots of business. It would all help towards regular pay rises at her annual appraisal. No-one at IBM knew David, or any of her past, and she had been able to reinvent herself. She chose a new gamine look, with a short, sharp haircut. It was businesslike and strong. Taking pride in her success, she felt that at last she was putting her past behind her.

She had heard rumours floating about that she was gay, not just because of her short hair but her lack of interest in flirting. She didn't care, at least it kept her safe from bloody men.

Andrew was introduced as a tennis partner by Tina. Just that. Phew, no pressure. Tina and Pete made up the foursome, part of Tina's continued therapy for Mouse's broken heart. "Exercise will do you good!"

Andrew, Scottish as his name implied, was a very clever doctor in the Royal College of Science, Imperial College, Physics Department. He was doing very important research into energy conversion that Mouse didn't fully understand. He was a good ten years older than the rest of them, but it didn't make any difference. He was quite quiet but had a great sense of wit and his green eyes would twinkle merrily when he found something amusing. He had a rather old-fashioned moustache and his dark hair was unfashionably long, which they all teased him about. He took it in good humour.

What was important was that he was good at tennis, quietly competitive, tall and strong. His lanky legs gave him an advantage when playing at the net.

As alumni of the university and, because Andrew was on the staff, they played at Imperial College's sports grounds way out of London, just off the runway at Heathrow. They could see and hear the planes landing and taking off as they played but were used to it. They were all able to admire the physics of the process of great hulks of metal taking to the air.

As plane after plane wasted gallons of fuel in their lumbering efforts to take off, Andrew would regale them on how his research would change all that. Something complicated about re-using the energy that was wasted as heat and noise and turning it instead to extra power. She didn't really get it.

It had become a weekend ritual. Tina and Pete versus Andrew and Mouse. Three sets of tennis, a drink and snack in the subsidised student bar, lots of natter and banter, and then back into town. The score was always close.

For months and months, Mouse only saw Andrew at tennis and was caught unawares when he casually asked her to the Royal School of Science Christmas Ball. She was pleasantly surprised and flattered.

*Does he think of me as more than a tennis partner? More to the point, do I think of him as more than a tennis partner?*

Her question was answered when he very gently kissed her on the lips when he came to pick her up.

"Is that okay?"

"Yes, it is more than okay."

*It is very much okay.*

They became an inseparable item. He took her to show off Scotland and share his passion for hill walking. She loved the Highlands, the space and rolling hills, the muted colours, all so different from the wooded Kent vales. She learnt to hike properly, a backpack on her back, appropriately sturdy boots and camping overnight, whatever the weather.

She laughed at his favourite woolly bobble hat that he had treasured since he was a young boy, worn throughout his school days, a memory of happy times with his late dad. They rambled up the bens and through the glens and setup camp in the wilderness, not another soul in sight.

She learnt to love the wild weather and revel in the wind and rain. Getting caught in a blizzard was an eye opener. For a moment, she was terrified that she was completely alone in the world, as she couldn't see anything at all, just a white blinding fog. Andrew laughed playfully when he heard her bleating in fear. "I am just here, you ninny! I will always be here for you." He was barely three feet away from her.

She loved the imposing grey, soaring buildings in Edinburgh, with their secret closes in contrast to the rich red brick and pantiles of her home town. She relished the strange Scottish vocabulary and was very confused when Andrew's mother mentioned that she was off to do "the messages" – shopping – and asked her, "Where are you staying?"

"What on earth does she mean, Andrew? She knows that I am staying at the B&B down the road, because she won't have unmarried lovers in her home. She is just as old fashioned as Mum!" Andrew laughingly explained that his mum was asking her where she lived.

He never moved in with Mouse in the house she still shared with Pete and Tina but stayed overnight. It seemed a bit pointless him paying rent elsewhere because he spent so much time there, but he was adamant and old fashioned in his own way.

She was super vigilant about contraception and, if there was any doubt that her pill wasn't having its full effect, antibiotics, dodgy tummy, she would firmly decline any activity. Andrew thought she was an over-cautious fuss pot. She didn't dare tell him why. She would never tell him why. She had learnt that lesson.

Andrew took her completely by surprise when he asked her to marry him on a wild hilltop in the Highlands on one of their expeditions. She thought that he had gone down on one knee to get the sandwiches from his backpack but, instead, he ceremoniously removed his old bobble hat, presented her with a beautiful sapphire ring, the box tiny against his big padded gloves, and quoted a poem.

*Ithers seek they ken na what,*
*Features, carriage, and a' that;*
*Gie me love in her I court,*
*Love to love makes a' the sport.*

*Let love sparkle in her e'e;*
*Let her lo'e nae man but me;*
*That's the tocher-gude I prize,*
*There the luver's treasure lies.*

"What on earth was that all about?"

"It's Rabby Burns – will you do me the honour of becoming my wife?"

"Yes, oh yes. Thank you so much. I do love you."

She hugged him so tight that he complained he was being suffocated.

Her mother was at last able to put on the wedding she had wanted. She was thrilled by the kilts, the bagpipes and the reeling that the MacLellan's brought with them. Dad happily did as he was told, marched her down the aisle, gave a sweet little speech and paid for everything without a murmur.

Mum confided in Mouse, "I know I wasn't happy at the time when you changed your mind over David, but I am so glad that you waited. You were right, twenty-one was far too young. We like Andrew, such a clever chap. Twenty-five is perfect, plenty of time for babies before the biological clock stops."

*Babies. Oh yes, babies.*

# Mouse 10

**Who would have thought that she would be eating in the Polo Lounge on Sunset Boulevard on her thirtieth birthday?**

It seemed light years away from the days when a good meal out was the Chinese takeaway in Tunbridge Wells with her mates from school.

Andrew gave her a digital camera, gift wrapped, she could tell; Andrew was inept at wrapping anything. It was something that she appreciated about living in the States; gift wrapping was the rule rather than the question.

She immediately used the camera to take pictures as they tucked into their very fancy lunch, enjoying the novelty of being able to see them immediately. The waiter obliged by taking some photos of them together, raising their cocktails to the camera. He proved rather clumsy, obviously not used to this hot off the press technology.

They had settled cosily into their California ranch house in the Altadena Foothills. It had looked like a large garden shed to Mouse on the outside when she first saw it but inside it was all very modern, an open plan kitchen, dining room and a lounge with three bedrooms, for the children 'when they arrived', and two and a half bathrooms. Half a bathroom always made her want to giggle.

The property was equipped with air conditioning, every kitchen gadget you could dream up, a giant laundry room with an enormous top-loading washing machine and dryer and the fiercest showers that she had ever come across. The plasma TV that they acquired was enormous and there were hundreds of channels to choose from, although it was mostly rubbish.

The enclosed back yard wasn't much, just a sort of lawn with strange spiky grass, a few straggly trees and a brick barbecue, but with amazing views of the Altadena hills; 'loads of room for the kids to play'. They were close to miles of hiking trails, which was the main magnet for Andrew.

Andrew had transformed from Imperial College geek to LA celebrated super-scientist. The research that he had undertaken and had tried so hard to explain to them all as he watched the airplanes at Heathrow, had turned out to be a global breakthrough in the efficient use of power. She still didn't understand it. His new role at NASA was very exciting and he was obviously loving it, although slightly reticent about the adulation that was being heaped upon him. He was self-effacing and found it hard to embrace the American 'hey, look at me, I'm so great' attitude.

They escaped for weekends and long hikes through Yosemite, Death Valley and north of San Francisco to Point Reyes where they could breathe easily and relax together, recapturing their familiar carefree days in Scotland.

She discovered that she wasn't very good at playing the 'fawning wife of brilliant scientist' either. Everyone always commented on how 'British' they were and begged for them to 'say something' because it was 'so cute'. As she was English and he was definitely Scottish this made them chuckle.

Mouse deliberately retained her accent and her own style. It was difficult to find a hairdresser prepared to maintain her sharp haircut and she refused to do anything more with her nails than keep them neat, tidy and clean, and at a length that she considered sensible. She loathed the high heels that many colleagues wore, and the masks of make-up.

As Andrew's fame increased, they found themselves invited everywhere, to gala evenings and charity events. Everything seemed very engineered and over excited to Mouse. She was much more used to the restrained and moderate ways of the Home Counties.

They ate out most of the time, it seemed that everyone did. They met up with Andrew's work colleagues and acolytes, who were thrilled to be in the presence of such genius. He continued to be his normal, modest self, which they found incredibly refreshing. She was very proud of him.

She wasn't used to not using her brain, so thank heavens there was an IBM office in LA. Wasn't there one in every major city throughout the world? They were very helpful about getting her green card. She had excellent references from the London office, and she had settled into her own familiar world of computing, commuting into town on the freeways in her automatic car. All so very American.

The only fly in the ointment was the fact that, although she had stopped taking the pill before the wedding, nothing had happened. Her recalcitrant body stubbornly refused to produce the longed-for baby. There was a nagging thought that something must have happened all those years ago. Tina had already produced two boys. She was the proud godmother of Christian, the first.

*Perhaps David was right. A mortal sin never to be forgiven. God's way of punishing her.*

# Mouse 11

**She was sitting at a sumptuous table, laden with gleaming silverware, sparkling glasses and an outrageously ebullient centrepiece of gaudy flowers offset by the blindingly white linen tablecloth.**

On her left was Gray Davis, Democratic Governor of California. This privileged table position was because of his interest in limiting auto emissions, the relevance being Andrew's research into energy optimisation in engines. Gray and Andrew were having an excited conversation across her. She leant back as far as she could to keep out of their way.

The Millennium. Such an amazing time to reflect, to look back and look ahead. There was so much right in her world. Andrew was a fantastic husband, she had certainly chosen well, and their lifestyle was incredible.

*How different my life would have been if I had married David.*

Here she was in the Beverley Hills Hotel, dressed up to the nines in America's best evening wear, her gamine-styled hair tinted to cover those annoying little greys, and make-up done by the beautician after manicuring her nails. She somehow looked more American than the native population. She didn't feel like herself at all, but she didn't want to let Andrew down in such auspicious company.

*Good heavens, what a long way we have come.*

Life was so good. Andrew was being paid a fortune as they had taken up his technological miracles for the Space Shuttle programme.

*Wow. What a high achiever. Could life be better?*

She inadvertently sighed. Gray and Andrew glanced at her and she smiled and flapped her hands for them to carry on.

***Life would be better if I could have a bloody baby.***

# Mouse 12

**The pristine doctor in the spotless clinic looked her in the eye.**

"Well, Mrs MacLean…"

*Why can't Americans get it right? Surely it wasn't too difficult. I have been practicing your bloody name for hours before I came to this appointment so that I could get it right – Doctor Pietruskzevwicz. And another thing. Why did he have to be a Reproductive Infertility Specialist? Wouldn't it be more positive if he was a Fertility Specialist?*

"Everything seems just fine. Your ovarian reserve and ovary volume are great. The blood flow to your uterus, ovaries and follicles are perfect. There are no other contraindications, no ovarian cysts, uterine fibroids and polyps. I can't see any reason why you wouldn't be getting pregnant at all. But tell me…" A pause. "Have you ever been pregnant before? It's just that…"

"No, no…" Mouse interjected hastily. She knew she was blushing. He must have known she was lying. He was a doctor after all. He looked at her oddly, head on one side. Took a breath.

"It would be a good thing. It would mean that we know that you are able to conceive?" It came out as a question.

*I am not going to admit it now. I would look extremely stupid… and I promised.*

He sighed with obvious total disbelief and went on. "Loads of couples wait several years before they get pregnant, particularly when the mom has been on the contraceptive pill for so long. Go home, relax, don't get so wound up about it."

*Of course I am wound up. I am getting desperate. I am thirty-two. The biological clock is ticking faster and faster. I have diligently researched every single nuance of conception. I know exactly how, when and why, every hormone, every biological function… but not why I am not getting pregnant… is this my punishment?*

She couldn't stop the tears tumbling down her cheeks.

*Why do I always end up crying?*

"You have had a lot going on in your life over the last five years. Don't underestimate what a toll it all takes: moving out here to California, a long way from home, having to play hostess to your husband after publication of his breakthrough paper for NASA. Yes, I know who he is. Don't we all? And I bet he is away a helluva lot presenting his papers? Maybe at all the wrong times?"

"He is so worried that I can't conceive. He has always dreamt of having kids. He even says so in interviews, which makes me feel even more of a failure. Every time my period starts, he goes into a total decline."

"I know. It is hard to face this so publicly. It must be quite distressing."

Mouse flinched and cried even harder.

***Quite** distressing… it was agony!*

In her distraught state, she had forgotten the alternative use that Americans gave to 'quite'.

"Look, honey," he looked more kindly at her and handed her a box of Kleenex, "just go home to your husband, relax, enjoy each other's company. Play some tennis at the Country Club, go to the ocean, get a tan, go hiking. Just don't try so hard. Make love not babies. It is so typical of such an eminent scientist like your husband to make it out to be one great big scientific procedure. Take it easy. It will happen. I promise you."

She shivered at the word 'Promise'. It was on the tip of her tongue to tell him about the termination. Perhaps it had wrecked her womb and it was some dreadful consequence of it that was stopping her from getting pregnant now.

*Shall I tell him? I should... I know it is all my fault. It is karma.*

**Mouse thanked him politely and left. So bloody British.**

# Mouse 13

**1st February 2003. It could not have been a more public disaster.**

The Space Shuttle burning up on re-entry, killing every single one of the seven crew. Just devastating. Andrew tried to explain it to Mouse when he arrived home, his face grey and drooping with the strain. He headed straight for the cocktail cabinet and filled a tumbler with Jack Daniels. He could barely speak he was so distressed.

He slumped on the couch with a groan. Mouse perched in a chair opposite him and waited for him to speak.

He started falteringly. Mouse sat patiently with a cup of tea.

"I was right there. I was right there in the vestibule of the Mission Control Centre. It was going great. Not an inkling of anything wrong."

Mouse sipped at her tea and waited for him to go on.

"The monitor picked up some high readings on the left-hand wing. Nothing alarming. Even when pressure readings were lost on both left landing gear tyres, no-one thought too much of it; it wasn't that bad. There was just no clue what was about to happen. It just bloody disintegrated. Jesus Christ, poor buggers. I can only hope and pray that the crew wouldn't have had any idea what was going on." He paused, grimaced, sucked in through gritted teeth. "Poor Mike. Poor Sandy, what is she going to tell those wee girls? They are only nine and eleven. Do you think I should call her? I had lunch with him the day before they took off. We were discussing the Physics experiments that he was going to do. Fascinating stuff. I can't believe that he has gone, just vanished."

Andrew sighed deeply, screwed up his eyes and rolled his head. "It was crazy that it took the guys so long to realise that it had disintegrated." He mimed an explosion with his hands slopping the Jack Daniels on the rug.

"We were all cocooned in that room. It was just so ridiculous when it suddenly began dawning on each of us that something had gone so horribly wrong. It took minutes. Everyone was exchanging glances, started whispering. We couldn't see what was going on. It was only when LeRoy solemnly told us to lock the doors, no-one was allowed to enter or leave, that we knew for sure that it was real."

Andrew threw back his head and a weird sound came out halfway to a howl.

**"Jesus Christ, Elizabeth. What a fucking disaster."**

# Mouse 14

**Every single day for weeks the TV was full of reports about the Shuttle disaster.**

They even had footage of the spacecraft breaking up. It was horrible.

The whole Shuttle Programme came to a complete, abrupt stop. Everyone was picking at details of every aspect. Unless you were involved in the inquiry, all staff were surplus to requirements. There was nothing else that needed to be done.

Everyone and everything about the mission was gone through with a fine-tooth comb. They had interviewed Andrew, under oath, and kept asking Andrew to verify his calculations for the effects of his technology on the fuel load. Had too much fuel remaining for re-entry contributed to the explosive and shocking outcome? Andrew took it personally and felt that somehow they might be trying to pin it on him, the Brit, the alien.

He kept going over and over his theorems, terrified that he had missed a "delta tending to zero" or "epsilon tending to infinity". He wrote out his formulae again and again, hunched over, biro poised, tracking every step.

Andrew became obsessed with the difference between UK gallons and US gallons. Had he got his sums wrong? Was he in some way culpable?

"It is so easy to get a tiny thing wrong, and it is all just nonsense, Elizabeth. Supposing it was because of me?"

He dropped his head into his hands and scrubbed at his eyes.

Andrew's contract was up for renewal. It wasn't renewed. No explanation, no debrief. The only time that he had been invited into work was for the interviews.

Andrew hadn't attempted to find a new job.

"Who the fuck would want to touch anybody associated with Columbia?"

At home all day, he read and watched and gleaned everything that he could about the inquiry. It seemed to be all about the foam damaging the wing when the Shuttle had originally launched. It took weeks for them to come to this conclusion. Even so Andrew wasn't coping.

He was quiet and uncommunicative but jittery, waggling his leg up and down compulsively. He snapped at her if she enquired gently, "My darling, what is wrong? Please talk to me."

"Stop bugging me!" He was becoming more American than the Americans, except it sounded strange with a Scottish accent. "For fuck's sake, isn't it enough that Mike and the rest of the crew have been torn apart and littered across Texas? I have been disgraced, no job, nowhere to go, nothing to do and it seems I can't even have children."

*Ouch.*

# Mouse 15

**It had been months.**

They were okay financially because Mouse was earning good money and Andrew had been rewarded very well for his clever ideas in the past, and for his lecture tours. He had a string of published books that brought in respectable royalties.

They hadn't 'eaten out' in ages. Everyone they had ever met had stopped asking them. If she suggested that they dined together, dressed up, had some fun, *held their heads high in public*, he would just look at her witheringly.

He picked at the suppers that she religiously cooked for him. She heard him scraping the remains into the waste disposal unit, preferring instead to drink red Californian wine straight from the bottle with Jack Daniels chasers. He hadn't been on one of his famed hiking expeditions in Yosemite since February.

Any hopeful mention of sex, with a hint of babies, was met with a stone wall. "Oh, for heaven's sake, enough, please give it a rest." It was getting rather late to remain optimistic, but she was still only thirty-four.

*When did we last make love?*

He claimed to be too tired for sex, but she could hear him in the dark, restlessly tossing and turning, obviously not able to get to sleep. He seemed to have given up on the whole parenthood mission. He seemed to have given up on life.

She googled obsessively and concluded that he was clinically depressed. She tried to raise it with him, but he shouted at her, swore at her. She didn't know what to do. She was so far away from her friends and her family. Dad was too frail to make the long flight over and Mum wouldn't come without him.

Since the move to the States, she had lost touch with most friends, other than Christmas missives. Liz? Where was she these days? Nikki? All those other Elizabeths from school days? At least she was still in touch with Tina.

They had driven up the Coastal Route to San Francisco with Tina and Pete only two years ago. BC – Before Columbia. It had been a great road trip and they had all got on so well together, laughing at the eccentricities of Hearst Castle, nonchalantly pretending to be very knowledgeable as they sauntered around the art galleries of Carmel, carefully avoiding children as a topic of conversation.

It was great seeing old friends. They even played tennis for old time's sake. It had been fun but not the same as the old days. Tina and Pete's kids, four of them by now, were typically American and very demanding. Their life revolved round their children's needs. It hurt to see Andrew's longing glances at them.

Perhaps she could ring Tina. She at least knew her number. But then would she have to confess the whole thing? The whole problem of not having babies, her deception over all these years…

Andrew inevitably and finally fell apart.

"It is colloquially known as a nervous breakdown, Mrs MacLean," explained the doctor gently to her when she had called him in a total panic when Andrew wouldn't, or couldn't, get out of bed and lay there sobbing and saying that he wished he was dead. It had been heart wrenching. "What is the point of it all? What is the point of life?"

**Mouse mumbled to the doctor, "I think it is all my fault. I can't have a baby and he so desperately wants one."**

# Mouse 16

**It was very odd to be back in the Kent countryside after so long away.**

It was all so very old and quaint. The roads seemed so narrow and bendy. She had almost forgotten about hedgerows, roundabouts and zebra crossings.

It was strange to take a fresh look at a village that she had taken for granted all her life. The houses with their top halves hung with orange-red tiles, pantiles, with warm brick below were so charming and friendly. Coggers Hall, that she had walked by, completely oblivious, on countless occasions, was a truly remarkable black and white, beautiful, ancient building, perched precariously on the edge of the river. It was centuries older than the United States.

It had definitely changed since she and Andrew had been away. Lamberhurst and its newly defined Conservation Area status, had finally acquired the bypass they had been promising it for years. The steep school hill, no longer harangued by streams of cars heading for the coast, was tranquil and utterly charming.

They took the right fork in Lamberhurst, climbed the steep hill, Mouse remarking out loud, "The Horse and Groom pub is a house now." Andrew drove on without replying and they traversed the Down, the wide-open green space where she had been to so many Bonfire Night parties as a child. She pointed out to Andrew where Maggie Thatcher used to live. He showed no interest.

They crossed the Kent and Sussex border and followed the road between hazel woods and then farmland tucked behind hedges. The hop gardens, with their distinctive rows of telegraph poles and spider's web of wire, had all vanished. The oast houses, with their strange dunce cap cowls on top of their round towers, were no longer used to roast the hops and all seemed to have been turned into bijou residences.

*The end of an era. The start of a new one.*

Mum, who seemed to know everybody, had heard of a part-time science teaching post at Tunbridge Wells Grammar School. It was a perfect job for Andrew, not too demanding but making use of his remarkable brain, and he would be a natural teacher. No-one round here would associate him with NASA, Columbia, or his momentous breakdown. They were all far too parochial.

They were renting an adorable cottage in Cousley Wood with a weatherboard face and tiny windows. It was totally antiquated after their ranch house in LA, and Mouse wondered what it would be like in the winter, with no proper heating, and the summer, with no air conditioning; if it were to ever get that hot, which was very doubtful in England.

She realised that she had become so accustomed to every modern convenience so easily available: the take outs, eating out, valet parking, the super-efficient medical system that treated you like a discerning customer.

*This is going to take some getting used to.*

The nearest decent supermarket was in Tunbridge Wells, perhaps for a bit of nostalgia she could go into town on the number 80 bus if it still runs. The only proper shopping mall of any note was the Bluewater Shopping

Centre at Rotherhithe, miles away in English terms, particularly driving a stick-shift car. She would just have to go and buy her meat at the local butchers, buy veg at the greengrocers and her bread at the bakers – if any of those existed any more.

*Yes, it is good to be back in England. A simpler life, more peaceful and gentle. A chance for Andrew to recover and get back to his old self. Fingers crossed.*

# Mouse 17

**In LA she had always been the wife of the eminent Doctor MacLellan**.

Always invited to the Country Club, encouraged to attend 'benefits' and at everyone's homes having bridge lunches, cocktails or a barbecue around the pool. At work she had been respected and given accolades in her own right for her diligence and hard work but, first and foremost, she was Doctor MacLellan's wife.

After being so busy and in demand, it was just so quiet around here – she didn't know what to do with herself. She didn't want to commute to London and take on a full-time job; she was too worried about being too far from Andrew. It was difficult to know where to begin in finding a life worth living and, worst of all, round here they played a weird system of bridge that she just did not get. She'd found herself a little job.

*To be honest, Mum has found me a job. Good old, Mum. She really does know everybody.*

The National Trust were opening the house at the centre of the Scotney Castle estate to the public. It was a beautiful house built from sandstone quarried in the grounds. All very local. She had visited the gardens as a child and had always been intrigued by the main building itself, which was made more mysterious by the fact that no-one was allowed inside.

Mum was a faithful National Trust member, knew the woman who was heading up the new team, and had heard all about it before it was general knowledge. Mouse had offered her services before anything official had been put in place and wangled her way in.

All that proposal writing at IBM had paid off and she worked part time in the office writing press releases, articles for the *Kent and Sussex Courier*, and material to be used on the websites. It wasn't much, paid peanuts, but she enjoyed it despite her mother's friend turning out to be a sanctimonious prig. "Call me Charmian," she had condescendingly allowed.

*As if I was going to call you Mrs Keswick in this day and age.*

It got her out of the house, she met some local people, other than Charmian, who were friendly, and she felt that she could have a laugh with in the office. It was always so quiet and sombre at home. She was always treading on egg shells.

*When did I last hear Andrew laugh? He used to all the time.*

Mouse had thought too that, by being part of the National Trust, she could encourage Andrew to take up hiking again. Her suggestions of weekends away at any manner of places described with great enthusiasm on her part were met with blank eyes.

She was asked to prepare an educational pack to encourage schools to visit and create a trail around the intriguing parts of the house. There was plenty to discover, priest holes and secret doors and a strange and eclectic mix of furniture and paintings. She innocently asked Charmian what age group they were targeting and what format was intended. They seemed perfectly valid businesslike questions.

"I think you may be worrying about this too much. I have tried to ignore the fact that you haven't had children yourself and thought that, with a bit of imagination, you would cope."

*Fuck you, Charmian.*

Sometimes the expletives that she had learned to use so freely in America were perfect.

It is difficult to make friends when you have no children. It is hard to find people to meet in the first place and then tricky to find things in common. Mouse was always happy to ask everybody about all their husbands and their kids, but she could sense the awkwardness when they didn't know what to ask in return.

Mouse was delighted to bump into an old friend, Charlotte, from school that she hadn't seen for years and years and they arranged to meet for coffee, to reminisce and have a gossip at the café at The Vineyard on the Down. It had become a major attraction, a bit Disneyfied in contrast to the Haselden's rather charming, old-fashioned mixed farm that Mouse had remembered from her youth.

All the customary enquiries had to be answered in turn. "Where do you live?", "What are you doing these days?", "Are you married?", "How many children do you have?"

Mouse wanted to change the subject quickly after baldly answering the last question, "None. Sadly. It wasn't to be." But Charlotte got in first. "Do you remember when we all went to that Halloween Disco and stayed at Liz's?"

*Ouch. How do people manage to punch me in the stomach and wind me with a simple question?*

Fixed smile back on her face, Mouse was able to reply in a jolly tone, "Oh, yes. That was the time that Liz told us that our lives would be mapped out by who we married. I think that has turned out to be true, don't you?"

"Definitely. You **are** married to Doctor MacLellan, aren't you?" Charlotte said it in a strange tone, with an odd emphasis.

"Yes, I am. Why… Is there…?"

"Oh, don't worry. It's nothing. You know what kids are like."

*I don't actually.*

Charlotte realised her mistake, blushed and looked embarrassed. Mouse prompted her, "No. What is it?"

"I shouldn't even have started this, please forget it. Another cuppa or a slice of that yummy cake?"

"No. No, thank you." Mouse hesitated. "Actually, Charlotte, I can't forget it. I am sorry to be pushy but..." Her learned American assertiveness was evident. She waited for Charlotte to reply. She did eventually, hesitantly.

"It is just that people have been saying... you know how they make something out of nothing..." Mouse nodded and stared, waiting for Charlotte to continue, and it all suddenly poured out in a rush.

"Doctor MacLellan has been seen giving a great deal of attention to one of the sixth form girls, Francesca Arbuthnott. My daughter is in the same year. They have been spotted on the number 80 bus together, quite openly... chatting and laughing... Perhaps they don't realise that they have been seen. I am sure it is nothing, probably very innocent... Perhaps you should have a word with him so that he realises that something perfectly harmless is being viewed with a bit of... you know... suspicion."

The first thing Mouse thought was ridiculous and totally inappropriate.

*How amazing that the number 80 bus still trundles its way through the villages after all this time.*

The second was very sad.

**Chatting and laughing? I can't remember the last time I chatted and laughed with Andrew. I can't remember the last time I saw him smile.**

# Mouse 18

**"Andrew?"**

"Yes…" He was rummaging around in his papers that he insisted on storing in neat piles on the dining room table and not paying attention to Mouse at all. "Have you seen my passport? I need it for identification for my CRB renewal and for the forms for the school trip."

"Andrew?"

"Yes, yes, I am listening."

"Francesca Arbuthnott?"

"Mm. Francesca, yes a lovely wee lass. Very bright. With a bit of help she should go far."

*That doesn't seem to sound like anything untoward. I won't be seeing gossipy Charlotte again in a hurry. He ought to know what people are saying behind his back. It's only fair.*

"People have mentioned…"

"Oh, for heaven's sake. Not you as well. What is it with everybody? I suppose people have commented about us on the bus. Why is everyone so obsessed? I suppose you are going to give me a lecture too, are you?"

Andrew seemed overly riled. Mouse stared in trepidation.

"From now on, I will just have to bloody cycle to school. That should shut everybody up."

Mouse waited. No further explanation seemed to be forthcoming.

**"Now have you seen my bloody passport or not?"**

# Mouse 19

*Andrew's late. It isn't like him to be this late.*

Mouse worried about him on his bike. He wasn't very experienced. It could even be said he was somewhat unstable, having always stomped along on his own two legs rather than using two wheels. For his safety, she had tried to get him to wear bright clothing, but he insisted on using his old navy cagoule and had somehow resurrected his old black bobble hat. He had been wearing it when he proposed all those years ago. She couldn't believe that he still had it. He looked a right old scruff.

She looked at the clock again. Seven o'clock. She had cooked lasagne for supper, his favourite. She would never stop trying in her endless endeavours to please him, to make him better, and was keeping it warm.

*He is always home by six thirty. Like clockwork. I wonder where he has got to.*

She phoned him but it went straight to the answerphone. She sat and fretted. She phoned him again and again, but it continued to go straight to the answerphone. He didn't come home.

At nine o'clock she was worried and thinking the most horrible thoughts. She phoned him again.

*Has he been more depressed recently? Have I missed something? Please God, make sure that he's okay.*

She decided to go looking for him, thoroughly, retrace his possible routes to and from school, casually look in all the pubs to see if he was there.

*But what if he comes home while I am out?*

She scribbled a note, grabbed her car keys and dashed out.

First stop was The Balaclava, only a footstep away from home but they had never actually used it. They wouldn't know him from Adam. She tried to look nonchalant as she frantically cast her eyes at every person in the sparsely populated pub while her heart raced. Old men clutching half pints stared back at her blankly. It was quiet for a Friday. Fear gave her the courage to ask the woman mopping down the bar if she had seen Andrew, but her description was a bit vague, she knew that. His moustache was his most distinguishing feature.

"No-one like that, ducks."

She checked out the Old Vine. She drove the short distance to the Old Vine, double parked, it was busy, and pushed her way in. She searched right through the cosy bar, checking carefully that he wasn't hidden in the inglenook fireplace and stared at everyone closely in the restaurant.

*They must think I am mad.*

She left trying to look nonchalant – and sane. Should she go even further afield, all the way to Lamberhurst? He would have no reason to go that far out of his way.

Very slowly, she drove to Tunbridge Wells, down Monk's Lane, Bartley Mill Road, Bayham Road through to Bells Yew Green. Her head swung constantly from right to left; it made her feel dizzy. She went extra slowly past any fields and hedges, searching, searching. She strained to see with the inadequate light of the headlamps.

On the outskirts of Tunbridge Wells, it was suddenly all built up and she crawled along Forest Road, her hands gripping the wheel, her nose pressed to the windscreen, looking about under the light of the street lights. She arrived right up at the locked gates of the school and tried to peer in. There was no-one to be seen. It was dead quiet.

She traced the same journey back, even more slowly, looking for anything at all, although she wasn't entirely sure what she was looking for. Her jaw ached from gritting her teeth.

She reached home, she had been out for ages, and scanned the garden for Andrew's bicycle and raced inside to see if he had returned. He hadn't. Her note glared at her from the table.

At ten thirty her hand hovered over the telephone.

*How do I find out if he has been in an accident? How long does someone have to be gone before I can report them missing? He'll be livid if he comes home and finds that I have reported him to the police.*

At eleven o'clock, she dialled 999 and hoped that she wouldn't look stupid if he walked in through the door announcing that he had decided to have a session at some other pub that she hadn't thought of.

Mouse found herself gabbling and unable to put her thoughts in order, but the call handler was very composed and professional and eventually nursed Mouse through to get the gist of her call. She explained calmly to Mouse that she had a list of questions that she needed to ask and that they would be used to assess the situation.

*It suddenly felt so real. Oh Jesus, where is he?*

Name, age, description was easy. Description of clothing was harder.

*What was he wearing? I don't notice; it is such an everyday thing, just chucking on your clothes to go to work.*

"I'm so sorry, I really am, but I need to check what is not in his wardrobe." She was panicking again. "He will definitely be wearing his navy cagoule and his bobble hat. He always wears them."

*He wouldn't be wearing his scruffy cagoule and bobble hat if he was somewhere respectable. Oh God, she must think I'm a terrible wife to not even know what my husband is wearing.*

She gave their address and added, "Yes, yes, of course, this is where he is missing from. I'm his wife. We live here… together."

The operator asked about the "circumstances of his going missing".

*What on earth does that mean?*

She tried her best. "He just hasn't come home and he is always home by now. His phone is saying that it is switched off and is going straight to answerphone. I can't check with school, where he works, because it is closed."

*Oh God, am I over-reacting. That sounds so lame.*

The list of questions seemed endless and started to get personal: medication, any reason to think why he might have disappeared, marital difficulties, any known risks, locations where he might have gone, people he might be in contact with.

Mouse answered them cautiously. She felt disloyal even mentioning his depression in the past and tried to play it down, he wasn't even taking medication these days – he had fastidiously weaned himself off anti-depressants. She wasn't sure whether she should get into the whole not having children thing. Surely it wasn't relevant?

At the back of her mind was a horrible little nagging thought. The girl at school. Wasn't that all just a silly rumour. She needn't say anything yet. The operator had come to the end of her questions and reassured Mouse that most people reported missing turned up within forty-eight hours.

A police officer called back and said that they would come round in the morning, more questions in more detail, just to be sure. If he were to turn up in the meantime, which they thought highly likely, then please contact them.

It was so late. It was past midnight.

**How was she going to sleep not knowing where Andrew was?**

# Mouse 20

**She awoke curled up on the sofa, stiff and freezing cold, all the lights still on.**

No Andrew. She felt awful, hungover, even though she hadn't had a drop to drink. She made coffee and turned the oven off. She had completely forgotten about the lasagne. It was burned to charcoal.

She sat there waiting for the police to come.

*When are they coming?*

She fidgeted and walked around the cottage, not knowing what she was doing. At a respectable hour, she phoned Mum.

"Of course he isn't here. Why on earth did you ring the police, darling? You will look so daft when he walks in through the door with a perfectly sensible explanation."

She could hear Dad in the background. Obviously his ears had pricked up at the word police.

"Shush, dear. Not you, Elizabeth. Can't you stop them? What are people going to say when they see the police turning up at your door?"

*Am I being daft?*

She went and had a look through all his things on the dining room table. Was there anything there that could shed any light on where he had gone? She noted that he had taken his laptop with him and his phone. He always did. Nothing unusual.

She looked in the garden shed. She couldn't think why but she had to check everywhere for clues.

She returned inside, went upstairs and, feeling a bit guilty, rummaged through all his clothes. She felt awful, feeling the backs of the drawers for something. Again, she didn't know what she was actually looking for. She carefully tidied everything so that he didn't think she was being nosey.

She had started going through all the kitchen cupboards when the police arrived.

The first question that they asked was, "Why was she worried?"

Why **was** she so worried? She was finding it difficult to put over just how worried she was and her real fear. She could barely acknowledge it to herself, but she knew that her first thought, second thought and last thought had been suicide.

She answered all their questions, trying to put this across subtly, but they weren't getting the message. She started telling them hesitantly about Andrew's breakdown. She was enormously embarrassed to be divulging such personal information and knew that Andrew would be too.

*But he hasn't left a note. He must be okay.*

"Does he pose a danger to other people?"

"Absolutely not!"

*A least they seem more interested now. Shouldn't they be out there looking for him?*

"Could he be intending to travel abroad?"

"No. Not until next month and that is with the school."

*But he does have his passport with him at school ready for the school trip.*

"What phone does he have, and does he have it with him?"

"Yes. I have tried to phone it, but it must be switched off because it goes straight to the answering machine. Look, here is the number… it's a Blackberry Curve."

"Model?"

"I'm not sure. Andrew is the one who is into his gadgets. Typical geeky scientist."

"When did he get it?"

"Does it matter?"

*Shouldn't you be out there looking for him? He has been missing for more than twelve hours. He didn't leave a note.*

"If it is the right model, we can find out where he last used it using GPS."

Suddenly excited for the first time, Mouse went and scrabbled around in Andrew's paperwork, making it untidy.

*I can tidy it up later, before he gets back and sees it.*

She returned triumphantly bearing the original box.

"A Blackberry Curve 8320."

"Oh." They were obviously disappointed. "Sorry, no GPS."

*Damn, damn, damn.*

"Is there any other information relevant to his absence?"

"No."

*But should I mention the girl?*

"It may be nothing, in fact I am sure that it is, but there have been rumours... gossip... about a girl... a girl at school..." She felt sick. "Her name is Francesca. I can't remember her surname, I am too upset... if I remember... but I am sure that they will be able to tell you when you speak to the school."

Their ears pricked up and they exchanged glances. Mouse suddenly wished she hadn't said anything.

*What will they think? Oh, Andrew, I am so sorry. Have I made you look like a predatory beast? It is all my fault. If only I could have given you your own daughter to cherish. How different things might have been.*

The police had a cursory look through all Andrew's things that were piled neatly across the dining room table, carefully noted the message that Mouse had left for him last night.

She showed them round the cottage, but they looked so enormous as they clambered up the stairs, their thick coats brushing against the paintwork on either side. She showed them their bedroom; the two spare rooms, one more of a storage dump; the bathroom. There wasn't anywhere else that he might be hiding. They searched through the cupboards and the drawers in their bedroom, but there wasn't anything to see. They took the opportunity to take his toothbrush, for DNA apparently. It sent shivers down her spine.

They left with the toothbrush, a photo, not a particularly good one but the only one that she could find that was printed, and a list of friends, relatives, people that they knew in England, Scotland and the US. Their next mission was to contact someone from school. They seemed rather eager to get on to that.

*Should I have said anything about the girl?*

As they left they reiterated that they were sure he would turn up.

She had better phone Tina before the police did. At least she would listen and not dismiss her fears like Mum had done. She was too far away to do anything, but she was good at listening.

It will make me feel better.

**Where are you Andrew? Come home.**

# Mouse 21

**It was Friday.**

The statutory forty-eight hours had passed. Andrew could now be registered as an official Missing Person on the national database. The police seemed surprised that he hadn't turned up.

Mouse was no less frantic than on Wednesday when Andrew had apparently vanished off the face of the earth. The police reported that they were following up with their enquiries, quite the most meaningless statement, and would keep her informed.

She had gathered that the suspicious Francesca Arbuthnott was at home and denied having anything to do with his disappearance. She would say that, wouldn't she? What about her parents? Could they have found out? It seemed very suspicious.

*Why aren't they telling me? Where is he? Why aren't they out there searching for him?*

Feeling helpless, she decided to recreate the list of all the people that they knew that she had given to the police and thought of a few more. She methodically looked up phone numbers for them all and started working her way down the list. It was excruciatingly embarrassing and increasingly hopeless.

She felt so frustrated. She decided to have another look around in daylight. She put the same note in a prominent place and cruised the route into school and out again. She went down each and every one of the back lanes that he might have decided to use instead of the usual route. There were so many of them threaded through the fields and woods. It was all so unlikely and if he had… well, he would be hidden away somewhere probably. But she had to do something.

*But he didn't leave a note. He would have left a note.*
Nothing. Nothing at all.

**I wonder if Tina will mind if I phone again.**

# Mouse 22

**Mouse felt worse than she had ever felt before.**

The whole thing of not being able to have children was an awful, hurtful obsession, but this was so much harder. It was the not knowing. The wondering. Going over and over every word said that day, that week, that month.

*What have I missed?*

Every noise made her jump, every slowing car, every speeding car, hearing someone call out. The doorbell made her jangle with paroxysms of terror. The telephone ringing made her leap out of her seat. It might be him.

She pounced on the postman. Perhaps there might be a letter from him?

Andrew had tried to explain to her what it felt like to be clinically depressed, being on constant alert, the surges of adrenalin at the very least thing, the paranoia, the unremitting fear of something nameless. She understood it now but was it too late?

Everywhere she went, when she ventured out at all, she constantly scanned faces. If she saw a blue cagoule, a black bobble hat, ruffled hair of just the same style, a glimpse of a moustache, she would run to catch up. Just in case.

*Oh, Andrew. Where are you?*

It was her fortieth birthday. She couldn't face anyone – not even her sister or parents. She was so alone. She couldn't bear to get out of bed. She trailed down to the kitchen, made herself a coffee and returned to curl up in a lonely ball. She wasn't hungry. She hadn't felt hungry since Andrew disappeared. The weight was dropping off her.

Mum rang and tried to persuade her to go over to them.

*I can't leave here. It's my birthday, perhaps he will come home today.*

Tina rang her to wish her a happy birthday. Such a good and loyal well-wisher. She let it go to the answerphone; she couldn't even face talking to her old friend.

**Andrew? Oh, Andrew.**

# Mouse 23

**Six weeks had passed**.

Mouse had run out of things to do to find Andrew.

The police had searched in the most obvious places, but a trawl of local waterways and the Bewl Bridge Reservoir had drawn a blank and, in all probability, cost an inordinate amount of money better spent trying to find the living. They were better equipped to find him than she could ever be and it seemed fruitless to keep looking along clearly empty roads and back lanes. It didn't stop her trying, combing every section for clues.

She had tried to get the *Kent and Sussex Courier* interested, but his story didn't catch their imagination. He wasn't a local hero, they didn't 'do' science, the association with Columbia was a red light and he had mental health problems. She hadn't dared mention Francesca Arbuthnott in case it was considered defamatory; they would have jumped on something salacious like that, but the girl must know something, surely. Or her parents.

Any newspaper stories had been confined to a few paragraphs in the middle of the paper hidden between coffee mornings and school OFSTED reports. There was never anything new, just a reiteration of his name, the fact that he spoke in a Scottish accent, a description that could be anyone at all with a moustache and the clothing he was last wearing: a tweed jacket, corduroys, a knitted tie, the navy cagoule and the scruffy bobble hat. They published his picture at first but only when they needed to fill the space. She had cut out any references and put them in a thin, essentially empty folder.

The story made the nationals as a miniscule paragraph. Apparently, it wasn't very hot news because hundreds of people went missing all the time and more of them were vulnerable young people not old fogeyish scientists. In any case, most turned up before they had even published the story.

The people that she spoke to at NASA were slightly more interested than people in Kent but realistically unable to do anything other than offer commiseration. They were so far away and Americans didn't like to be associated with the delicacies of mental health. You could hear in their voices what they were thinking.

*But he didn't leave a note. He would have left a note.*

She had phoned everyone she knew, even people that she didn't know but might know him. She had phoned them all again and received the distinct impression that, although very sympathetic, they wished she wouldn't call again.

She had leaflets printed and distributed them to everywhere she could think of, around all the local towns and villages. Their remains fluttered from lampposts, many torn down.

She had stood at the closest stations, handing out leaflets to embarrassed-looking commuters who wouldn't meet her eye. The ones in Wadhurst, their nearest station, knew who she was and she parted the stream of hurrying figures like Moses parted the Red Sea.

She had gone up to London on the train for three days on the trot, handing out leaflets at all their old haunts. She thought she would freeze to death in the wind tunnel of Exhibition Road as students at Imperial College took leaflets off her. Frustratingly, she could see them take a cursory look and chuck them away as soon as they had gone a few yards.

Andrew was an only child of only children, so it was difficult to find any relations, any threads to follow up. It was a relief in a way that his mum was dead; she would have been horrified by their dear son's negligent wife who appeared to have 'mislaid him'.

In desperation, she had spent a weekend in Edinburgh and handed out flyers on Princes Street and The Royal Mile, just in case, not knowing where else she could reach people that might have known Andrew in Scotland. She stayed in a chilly B&B. The owner didn't believe in wasting money on heating.

Everyone seemed to jump to the conclusion that it must be just a straightforward case of a depressed man taking his own life. It made it worse because truthfully, realistically, she had come to the same inevitable conclusion. She knew that the police thought that. She didn't want to believe it.

*If that was the case, we would find his body. Why would he have hidden himself? Where could he have hidden? And he would have left a note.*

Her mother most certainly did. "For heaven's sake, darling. Pull yourself together. You just have to accept reality. Go back to work. Charmian won't keep your job open forever."

Her frenzied campaign had been an utter failure in all respects and it had proved impossible to get anything going on the back of Andrew's previous eminence and short-lived worldwide fame. The only individuals who held out any hope to her were the lovely volunteers at the Missing People charity. She found herself going along with their theories, almost believing that he could be out there somewhere, alive, but only because she didn't want to dash their optimism.

**Andrew, where are you? I do love you. I am so sorry that I couldn't give you babies. Perhaps you should have married someone who could.**

# Mouse 24

**Mouse couldn't believe it.**

Nearly four years had passed. The ache, the longing to know what happened to Andrew still ate at her very being every day. She tried to imagine what it would have been like if they had had their two point four children and were living like a normal loving family. *Would he still be here?*

*Will it ever get better?*

Dad had died and Mum had moved two years ago, settling into Susie's granny annexe. It was indeed a granny annexe, as Susie had so conveniently provided her mother with the yearned for grandchildren. She had married well and happily and had become a happy housewife with chickens in the garden and fat ponies for the children in the paddock behind their home.

*Well done, Susie. At least one of us has managed to do the right thing, marry the right person and live the right sort of life.*

It was ironic that Mum had then died so shortly afterwards. In a way, it was a blessing. A stroke is a nasty thing and robs you of your dignity as well as your ability to control your body. Susie was not very happy coping with adult nappies.

*I shouldn't think that Mum was too chuffed either. So horribly undignified.*

It was odd to be in the crematorium in a strange town far from home. None of Mum's old friends had bothered to make the trek. It was a long way. It was horribly impersonal.

Mouse stood beside Susie and realised that she didn't know her anymore. Susie had never bothered to come out and visit them for all the years that they were in the States. "Andrew is so important these days, I would bore him to death, just a happy housewife and mum. What would we talk about? I only ever talk about the children and I can't do that can I?"

*Ouch.*

She had sometimes come down to Kent but had always come to see her at Mum and Dad's – and then for only a short, cursory visit. Susie found Andrew's breakdown embarrassing and "didn't like to intrude" and when he went missing she seemed to be totally detached and didn't know what to do or what to say. Susie seemed more uncomfortable than sympathetic that Andrew had gone missing and had seemingly run out of things to say. She had thought it "Better to leave it to Mum being 'on the ground' so to speak."

Mouse was amazed at Mum's funeral when Susie confessed that she had always been jealous of Mouse and Mum's relationship. "Mum and you were always so close. It was as if you had a big secret. I always felt shut out."

*If only you knew. Oh, Mum, you took our secret to the grave. I will too.*

Mum's house, their childhood home in Lamberhurst, was sold when she had moved to Susie's. Mouse definitely didn't want to move into it. She had to stay where she was, just in case. Supposing Andrew came home and she wasn't there, some stranger opening the door to him.

*I can't let that happen.*

She was glad of the cash that they received for it as without Andrew she would have struggled to pay the rent and the bills on her trivial little job. Fortunately, they had a joint bank account so she could at least access their funds.

*Imagine if we hadn't? I would be left in limbo.*

She knew from Missing People that many were.

For heaven's sake, she was not even forty-four but she felt like an old, reclusive, obsessed woman. She had even adopted a mad, fluffy dog of indeterminate parentage. She decided to call him William. Echoes of the schoolgirl joke years ago, and the final acceptance that the promise of a child had now gone. In any case, her periods were becoming more and more erratic these days, so her potential childbearing years were clearly over.

William cheered her up, gave her a reason to live. He was cute but a bit of a handful and had her eating out of his paw. He was oblivious to anything other than where the next meal and cuddle were going to come from. She actually found herself eating a bit more because she couldn't resist sharing her lunch with him. He was more than a bit chubby as a result, she was less of a skeleton and more a twig. She chatted to him as if he were a child. The child she had never had. He slept on her bed.

*For God's sake, don't tell Mum how much I spoil him – she will have a fit.*

She often forgot that her mum was dead. She never forgot that Andrew was missing.

Taking William for long walks around Bewl Bridge Reservoir made them both happy. She let him wander off into the woods.

*Who knows, perhaps he might sniff out Andrew's remains.*

William also provided the perfect excuse not to go anywhere for more than a few hours.

Tina had nagged her about meeting her halfway and flying to New York, promising shows on Broadway, shopping in Macy's, climbing the Statue of Liberty, paying their respects at Ground Zero. She had resisted. She couldn't be away just in case.

*Is he out there somewhere, lost and unhappy, mourning for the children I couldn't give him? If only… or is he like all those poor souls at the World Trade Centre? Is he permanently lost?*

***He must be dead… but there was no note.***

# Mouse 25

**The police were at Mouse's door.**

They hadn't been in touch in years. She had stopped pestering them, or that is how it felt, after several years of absolutely nothing. Mouse was surprised by the way her skin prickled and all the old feelings of fear welled up.

William barked at them suspiciously and jumped at one of them leaving dog hair and a bit of mud on his immaculately clean uniform. He stared straight ahead, totally ignoring it.

"Mrs MacLellan?"

"Yes?" She had never seen these particular policemen before.

"Good afternoon. I am Detective Inspector Fuggle." The plain clothed man stated, thrusting a warrant card at them, although it was rather obvious that they were real policemen. "This is PC Thompson and this is PC Stemp. I wonder if we could come in for a moment."

She didn't recognise their names but waved them into the lounge. There wasn't enough room in the hall for all of them.

"We are here to let you know that there has been a development in the case of your missing husband. A Doctor Andrew Angus MacLellan."

"What?"

*After all this time?*

Mouse went rigid.

*What? They have found him? Where is he? Why isn't he here? Missing People warned me that he might not want to come back. He's alive. Thank God.*

"As part of another investigation, we have found items that we believe may belong to your husband…"

*Items? What can they mean items? Just items?*

Her hot eagerness burst and drained away leaving her cold. "Where? When…?"

"Last night we had reports of a woman who had been involved in a collision with a vehicle. On attendance at the scene, we discovered items not associated with the victim and obviously from some time ago. Do you know Sweetings Lane?"

"No. Where is it?"

"Just over half a mile from here, a back lane, in the direction of Lamberhurst."

"I didn't look there. I should have looked there. I only looked between Tunbridge Wells, the school, and home. Oh God, why didn't I look further afield? He was only half a mile away all that time." She started sobbing hysterically. "Have you found him? You should have searched the lanes. Poor Andrew… we made all sorts of assumptions…"

But they had only found a bicycle, bent and buckled, and a rucksack… not Andrew himself. Mouse collapsed in agony at the thoughts that swept over her.

*Oh my God, he is dead. All this time.*

She found herself guided to an armchair and handed a glass of water. As if that could make any difference.

*His bike had been totally buckled. How had it become buckled? Was it deliberately hidden? Where was Andrew?*

Once she had calmed down sufficiently, the police politely explained that they would be looking further afield tomorrow for any other 'evidence'. The implication made a wave of sickness rush through her. She staggered to her feet, her head swimming.

They advised her not to tell anyone about their suspicions and not to jump to any conclusions until the items had been fully examined and a further search made.

*How can I not?*

**As soon as they had left, she phoned Tina.**

# Mouse 26

**They came back again the next day.**

They had carefully examined the items that they had found, listing them as his laptop, his phone, a package containing an iPad with a receipt from the day it was purchased with *This is Francesca Arbuthnott's. Please give it to her.*

*What is that all about? She is the girl...*

It was scribbled in biro, definitely in Andrew's writing, she could see that. It was all perfectly preserved, as if it had only been placed there the previous day, all wrapped in plastic bags.

There was also a note, not a note exactly, actually a poem. They handed it to her in a plastic folder. It was definitely his handwriting too.

> *But Mousie, thou are no thy-lane,*
> *In proving foresight may be vain:*
> *The best laid schemes o' Mice an' Men,*
> *Gang aft agley,*
> *An' lea'e us nought but grief an' pain,*
> *Still, thou art blest, compar'd wi' me!*
> *The present only toucheth thee:*
> *But Och! I backward cast my e'e,*
> *On prospects drear!*
> *An' forward, tho' I canna see,*
> *I guess an' fear!*

It made her skin crawl.

"Do you know what it means?"

"It's a poem by Robert Burns. It is about a mouse that he steps on. My dad called me Mouse. Andrew thought it was cute, so he did too. He was always quoting Robert Burns – he was Scottish. Andrew, I mean – and Robert Burns too."

She knew she wasn't making a lot of sense.

*Was this his suicide note? I don't understand what it means. But no-one mangles their own bike, staggers over to another part of the rubbish dump and commits suicide. Or do they? Was it something to do with that girl, Francesca Arbuthnott? Why did he leave her that iPad?*

"There may be some other help that you can give us."

She nodded. Detective Inspector Fuggle hesitated.

"The woman injured in the collision was a Mrs Arbuthnott. Do you know Elizabeth Arbuthnott?"

Mouse was shocked and baffled. Was it an appalling coincidence or was it of relevance that Francesca's mum had been found with his stuff? With a note to Francesca?

"No. No, I have never met her, ever." It seemed important to make this absolutely clear.

*What the fuck is going on?*

She shuddered. She had surmised that the poor woman was in a very bad way, although everyone was very cagey about telling anyone anything it seemed. Gossip was rife. Her family were keeping a twenty-four-hour vigil at the hospital. Mouse's instinct was to keep well away although she had so many questions. She took William for a very long walk right round the reservoir. He was exhausted by the time they returned.

**So was she, physically and mentally.**

# Mouse 27

**They had searched everywhere, apparently, and very thoroughly, but had found nothing more.**

They hadn't found his body.

*Were they looking in the right place? They'd been totally wrong before.*

All the forensics tied together with the statements given when he disappeared. Phone records were consistent on his retrieved phone. The story given by Francesca of Andrew buying an iPad for her mum's birthday turned out to be the truth. There it was. Unopened. Unused. All those years of judging the girl, the rumours, the gossip, the ostracising.

*I wonder if everyone else feels as guilty as I do.*

It gave her a very clear picture of his last movements but what had happened next? Her intense, continuous need to know where he was that had plagued her for the last five years had stirred up again. Tantalising clues but no nearer the truth of his disappearance.

She knew she should be satisfied that the perpetrator had been tracked down, arrested, and held on remand for killing Elizabeth Arbuthnott, and for so cowardly and callously dumping her mortally injured body right on top of Andrew's belongings, but were they connected?

Elizabeth Arbuthnott's inquest had been held. It was absolutely clear what had happened in her case. There were specks of paint on her clothes, and they had been able to test them so thoroughly that they could give the make and year of the vehicle. Tiny fragments of glass and debris on the lane were also embedded in her clothes and her hair.

The accused's phone had been tracked to the exact spot in Sweetings Lane.

His battered old Volvo had been mended after 'hitting a deer' and the garage where he had had it mended had been tracked down and had recorded conclusive damage not only to the front of the vehicle but the roof too, and 'fibres' from her horse were found on the discarded parts that had been replaced.

He had been spotted in the off licence in Wadhurst High Street where he had bought cheap vodka. The lady behind the counter knew him well, he was a regular customer. She remembered exactly what he was wearing because he had had a smear of egg down the front of his navy-blue cashmere jersey and his striped shirt was untucked from his red corduroy trousers. "I thought to myself, what has become of him? So sad to see him come to this. I've known him since he was a boy. He was trying to appear sober, but he didn't make a very good job of it." She swore she wasn't "mistaken about the day in question" as claimed later by the defence.

The clothes identified by the lady in the shop had apparently disappeared, or never existed, "she must have been mistaken, I don't have any clothes like that", or had been shrunk in the wash and thrown away "by my mother, she isn't all there you know", or had somehow ended up burnt to ashes in the log burner. "I have no idea why mother did that."

"I have already told you, I hit a deer years ago and, of course, there was debris from the car on the lane. She must have been hit in exactly the same spot; it is on a blind bend just there."

He was a smooth, lying bastard telling wild tales about how others had come to be using his car that fateful day: "it must have been taken by a joyrider or one of the children."

And how he had left his phone in the car so, of course, it would be traced to the same place.

Trying to involve his children? That was truly despicable. "They are the only other people who could possibly have been using my vehicle... or the gardener?"

He even tried to blame it on his mother, even though she is so old and frail she can barely put one foot in front of the other and could not have moved poor Elizabeth from the road to where he had dumped her. He tried nailing it on his 'wife', who it transpired was his 'ex-wife', claiming that she was trying to frame him to get her hands on his money and his mother's house. She wasn't there to hear him weave his fantastic tales. Neither was his mother, fortunately. What must she be feeling?

It was quite obvious that he was an alcoholic, as well as a despicable, cowardly, evil... she couldn't think of a word horrible enough to describe his vileness.

He would not admit it.

It would be some time before it came to trial because they had to thoroughly examine every tiny piece of evidence. They had to counter every claim.

He had obviously worked out that, after all this time, there was insufficient evidence to link him to Andrew's disappearance. "I don't know what you are talking about. Of course there are fragments of the same vehicle on his rucksack, they were contaminated by the other body."

*No, you fucking, lying bastard. She was alive when you dumped her.*

He must have been involved with Andrew's disappearance somehow.

*The buckled bike? Why the poem? What was the message to Francesca? Where was his body? Where are you, Andrew?*

She asked the questions out loud, ending in soggy tears. William looked at her eagerly, wagged his tail, and leapt into her lap.

**She hugged him tight.**

# Mouse 28

**She went to the murder trial.**

She felt that, somehow, he must have something to do with Andrew's disappearance. He must.

She sat in the visitor's gallery on the days that she could spare from work and glared at him. It made her feel better. Despite every bit of evidence, painstakingly proving his guilt, he still tried to wriggle out of it. His defence barrister took turns at playing at being indignant, incredulous, confused. His favourite word was 'circumstantial'. He deserved an Oscar. They both did.

She couldn't help but be drawn to the agonised faces of Elizabeth's family. She felt embarrassed; it seemed intrusive. Elizabeth's husband, James, sat solemnly, his arresting face without expression, no reactions visible to the unfolding testimony as if listening to a boring sermon. A very handsome man. Dignified. A vague memory niggled. His folded arms were the only sign of antagonism.

His children sat either side of him. His son was the absolute spitting image of his father, well built, good looking, but obviously a younger version with his curly hair still dark, almost black. His daughter, the notorious Francesca, seemed to be permanently in pain, her face distorted. Many times over the days a trickle of tears would run unchecked down her cheeks, her dad would instinctively take her hand and comfort her. She must look like her mum – you would never have guessed that he was her father.

*The girl that Andrew said was the daughter he had never had.*

The jury only took fifty minutes to return their verdict. "Guilty."

*Thank God.*

As soon as the judgement was given, she slipped away.

Now that it was over, she had an intense need to do something to move on. She decided it was time to bury any hope of finding Andrew alive. She chose Lamberhurst as his final resting place. The vicar was understanding and seemed to be quite au fait with the process of burying something – anything – associated with Andrew. She chose his rucksack and his final poem.

The view from the church was incredible and she felt that he would like that, looking out over fields and countryside where he had loved to stride, his bobble hat on his head, his knapsack on his back. It was all very odd, but it was cathartic.

She needed to know where he was. She would never know what happened to her child – she assumed that its minute body had been burnt or thrown away or just flushed down a drain – so it was important that she could at least mark Andrew's passing.

She chose a poem to be engraved on his memorial stone:

*A fond kiss, and then we sever;*
*A farewell, alas, forever!*

**Good old Robert Burns… he has something for every occasion.**

# Mouse 29

**She adopted Lamberhurst as her local church.**

She didn't come very often but she felt that it was congenial to be able to come and visit Andrew in his final 'resting place'. She came every time her thoughts wandered to imagining that he might still be alive, and she liked to keep his 'grave' tidy. Over the last eight months she had visited at least a dozen times.

It seemed appropriate to go there for the Christmas Eve midnight service. She was late. She had completely misjudged the time it would take from her new abode in Tunbridge Wells. Now that Andrew had been given a dignified farewell, there was no good reason for her to stay in the Cousley Wood cottage. She had at last accepted that he was never coming back, and physically moving away seemed a good way to prove it to herself.

She slipped in as quietly as she could and slid into the nearest vacant pew to find herself next to James Arbuthnott. Francesca and his lookalike son were beyond him. Beyond them was a sprightly looking old lady with bouncy curls.

*Awkward, but hopefully he won't recognise me.*

He obviously did. She caught him looking at her oddly. She looked ahead, trying to appear nonchalant but couldn't help glancing sideways. He kept looking at her, a puzzled look on his face. He had obviously known that she was Andrew's wife.

He sang spiritedly but out of tune and not in time with the music. It made Mouse chuckle inside. Beyond him Francesca sang out beautifully, tunefully.

When it came to Sharing the Peace she had to turn to him, it would be rude not to, and warmly shook his hand. He looked her in the eye. She looked away but smiled so that he didn't think she was being unfriendly.

The service over, she was about to flee when he touched her lightly on the shoulder. "Look, I know it may not be appropriate to say this now, but it would be good to get together for a chat sometime."

"That would be nice."

She fled. She could feel that her face had gone very red.

***How ridiculous, anyone would think I fancied him.***

# Mouse 30

*How did he get my number?*

She hit the play button again on her answerphone and listened to James's message again. And again. She now had to find the courage to ring back. The ball was firmly in her court. She went to ponder this development with a brisk walk.

*Come on, William. Walkies.*

She didn't want to come over as too eager, like the deliriously happy William.

*A dog is so easily pleased. Come on, my little boy!*

**She waited a couple of days.**

# Mouse 31

**They arranged to meet at the pub on the Pantiles.**

Mouse was mortified that she was so het up about a simple 'meeting for a chat' and had gone over and over what he might want to 'chat' about.

She couldn't think what to wear. Everything seemed to look so dowdy and grey. It made the white hairs in her neat short hair shine out.

*Don't be ridiculous. It doesn't matter what I wear and how I look, it's only a chat.*

She deliberately arrived a bit late so that she wasn't the one sitting there looking all alone, waiting. It also gave her a chance to pull herself together and persuade her face into an everyday, relaxed arrangement.

Tentatively, she broached the door of the bar, the heat emanating making her red in the face, or was it a hot flush? James was there and proved to be a perfect gentleman, rising from the table on her approach, giving her a polite kiss on each cheek; it was just a respectful greeting, but it was like an electric shock.

*Get a grip.*

He eased her in with him by solicitously buying her a glass of wine, and courteous enquiries about her new home. They both knew that there was a giant-sized elephant, in fact two elephants, in the room. Almost a herd of them. At least they were in neutral territory, their surroundings suitably mundane and down to earth.

He managed to gently introduce the whole topic smoothly. "Let's get it out of the way." She had become so used to the awkwardness of people whenever she was unmasked as the 'wife of the man that disappeared in dodgy circumstances (did you hear about the girl?)'. It was in such contrast to the days when she was greeted with delight when they found that she was the 'wife of the famous Andrew MacLellan who had changed the world with his genius discovery'.

She guessed that James encountered the same problem being the 'husband of the woman killed in a hit and run by a mad, drunk driver' and, more unfortunately, the father of the 'girl involved with Andrew MacLellan'.

Tentatively, she was able to haul out the story from the deep depths of her core, where it had weighed so heavily and dragged her down for so many long years. The fun of being the wife of a C-list celebrity, the glamorous lifestyle, the devastation at not being able to have children, the decline of Andrew into an empty shell, their return to the area where she had been brought up, his disappearance. And on and on about his disappearance. And finding his bits and pieces. The despair of not getting justice for him.

James was an excellent listener. He gently asked encouraging questions when she hesitated, didn't interrupt when she was in full flow, and held her gaze when she found herself staring into his concerned eyes. Horrified by her endless outpourings, she stopped herself. Pulled herself together. She found that he was gently holding her hand. They hadn't touched their drinks.

"And you, James. I am so sorry for going on and on about me. Tell me your story."

She wasn't sure whether to withdraw her hand, but she liked the feel of his rough, workmanlike skin and the warmth that it brought to her soul. She painstakingly kept her hand still so that he would carry on.

She hung on every word. He was so eloquent; his love for Elizabeth, who he affectionately called Moo, and his beloved family radiated from him. He was so proud of them all. He loved them all deeply, solidly, fundamentally.

He wasn't afraid of telling her that he was absolutely certain that Andrew and Francesca's relationship was truly innocent, had always been certain, not just the discovery of the iPad but his complete faith that Francesca was telling the whole truth. He was grateful to Andrew for coaching Francesca to an A grade level, setting her out on an incredible academic journey. She was doing a PhD at Edinburgh University now and he was looking forward to her becoming Doctor Arbuthnott.

For the first time, she truly believed Andrew's innocence. Another weight lifted, but there remained a sorrow that it was her fault that she hadn't been able to give him a daughter of his own to love and encourage.

*How different things might have been if we had been able to have children. It could have been a completely different story, our daughter with a PhD at his alumni university.*

He spoke about the agony of watching Elizabeth dying. He was very practical and dry-eyed so she had to hold in her own tears. She had no right to cry. He disclosed how every day he missed her. He hadn't realised how she was so much an essential part of his whole.

"My biggest regret is that I never told her how much I loved her. We were thrown together and just never got round to it. I never actually said those words… I love you. That is so sad. I did though. I loved her utterly and completely."

He stared into space. She stayed silent, hoping that her empathy was evident. He suddenly started talking again.

"I know that this sounds crazy but, in many ways, you remind me of her. The way your face is put together, your eyes, your lopsided smile but, of course, there was a lot more of her than you. My darling old Moo. She had a permanent war with her weight and her hair was all over the place, but I never cared one jot what she looked like. I just loved her the way she was."

*I didn't know I had a lopsided smile.*

They seemed to be unable to stop talking. It felt so beneficial, she couldn't remember when she had last felt this good. She felt more positive than she had for years and years. The ache and agony of missing Andrew was being gently soothed and diluted into something she felt she could cope with. She was able to remember the good times when they had been happy and had walked and laughed and played and smiled and kissed.

They agreed that they should go and take a purposeful walk in Sweetings Lane to lay more ghosts to rest and reminisce about the good times they had with their respective spouses. It seemed to be doing them good.

"Is tomorrow too soon?" James asked.

"No," Mouse replied.

It was hard to leave but James had to get back for milking and she had to return to reality. It felt strange to say goodbye.

**He gave her a kiss on both cheeks, as he had for his greeting, but this time it felt different.**

# Mouse 32

**"It is absolutely ridiculous at our age to be snogging on the sofa!"**

James had declared, shoving William on to the floor. He liked to join in the fun. Mouse had giggled childishly.

"I don't know why you don't just move in with me."

Mouse resisted for one whole month.

Mouse felt odd about moving in to someone else's home, with someone else's things everywhere, their photographs, their apron, things that they had chosen together as a couple. It was hard not to feel that Elizabeth had just stepped out for a moment and was going to be back at any second. "Don't you think it is too soon? It is only fourteen months since Elizabeth died."

"No. I feel that I have known you forever, and what on earth is the point in waiting? How do we decide how long is enough?" was James's blunt reply.

*I wonder what my life would have been like if I had met and married you when I was still a girl. My life would have been very different.*

James was very understanding and came up with a brilliant idea. Before she actually moved in, they stripped out his mum and dad's old bedroom and painted it together. They spent a morning at John Lewis in Tunbridge Wells, buying new curtains, new rugs, new bed linen.

It had been a long time since she had made a joint decision, and she was scared that she might have become set in her ways and unable to negotiate with someone else's taste. She was also concerned that she might be stepping on his mum's toes. She kept checking with James.

"For heaven's sake, woman, you choose – that is your department. Mum won't give a toss and I don't have a clue. Never have."

*Phew.*

When they set to with decorating she discovered more about him. He was very impatient and reluctant to put on enough coats of emulsion, particularly on the dark feature wall. "It is fine. Don't fuss." He didn't have the patience to do the gloss 'Too fiddly', but he was excellent at putting up a picture rail, the curtain poles, and made an incredible headboard out of an old door.

She moved in and they carried her suitcases up to 'their bedroom'.

"There you are, we are both moving in somewhere new," he declared and insisted on carrying her over the threshold before plonking her on the bed and eagerly leaping on her.

*I love this man.*

# Mouse 33

**Mouse was changing into more suitable clothes to go and get her mammogram done.**

She had a scheduled slot at the travelling clinic parked up behind the Village Hall and knew that she would need to whip her top off before the humiliating squelching of her boobs between two slabs of metal that followed. Mouse turned sideways to the mirror and was shocked by her bulging belly.

*I must cut down. This is ridiculous.*

She was eating far more than she had for years and 'they' always say that you fill out when you are horribly content. Her clothes were all getting tight, very tight, and she was reluctant to give in to it after so many years of being Hollywood thin.

Barbara insisted on baking cakes at every opportunity and Mouse found it very hard to refuse. She would have a nibble, *like a mouse indeed*, and try and crumble the rest to make it look as if she had eaten more.

She always carefully gave herself tiny portions of carbs as she loaded up James's plate. She cut out wine in the evenings to reduce her calorie intake. In any case, she had rather gone off it; it tasted metallic, but she didn't like to say so to James. It was his choice of wine and he rather prided himself on his discerning selections.

She found the prosaic white caravan and hopped up the functional metal steps to be greeted by a bored looking nurse. "Name? Date of birth? Address? Is there any possibility that you are pregnant?"

*Fat chance.*

It still hurt when people asked her that. They weren't to know about her years of yearning. She went into a white Formica-lined cupboard, took off her top and put on a well-chilled gown and stood there, feeling somewhat cool as well as claustrophobic, until a knock came on the door and in she went.

A different nurse, marginally friendlier, welcomed her in and looked at her boobs rather than her eyes as she slipped off her gown. She frowned. She looked up at Mouse. "Were you asked if you might be pregnant?"

"Yes," said through gritted teeth.

"Are you sure that you are not, because your breasts look very much like you are."

*How can breasts **look** pregnant?*

"Do you see all these veins? They are raised and very prominent. And these little pimples? We call those Montgomery's tubercles. They tend to enlarge in pregnancy."

Mouse burst into tears.

*What a horrible, horrible thing for this woman to say… for her to presume… just so unfair…*

"What on earth is the matter?"

Mouse tried to explain through the sobs. The nurse seemed to get the gist of what she was saying and suddenly turned from an efficient automaton into a caring human being.

"Look, my dear, I am sorry for all your anguish and heartache, but I can't go ahead with the mammogram while I have these doubts. Please could you go and establish it for certain. I may be wrong and I am sincerely sorry if I am. The X-rays may be low-energy but the risk to a foetus is still unacceptable."

Mouse returned to the cubicle, pulled on her clothes and scurried out of the caravan still in distress.

*There isn't a bloody pharmacy in Lamberhurst. I'll have to go to Wadhurst.*

She raced to Wadhurst, parked erratically in the High Street, dashed in and found herself pink with embarrassment at having to ask for a pregnancy test. She felt a complete fool and didn't know where to look. The woman behind the counter looked at her with open astonishment and managed to mix it in with a good degree of disgust.

*It is obvious that she knows who I am, I am notorious. The 'scarlet woman who lost her husband and moved in with James Arbuthnott, his wife barely cold'.*

She had heard all the backbiting gossip. It was impossible not to when you lived in the country. She tried to look normal, kept calm when asked all sorts of questions about what sort of pregnancy test she wanted (who knew there were so many to choose from?), paid for her 'Pregnancy Test with Weeks Indicator' and legged it as quickly as she could. She drove like a mad woman back to the farmhouse wanting to tell James all about it, share her distress, her confusion.

*What on earth is he going to say? He'll think I am having a phantom pregnancy like one of his cows. He'll think I have gone nuts and that I'm imagining things because I've yearned for babies for so long. I'll have to tell him about the termination. He'll ditch me like David did.*

She slowed down. Pulled in to the side of the road, hazard lights on, pretended to use her phone so anyone passing would not think her too crazy, took a deep breath and had a good think.

*What if I am? What if I am not? Calm down, calm down, you old fool. For God's sake, I'm supposedly an intelligent woman. The first thing is to establish the facts and I now have the wherewithal to do that. Whether James is in or not, I can go straight to the downstairs loo and do the test. Even if Barbara is pottering about, I can just say I am desperate for a pee.*

She took the kit out of her bag, unwrapped the packaging and read the instructions three times. It seemed straightforward enough. She was prepared.

It was always difficult to tell whether James would be inside or not between the two daily milkings. The first indication was whether his wellies were in the boot room.

*Phew, no wellies, he isn't in.*

She listened carefully for any sounds of Barbara, who was often discovered clattering things in the kitchen, ironing everything in sight or baking.

*No. Nothing.*

She scuttled through into the loo, whipped out the testing stick and pushed out a pee hoping that she was hitting the right bit of the apparatus. Some wee splashed on her hand.

*Yuck!*

She then extracted it from between her legs, placed it on the windowsill, washed her hands very thoroughly and spent the next two minutes with her gaze flicking anxiously between her watch and the window on the device.

*Probably the longest two minutes in anyone's life.*

She could hear William scrabbling at the door to get into the boot room and shouted, "Be with you in a minute."

*Ridiculous – he is a dog! Why do I talk to him like a human?*

'Pregnant 3+' appeared.

She looked again. And again. She was peering at it as if it might suddenly disappear.

*Oh my God, oh my God. Oh my God. I didn't think I could conceive, but I'm bloody pregnant. That bloody woman was right. What the hell is James going to think? He will think I lied.*

At exactly the same time, she heard the back door rattle open and the clattering of James and his dog, Strumpet. William barked. James shouted jauntily, "Shut up, William, you apology for a dog!"

He set to with his usual well-practiced routine, cap off and onto the top peg, coat off and onto the second peg, boots off. He had obviously seen her car because he cheerfully called towards the kitchen, "Hello, my darling. I'm home. How did your boob squashing go?"

She hesitated for a moment and then opened the loo door. Suddenly she couldn't think what to say, so just stood there gawping, her mouth flapping open and closed.

"Goodness me, you look horrified. What's happened? Are you alright? What did they find?"

She rushed at him, shoving him back against the mound of coats, wrapped her arms round his neck, hid her face in his chest and squeaked, "I'm pregnant."

"What did you say? Did I hear that right?"

She leant back, looked up at him, her face a picture of horror. "I'm pregnant."

"Well tickle my arse with a feather. What a wonderful surprise." He enfolded her in his woolly jumper, rocked her from side to side. "Bloody hell. A miracle. You clever old thing."

*He doesn't seem to be angry.*

"Well, well, well… Goodness me… Holy mackerel… It seems it wasn't your problem after all."

*He actually looks quite pleased.*

"I think I've run out of clichés now. Let's put the kettle on, sit down and have a good natter about this."

**He gave her a long, firm kiss on the mouth, patted her bottom and led her by the hand into the kitchen, with a skip and a whoop.**

# Mouse 34

**James was useless when the time came to have the first scan.**

Firstly, he found it hilarious that Mouse was having her tummy rubbed with jelly, 'very fifty shades', and secondly he proclaimed that he had thought that all scans were done rectally these days, like they were with his cows. He also professed that he had been told that it was a 'dating' scan and was therefore somewhat disappointed to find out that it was nothing like the tryst he was expecting.

*I suppose his daft remarks are meant to be keeping me from being nervous. They're not.*

She was so uptight that her neck ached. It was bad enough that her full bladder was shouting to be emptied. The sonographer whizzed all over her stomach with the 'mouse' as if playing some shooting game on a console and didn't say anything at all for ages. All sorts of shapes appeared on the screen, but Mouse couldn't make out what they were, certainly nothing that looked anything like a baby.

When the sonographer suddenly declared "Right!" Mouse nearly jumped out of her skin she was so on edge, crushing James's hand in a nervously clenched grip.

"Firstly, I must tell you that everything is looking splendid, your liquor levels, pelvis and everything. So now I want to show you baby's beating heart." She wiggled the 'mouse' and Mouse could see on the screen a pulsating blob with what looked like a pair of wiggling tentacles.

*Oh my God, that is wonderful. A baby's heart. It is alive. It is real. Don't worry, tiny little thing, I will do everything and anything to make sure that I keep you safe.*

Mouse could feel the tears starting.

"There we are. A healthy spine. And if I measure the little legs – if it will stay still long enough – a real wriggler this one – we can see that baby has a gestational age of fifteen weeks, so we are too late to do a nuchal fold test, but don't worry; there is a blood test that we can do to screen for Down's syndrome."

James squeezed her hand.

"And now I need to just manoeuvre over here…" the radiographer paused. "And here is the second baby and you can see that little heart beating too. Don't worry, by the way, I have checked very carefully and there are just the two."

Mouse gasped. James threw back his head and made a sound that sounded like a bull bellowing before roaring with laughter.

"That is hilarious. After all this time of you waiting for a baby and two come along at once."

He threw his arms awkwardly around Mouse, not caring that a streak of jelly splurged itself down his sleeve, and kissed the top of her head.

*Thank you, God. Thank you.*

"Wait until I tell Francesca and Little Willy. They will be delighted."

**He threw back his head and whooped.**

# Mouse 35

**It is not straightforward when you are an 'elderly primigravida'.**

Mouse obsessively poured over all the data on pregnancy that she could find on the internet. She discovered tests that she had never heard of, like 'Chorionic villus sampling', and chromosome disorders other than Down's syndrome that were a complete revelation: Edward's, Patau's. She carefully noted every test that was possible, how it was performed, at what stage of the pregnancy, the pros and cons, the risks and statistics on outcomes.

She started on a health regime, eating well and sleeping to a strict routine to make sure her health was in tip-top condition. William Dog, to distinguish him from Little Willy, had more walks so that she could exercise gently. She bought a blood pressure monitor to make sure that she picked up any hint of pre-eclampsia. She took all the iron and folic acid tablets that she was given.

The more she read, the more she worried about her babies turning out to have 'neural tube defects' and 'chromosomal disorders'. It seemed that to find out what was going on for certain you had to have 'diagnostic tests' that risked losing the babies. As a result, Mouse was finding the whole pregnancy more and more alarming. She was getting so anxious for her two little precious charges and there was nothing more that she could do. After hours of studious research, she presented her prolific findings to James.

"It seems to me that what you want to ask yourself is 'what would we do if we found out that something was wrong with either of them?'."

"Nothing, nothing at all," Mouse protested loudly. "I would never, never, ever countenance a termination."

*Should I tell him? No… no…*

"So we are we happy to love them however they turn out, Down's, ups or in between?"

"Of course!"

"Then stop worrying yourself to death then. If you want to do some research, go and find out some decent names… and be prepared for me to veto any that I think are ridiculous. I quite fancy Demelza for a girl, don't you?"

She swiped at his head with her sheaf of papers, leant down and gave him a kiss. He patted her bottom.

"Or I was thinking Maud Gertrude after my great-grandmother."

Mouse laughed again, relaxed.

***Oh, James, I do love you.***

# Mouse 36

**She felt enormous.**

Her waist was forty-four inches, her back ached, her boobs swung like one of James's cow's udders and her belly was hanging around her knees when she went into labour at thirty-eight weeks. She knew from her research that this was perfectly normal and ideal from the babies' development point of view. The 'going to hospital' bag had been packed for weeks, 'just in case'.

It started as cramps at breakfast and built up during the morning. They felt horribly like the twinges that she had for days after her termination. She tried to put that out of her mind. This was clearly the Latent Phase, as described in her books and in her prenatal classes.

At lunchtime, James told her with a grin that she must be on her way because she was "behaving like a restless cow." When she glared at him, difficult to do as a spasm rolled through her, he retorted, "That is a good sign, my love. Nature is doing its thing. Our babies are on their way."

Barbara added, "It is all perfectly natural, ducks. It's very early days. Have a cup of tea, put your feet up, have a little rest; you need to keep up your strength for later." She did try to do as Barbara had suggested, but it was very difficult to relax when such a monumental thing was happening.

Things started building to what she assumed were contractions by tea time, and she suddenly started getting very anxious. She had read that it could all take a long time for a first-time mother; her waters hadn't broken, and she didn't want to come over as an over-anxious mummy, so she waited patiently.

*I will wait until James has completed milking. Perhaps I ought to get Barbara, but she will think that I'm making a fuss.*

She was desperate for James to finish and getting terrified by the increasing strength of the contractions. They seemed to be coming more often. As James stepped in through the door, she pounced on him, fed him a messy, hastily assembled cheese sandwich, rushed him through a shower to reduce the ever-present odour of cow manure, and herded him out of the door. James drove her into Tunbridge Wells, belching pointedly. Mouse was too wrapped up in the latest contraction to comment.

She was excited to find that she was already seven centimetres dilated when she was examined.

*Wow. I'm in Active Labour.*

She was relieved to be able to get at the machinery to check that both the babies' little hearts were beating well, not too fast, not too slow. She checked as carefully as the nurses that the two machines were recording two different babies. The printouts were fittingly not in synch.

Her birth plan included having an epidural so that, should she need an emergency section, as happened forty per cent of the time, she would be ready for them to do it straight away, and she was prepared to move into an operating room to do this. It was all very clinical and, as a scientist, she found it reassuring.

Labour progressed to plan, and the epidural proved a godsend; she was aware of contractions in a vague sort of detached way, but they didn't hurt like they had done before. Being competitive, she listened very carefully to the cervix dilation countdown and fist pumped when she reached ten.

*I may be an elderly primigravida, but I can do this.*

The midwives, there were two of them because they had responsibility for one baby each, looked very surprised.

Mouse continued to carefully scrutinise the heart monitors. The babies seemed fine, despite being squeezed and crushed.

James proved a good coach when it came to pushing, although his choice of vernacular also had the midwives wincing. "Come on, old girl, you can do better than that. Show us what you've got. Give it some welly." He obviously thought he was coaching a rugger match.

The first baby slithered out, the cord cut, and was bundled up by the first midwife and taken away. The second midwife leapt on her stomach and grabbed at the second baby. "You'd make a good prop forward," laughed James.

Forewarned, Mouse wasn't too alarmed, knowing that this was to keep the baby's head down and bum up, ready for delivery, but it was a bit more intrusive than she had expected. Someone else jabbed her with a needle to keep the contractions going for the second baby.

She heard the midwife exclaim "It's a boy" as she laid him on a tray, before rustling around, mopping him up before he let out a feeble little cry. Mouse's heart nearly exploded with joy and she looked at James over the determined midwife who was keeping a firm hold of baby number two. He looked equally delighted.

"Two point five kilograms, ten fingers, ten toes and perfect," the midwife said as she handed him, wrapped in a blanket with a little blue hat on, into James's arms. She couldn't reach Mouse because of the midwife in the way, looking as if she was kneading dough.

*Oh my God, here come the tears again. I always seem to be crying.*

At least this time they were tears of joy as her adorable son lay in the arms of his handsome father. He looked exactly like his father after a few beers, a bit red in the face and his eyes screwed up. "Do we have a name for him?" asked the midwife.

"His mother thinks that he is going to be called Theodore, meaning divine gift, but I am going to be calling him Ted after Tractor Ted." The midwives laughed politely.

"Here comes the other one…" Theodore was whisked away as the second baby made its presence felt. Making a very rapid entry into the world, out popped a skinny little girl. The midwife nearly dropped her as she shot out. The baby protested loudly at the indignity of it all.

Her bawling little girl was whisked away and the same rustling ensued before she was returned to Mouse wrapped in a blanket with a pink hat on. "You can't hold her for long. She is a bit on the small size so we would like to pop her into the neonatal unit just to keep an eye on her. She is weighing in at 1.8 kilograms, low weight but perfectly formed. Does she have a name?"

Mouse cradled her in her arms, she was ecstatic, "Hannah. Hannah Elizabeth. It means God has shown mercy."

**"She looks exactly like Francesca did when she was born."**

# Mouse 37

**James, in his down to earth common-sense way, had persuaded her to have a doula to come and live in and help out.**

"If Ted turns out to be anything like Little Willy, you will have your work cut out. He used to drive poor old Moo to a complete frazzle and was a real little bugger. Bless her, she coped so well for such a young thing. And let's face it, you have twice as many babies and you are more than twice the age of his mother."

*Thanks for reminding me about how old I am. I bloody feel it.*

The doula, Jenny, was a kind woman and was brilliant with the babies, and with Mouse. She knew what she was doing, whilst Mouse found that she didn't, despite so much research. How could babies be so complicated?

Jenny changed them, bathed them, swaddled them, leapt up and brought them to her in the night and somehow settled them down again so that Mouse managed to get plenty of sleep. She seemed to be quite happy to spend hours jiggling Ted up and down while he squawked his little head off.

"Told you – just like Little Willy, you see," proclaimed a proud James smiling with delight at his bumptious son.

When Jenny wasn't helping, Barbara was on hand with a fresh cup of tea and home-baked goodies. She adored the babies and spent hours cradling them and crooning to them and telling them all about their daddy and the farm. She regularly called them William and Francesca, but she was such a dear, kind and gentle soul, Mouse couldn't bear to put her right.

Jenny taught Mouse how to nurse her babies – not as easy as it sounded, it turned out. She even managed to find time to stick the washing in. The woman was a saintly Mary Poppins and she was happy and smiling all the time. She seemed to survive on cat naps whenever the babies were snuggled down to rest.

Mouse couldn't have managed without Jenny. She felt a bit guilty that she was getting so much help, knowing that she wouldn't have been able to cope on her own. All the same, despite being waited on hand and foot and having lots of fantastic cuddles with her new-borns, most of all she felt guilty for feeling very weepy all the time.

*Was this just hormones? I should be ecstatic, but I just can't stop thinking about how my other baby would have been. Was it a boy like Ted or a girl like Hannah? I'll never know.*

Staring avidly at their tiny faces, watching them wriggle and squirm and nuzzle, it preyed on her mind continuously. The only person in the whole world who she felt would be able to put her mind at rest was James, but what would he say? Wasn't it too late to suddenly confess? Would he walk away like David or even worse stay but despise her forever? Did she dare?

**She obsessed about it, her stomach churning until she thought she would be sick.**

# Mouse 38

**James saw it first in the newspaper.**

"Hey, listen to this. They are making new legislation about missing people."

Mouse cringed, caught on the hop.

"It looks as if you can apply for Presumption of Death. They check out all the usual things, like bank accounts, passport applications and such to make sure, and then give you a certificate. It is scheduled to become law in October 2014."

Mouse felt strangely giddy. All the thoughts that she had settled like sludge in a pond were stirred up into a horrible dirty fog.

*Supposing that their enquiries find that he is alive after all this time. Hiding. Hiding from me. It can happen. Missing People said it could.*

Her heart was pounding.

"Might as well give it a go, love. It would settle things once and for all. I'd be able to make an honest woman of you. Can't have our children growing up as little bastards."

*Marry James? He wants to marry me? But… the baby, the mortal sin…*

It was the trigger that Mouse had needed. Her whole mind was swirling with the mud. She realised that, before she could say anything more, she would have to confess. She trembled with nerves and tried to find the courage to speak.

"I thought I might get a slightly more ecstatic reaction than that," laughed James.

Mouse burst into tears.

"Whoa, that is even worse. Surely marriage to me can't be as bad as that."

"You won't want to marry me once I tell you what I have done."

"What on earth is all this about?"

"I am a wicked and terrible person. I should never have been allowed to be a mother. I committed a mortal sin…"

She sobbed wildly.

"When I was at school… I aborted my baby."

More wails.

"Please don't leave me… please don't… I love you so much."

James wrapped his arms round her and rocked her like a small child, stroked her hair. He waited until the worst of the outburst had quietened to whimpers.

"Now listen to me, you old fool. I carry my own guilt too. Let me tell you a story. It is a long one from a long time ago.

"I was sitting at the kitchen table after afternoon milking, mug of tea and a newspaper at hand when the front door knocker sounded. I slopped in my socks to the door, leant down and shouted through the letterbox to go round to the back because the door didn't open. I couldn't see who it was because it was dark.

"I went to the back door and opened it to see a slip of a girl creep round the corner. I instantly recognised her and my heart dropped. I felt so bad because we had got together at the Young Farmers' Halloween Disco. I had seen her many times at previous events, fancied her, chatted to her. She was a lovely, cheerful girl, a bit shy and I liked her a lot. I thought that she liked me too, but I felt that she was a bit young, seventeen and still at school, to get too involved with an old bloke like me. I was twenty-five, which felt ancient. I thought I would wait until she had left school before I started dating her properly.

"On the night of the disco, I was very, very pissed after a calving had gone badly wrong. The cow had died, the calf was not at all well and it was entirely my fault, well I thought so anyway. She was adorably sympathetic and let me cry on her shoulder, literally, a drunken outpouring. One thing turned into another and we got carried away. It was my responsibility to manage the situation and I was fantastically stupid. I thought I had made a date to see her again, I wanted to, I liked her even more than I had realised, but I was so pissed that it was all a bit of a blur and I couldn't remember.

"And suddenly there she was. I couldn't think why she had come but, after the niceties of 'How are you? Do come in. Would you like a cup of tea? Do take a seat...', she blurted it out. Poor thing was terrified. I leant over to put my hand over hers and she flinched, a look of terror on her face.

"My initial reaction was 'is it mine?' Crass I know. Obviously, it was. My second thought was that she had come to talk to me about having an abortion. As soon as possible. I would pay or whatever it was that she wanted. I said so.

"She looked at me like a rabbit in the headlights with tears streaming down her face. I didn't dare try and touch her again. She hiccupped and sniffed but didn't say anything for ages. She kept looking as if she was about to say something but then just let out another sob instead.

"Eventually, she mouthed, 'I don't think I can.'

"I was horrified at the thought that she might want to go ahead and have a baby. It didn't seem like a real thing to me, not a human being, just the result of a stupid, drunken, careless mistake. I can't remember what I said next, but I tried to persuade her that it was the right thing to do, for her, for me and, in a perverse way, it seemed right for the baby too.

"I think I looked questioningly at her because she took a deep breath and whispered, 'Mum wants me to get rid of it… as you do… I don't know, but I can't help thinking that for the rest of my life I might always wonder about that baby. Suppose it was the only one that I ever had?'"

James paused. Looked straight at Mouse. Mouse flinched. Pursed her lips to stop crying again. James continued.

"She said, 'Don't worry, James. I won't expect you to have anything to do with it. I haven't told anyone whose it is, although my friends will have a pretty good idea. I just thought I should tell you.'

She leant forward, about to leave.

"And I let her go. Unbelievable I know, but I did. What a shit."

Mouse went to speak but James hushed her, placing a firm hand over hers.

"Five weeks later, I got a phone call from her. 'I have been chucked out by Mum. I don't know where else I can go.' Of course, I came to my senses and said that I would help her with the baby. I would marry her if that was what she wanted. I collected her from her doorstep where she stood, this little girl, surrounded by a pathetically small suitcase and a heap of carrier bags.

"We did get married. We had William. I loved William deeply. I used to look at William and think that he might never have lived and I might never have known him if I had had my way."

James looked at Mouse. His eyes were brimming too.

"As you know, we went on and had Francesca. We had the most wonderful, happy marriage and a perfectly formed family. It was as if we were destined to be together, and I loved her so much. I never told her that. Before her senseless murder."

He looked so sad. Mouse squeezed him to show understanding.

"But don't forget what my first reaction was. If that had been you, I would have commended you on your decision. I would have been relieved. I would have agreed with you. I would have said that you and your mum were doing the right thing. I would have let you carry on your life as if nothing had happened. I would never have married you. Do you see?"

Mouse nodded, unable to speak.

"Let me help you get through this. I love you. I love Ted and Hannah just as I love Willy and Francesca. We must let that little soul go. We could even name him or her, something like Alex or Charlie, so it doesn't matter whether it was a girl or a boy. We can mourn the loss together."

Mouse dabbed at her eyes and nodded again.

"We could even go to church and give you a chance to say goodbye properly, like you did with Andrew."

Mouse managed to squeeze out a weak, "Thank you, James, thank you, thank you."

"More than anything, I love you. I want you with me for the rest of my life. Elizabeth MacLellan, I would be so honoured if you were to be my wife."

She didn't know what to say. Just nodded through the tears and turned her face to seek his mouth.

**He didn't seem to mind the tears and the snot when he kissed her back.**

# Mouse 39

**Mouse wasn't sure what to think when she received the certificate stating that Andrew Angus MacLellan was Presumed Dead.**

In a way it was a relief. She had permission to stop speculating and wondering. He genuinely wasn't out there somewhere living a new life. It would have shown up in their searches. There were no applications for passports, birth certificates or entries on Electoral Rolls for Andrew Angus MacLellan. It wasn't always the case. She knew that others at Missing People had had to face the horrendous thought that their loved one was alive and well but just didn't want to come home. Somehow that would have been worse.

*But where is his body?*

She went and visited his grave, on her own, and quietly said goodbye. She read a poem that she was certain he would have liked, although she didn't think it fitted completely:

> *An honest man here lies at rest,*
> *As e'er God with His image blest:*
> *The friend of man, the friend of truth;*
> *The friend of age, and guide of youth:*

So true.

> *Few hearts like his, with virtue warm'd,*
> *Few heads with knowledge so inform'd:*

That is the bit I like best.

*If there's another world, he lives in bliss;*
*If there is none, he made the best of this.*

She allowed herself to weep, discreetly and whispered "he **has** gone."

She could now marry James openly and honestly. There was no reason in law not to marry.

**'Be careful who you marry'. It feels so very right to be marrying James.**

# Mouse 40

**Mouse received an email forwarded from Tina.**

There was going to be a school reunion. Tina was definitely going. "Would you come? It will be a laugh."

*Would I?*

Echoing in her mind was that ridiculous day when Liz had stood in the science lab spouting forth about where they all might be when they were fifty. And here we are. She couldn't quite remember how it had gone but she recalled the portentous words, 'Be careful who you marry, girls.' She had so recently brought them to mind as she married James. She snorted out loud.

She thought about it. Did she want to put herself out there, tell her story? Could she face those girls and not tell them her dreadful past secret and how it had messed up so much of her life? Should she have had that little baby and perhaps even married the father? She could have married David if she hadn't told him what she had done. She had married Andrew. She wasn't sure that she wanted to get into the whole Andrew being famous and then having a breakdown and committing suicide, or whatever it was. Those that had stayed in the area would know all about it. Those that hadn't would no doubt enjoy the whole juicy scandal of it all.

Then there was all the stuff around her having babies at such an ancient age and marrying James. The whispers of 'too old', 'too soon', 'slut' all whirring round her head.

*I wonder how different my life would have been if I had met and married James in the first place.*

She made up her mind, was resolute.

*No, I'll stay at home, take Ted and Hannah on a lovely outing with their daddy and William Dog. It'd probably be a bit too much for Nanny Bap, but perhaps Francesca and Little William would like to come too? They adore their little sister and brother. We can go to Bodiam Castle and play at being knights or Bedgebury Pinetum and follow the Gruffalo Trail.*

**They love the Gruffalo – perfect when you are four.**

# Lizzy 1

**She sat slumped on the edge of a wooden chair in the dreadfully old-fashioned Commemoration Hall.**

Staring wretchedly into the distance, sipping warm, flat cider from a plastic cup, her gaze was focused hopelessly on Patrick Shepley-Botham.

Unfortunately, he was draped over Anne Finlayson, let out for half term from the renowned and distinguished Benenden School. Letting one hand wander casually over her back, he was clutching both a bottle of wine and a cigarette in the other.

She was feeling a bit stupid. She had escaped from unwanted attentions from one of the young farmers. He was an amusing guy, attractive, rather old, she had chatted to him before, ideal husband material but very drunk. She knew who she wanted (it wasn't a farmer), and despite being very pissed herself, it had suddenly dawned on her that she was being totally unreasonable, a bit of a prick teaser. She could only go back to stare at her unrequited love.

"Shit, shit, bugger, shit," she murmured under her breath. What did she have to do to get Patrick to notice her? She studied Anne's considered sinewy movements, the way she looked – fastidiously aloof; her long blonde hair, cut into a classy, private school style; her adroit make-up; her ingeniously trendy but upmarket clothes. Anne's whole demeanour was subtly different from her own. A siren not a witch. She studied her very, very carefully.

Suddenly Tina and Nikki descended.

"Come on, you twit. Stop drooling. Time to go."

**"If we can drag you away…"**

# Lizzy 2

**She opened her A Level results with trepidation.**

All this mooning about unrequited love had definitely disturbed her studies. She had spent more time studying how those other girls, the ones that he was attracted to, were different, what they did, how they looked, how they behaved.

She definitely had to go blonde. She wanted to dye her hair but knew she could wait until university. She could start growing her hair, though, despite the nagging from Mum to go to her dreadful hairdresser in Wadhurst for a tidy up. She would end up with a perm if she wasn't careful, emerging from the domed hairdryers like a poodle. How come they still have those old-fashioned things? It was 1987, for God's sake.

*Phew. Two Bs and a C. Enough to get into City University, way down the list but it will do.*

She needed to be in London, not some provincial university, and she hadn't been certain that she would get the grades that she needed for Imperial.

*Mum looks a bit disappointed.*

"Mum, can I phone the others please? I want to see who is going where. I bet Nikki would have got her grades for Edinburgh and Tina is sure to have got into Imperial College. She is so clever."

*I hope Liz got her grades and is still on for City.*

# Lizzy 3

**City University was a revelation.**

Who knew that there were so many people their age in the world? As she walked into her designated Hall of Residence, dragging her far too heavy suitcase, the two bags over her shoulder slipping awkwardly, she was greeted by a smiley boy who was a Hall Monitor – a third year who was designated to help them feel at home and answer any questions she might have. She was nervous but decided to practice acting cool. He was over-hearty and far too loud.

She was given her room key. She realised that she had never had a key to look after before. Their lockers at school had all had combination locks and the doors at home were all always open.

"I wonder if you could tell me, has Liz Woodhall arrived yet? She is a friend from school…" Oh God, that made her sound feeble and childlike all at the same time.

"No, not yet. I am sure she'll be here soon."

*Oh God, that was so patronising. I must have sounded pathetically needy.*

"Come down to the Common Room, once you have settled in, for tea and coffee! I am sure your friend will be there soon enough! Meet your other inmates!" He spoke with over enthusiastic exclamation marks at the end of every sentence.

She flung her bags over her shoulder and lugged her case to the lift, which had two other students in it. One a Chinese girl and the other a very spotty boy. She nodded a greeting but couldn't think of anything sensible to say. They stayed awkwardly silent too. She ascended to the giddy heights of the fourteenth floor to find her room. She had never been that high up before; there were no skyscrapers in Tunbridge Wells.

She found her room, 1409, and turned the key in the lock. The door swung open but was heavy and wanted to close on her, like being caught in a Venus flytrap. The room was very small and very bare, with the minimum necessary furniture to justify calling it a bedroom. The curtains were snot green. A sign on the back of the door telling her what to do in case of a fire made it even more institutional.

*I hope there won't be a fire, not when I'm so high up in a tower block.*

The view from her window was astonishing; she gingerly opened it and hardly dared to look down. Loads of flaky, grimy modern buildings far below and traffic whizzing by. She could hear the hysterical squeals of the black cabs' brakes from right up here. It was oddly windy and there were plastic bags and other debris wafting around in a lazy tornado swirling around. It smelt dirty in a distinctly urban way.

Should she unpack now? It was all a bit uncertain. She wanted to find Liz, but she had one vital thing to do. If she was going to reinvent herself, she had to do it now before she met anyone properly. She scrabbled in her case for her hair dye and carefully read the directions. Liz was going to be amazed.

Mission accomplished, she headed down to the Common Room and looked around, trying to look composed. There was a loud shriek and Liz came hurtling towards her. She stopped dead, stared and then burst out laughing. "Oh my God, what on earth have you done to your hair?" Lizzy practiced looking nonchalant and superior.

**It wasn't quite the impact that she had hoped to have**.

# Lizzy 4

**The other people on their course were very amiable.**

They were a much smaller group than Lizzy had imagined and largely made up of boys who were on bursaries from the services. They were all officers on some sort of graduate scheme from the Army, the Navy and the RAF. It explained why they were all so clean-cut and smartly dressed. Their group stood out from the rest of the City students. This was a good thing, Lizzy decided, and an unexpected bonus.

Liz commented, "Plenty of husband material here" – but Lizzy still had her sights set elsewhere.

Their lecture rooms were very like school classrooms, with whiteboards and overhead projectors, but less stuff on the walls. They obviously didn't have to impress any school inspectors with superfluous bright posters. They weren't children now after all.

No-one, other than Liz, turned a hair at her blonde locks. Why would they? The colour had turned out rather yellow, a bit brassy, a monotone colour, not what she had hoped for. She would find a good hairdresser and get it made more natural. Everyone was far too polite to mention it, except for Liz who kept singing 'One Way or Another' by Blondie. She rose above it.

After going out with a few others, Liz finally plumped for Jim, a handsome chisel-jawed army officer, but Lizzy kept the boys at a safe distance. She was a woman on a mission.

Lizzy let it be known that she intended to be a virgin when she married. Rather than attracting ridicule, she was surprised to receive respect. "We are far too young to get serious," she declared, and the boys seemed to accept it in a gentlemanly way.

*I'm saving myself for Patrick, but they don't need to know that.*

She had plenty of time. Three years at university would be just right, she would then be 21, a most eligible age.

**In the meantime, she could practice on these well-mannered boys.**

# Lizzy 5

**In the second year, the boys on the course found a mews flat off Holland Park.**

It was a real house, very posh but they were all on military allowances and could afford it.

Lizzy and Liz found a perfect flat near Earl's Court. It was very small but very cheap and they shared a room. Lizzy was very careful about turning off lights as she left a room and paranoid about Liz's profligate use of the heating. She bought Liz a woolly jumper and gloves for Christmas as a hint.

The boys had the wherewithal to have great parties, drive in fancy sports cars and eat extravagantly. They were very sweet and took Liz and Lizzy out to dinner and even to their fancy balls when they couldn't find anyone of potential girlfriend material to go with them.

Lizzy didn't want to eat lavishly. It was firstly a waste of money and, secondly, it was a foundation stone of her grand plan that she became willowy, i.e. thin. She took up jogging to tone her muscles, and use up calories, and invested in a Green Goddess yoga video to sculpt her shape. Liz started nagging her about being too skinny but Lizzy concluded that she was just jealous.

The money she saved from frugal catering and healthy, free exercise, she spent on getting her hair sorted out – it was now a shiny, highlighted natural-looking blonde. Liz didn't laugh at her now, but she still sang 'One Way or Another' under her breath. She wasn't entirely sure whether she was just referring to the hair colouring or the references to stalking, of Patrick Shepley-Botham, of course.

During the long summer holidays, she found a job at Harrods, in the ladies' shoe department, which proved an excellent place for research purposes. She learned the delicate art of customer service without being obsequious and observed how to be a gracious customer. Her boss liked her refinement, which was coming on nicely with lots of practice, and they happily employed her again and again for the Christmas rush and the tourist season.

She became very friendly with the girls on the make-up counter and they were happy to use her as a demonstration model. They couldn't do anything else with the opened pots and used lipsticks other than use them themselves or give them away to friends. Lizzy accumulated a little stash of Mac, Christian Dior and Elizabeth Arden and was learning how to apply the stuff to her best advantage.

The hairdressing department were also keen to use her as a model, although she refused to oblige if they wanted to cut her long hair. It had taken forever to grow, it wasn't very cooperative, and she was hanging on to it. It did mean that she could keep it blonde, though, and her roots rarely showed.

She used her staff discount to buy choice, classic pieces from the ladies' fashion department, items that would never go out of fashion. For birthdays and Christmas, she asked for money, which she spent on Russell & Bromley shoes and carefully chosen co-ordinates from Fenwick's and Harvey Nichols.

Her wardrobe was beginning to look very exclusive and sophisticated. She decided to invest in a fabulous, understated dress when invited to a naval function by Nick, a jolly, rotund, naval chap on the course. He kindly asked Lizzy to the annual ball at the Royal Naval College Greenwich, making up a party with Liz and Jim. She wasn't entirely clear what he felt about her. She hoped that accepting his invitation wasn't too much of a 'come on'; she liked him but not in *that* way. Perhaps her well known virginal status would keep her safe from unwanted advances.

From the moment they entered through the imposing gates of the College, it was spectacular. The beautiful, long vaulted rooms had incredibly detailed painted ceilings. Everything about it was just perfect: the chandeliers, the fluted columns, the vast marble fireplaces with enormous flower arrangements burgeoning from their mantelpieces. Lizzy hadn't seen anything like it before. She liked it. Very much.

It seemed very grown up to be waited upon so vigilantly by uniformed butlers and waiters, all so deferential and polite, who were clearly older and more sophisticated than their 'pretending to be adult' guests.

The boys looked twice as handsome in their uniforms, older and more sophisticated than they ever did in their everyday student jeans and sweaters. It seemed that being all dressed up made them come over all very old fashioned, complimenting the girls on their dresses and solicitously filling empty glasses.

Thank heavens she had pushed the boat out and bought a slinky long dress to wear. She had felt a bit daft putting on such a glamorous creation in their dingy flat but had been relieved that Liz was wearing 'long' too. Liz's was a very girly creation, floral with a pie crust collar. Hers was black with clingy long sleeves, an empire waist and a plunging neckline that showed off her cleavage, albeit assisted with some 'chicken fillets' in her bra. Her boobs had all but disappeared with the weight loss. Her hair was designed to look casual, diamante hair clips holding it back on each side, but had taken her ages to get just right.

Nick attentively accompanied her to their table, deftly held out her chair and settled her to her place. The tables were fabulous, with down to the floor linen tablecloths, old-fashioned silver candelabra, a family of glasses of all different sizes, and regimented rows of silver cutlery. Wow.

She looked casually around the table, admiring the precision, the wonderful formality of the uniformed boys, and the girls in their dresses, all looking very glamorous. Her eye came to Patrick Shepley-Botham. Her tummy flipped followed by a wave of tingling nerves that made her hair feel all tight.

*What the hell is he doing here? What do I do? How do I play this? I mustn't be seen looking at him.*

Nick took his place and, with huge relief, she turned to him and made innocuous remarks about how lovely it all was. He busied himself getting her a bread roll, filling her glass, passing the butter. She wasn't going to touch the bread roll and certainly wouldn't be using the butter, but it seemed the right thing to do to take it politely.

She concentrated on Nick with her eyes, but the back of her neck was prickling and her head was having a completely different conversation than her mouth. Should she acknowledge Patrick? It was far too soon to make a move. Should she wait for him to acknowledge her? What should she do? Had Liz noticed? Could she get Liz's attention?

*I must play this very cool.*

While answering Nick's considerate conversation, and then turning to her other dinner companion for the main course, she formulated her strategy as she pushed her food around the plate.

He didn't approach her until after dinner and caught her on the way back from the Ladies'.

"I believe that we have met before."

She looked at him, appeared to study his face slowly, as if deciding.

*Oh my God. Ignore the fireworks that are going on in my head. Keep cool.*

"I think that might be right. You are from Wadhurst, aren't you?"

"Yes, yes, Patrick Shepley-Botham. You look familiar but different."

She kept quiet, deliberately, and did her best to look quizzical.

"In a good way. I mean, I hope you don't mind me saying so, but you look enchanting." He looked her up and down. She continued to hold out.

*Keep cool.*

"I'm so sorry, that must sound ridiculously callow. Would you care to join me for a drink? We should catch up."

*I would love to more than you could ever know. Stay cool. Keep him interested.*

"That would be fun, but I must get back to my partner. I would hate to be rude. It has been great to see you. Perhaps we will meet again."

She walked away, her heart beating, her face burning.

*Oh God, I hope I have done the right thing. Should I have said yes? I mustn't appear too keen.*

She cornered Liz in the Ladies' and established that Jim had been at Sandhurst with Patrick and had become a good friend. Liz reported that Patrick had been the life and soul of every get together throughout and was well known for being the party animal.

*He would be, wouldn't he? This is an ideal connection. How can I use it to my advantage?*

For the rest of the evening, she danced with Nick, Jim and the other boys in their party. She pointedly looked anywhere but where Patrick was. She followed him out of the corner of her eye and caught him looking at her. He wasn't with anyone in particular and certainly wasn't intimately entwined on the dance floor.

*Yes!*

# Lizzy 6

**When you are all together as a peer group everyone turns twenty-one all at the same time**.

The invitations were flooding in for parties and Lizzy realised that she could be picky without causing offence. She decided to go to the smart ones: the tasteful dinner parties, a picnic in Hyde Park, a weekend on the coast in one of the naval chap's family holiday homes. She turned down the less enticing. Who after all wanted to go to a Bad Taste party where you had to dress up and look awful?

She also carefully connived to find the ones that Patrick Shepley-Botham would be attending. She knew he would be at Jim's at The Hurlingham Club.

She scoured Bond Street for something suitable to wear and ended up in Fenwick's, where she bought a dark-green velvet dress with a little bolero. It suited her and matched her eyes. With the bolero on it looked very chaste, but without it the halter neck dress showed off her lean back right down to her waist. She knew she looked sexy and intended to do the reveal after dinner as the dancing started.

She splashed out and took a cab. Her high heels gave her that suitably gracious height but were a bit tricky on the bus or the tube, let alone the whole outfit. She swept in along the grand drive and felt very smart as she carefully alighted with the aid of the uniformed doorman. She gave her name on the door and checked down the list, and there was Patrick Shepley-Botham's name. He hadn't arrived yet.

She sauntered in, took a glass of bubbly and went in search of Liz, Jim, Nick and other friendly faces. She found all her course mates in a gaggle and they had a good catch up as old friends do. She was facing the door when Patrick came in with a drop-dead gorgeous, lanky blonde on his arm. He looked very pleased with himself.

*Shit. Shit. Shit.*

"Liz, who is the blonde attached like a limpet to Patrick?"

"Oh, that is his fiancée. She has a ridiculous name, Ploppy or something drippy like that."

Fortunately, Liz was so busy laughing at her own joke that she didn't see Lizzy's face fall before she sped off to the loo.

**She cried her eyes out in the Ladies', ruining the hours spent carefully painting her face.**

# Lizzy 7

**Lizzy was thrilled when Liz asked her to be a bridesmaid at her marriage to Jim.**

She wasn't quite so pleased when she saw the dress that she was expected to wear. It was pastel orange and she was to wear a straw hat with it. It may well have done something for Liz's dark-haired sister, but it looked awful as a blonde.

"You could always go back to your real colour," Liz had laughed.

*I've forgotten what colour I used to be.*

They all got ready at Liz's family home, where they had all stayed that Halloween evening. It seemed a lifetime ago. Instead of sickly-sweet mead they were sipping champagne.

"Well, here I am, and I know who I am going to marry. What about you, Lizzy?"

"I don't know. I have totally blown my chances. I will either marry Nick, he keeps asking and I keep turning him down, or be an old maid and live with a hundred cats in a pokey old cottage behind the high street."

"There is someone out there for all of us. You'll see." She was smirking.

*Why was she smirking?*

The service was at Wadhurst Church, a stone's throw away but still requiring fancy cars. They had a giggly time in the porch, sorting out Liz's voluminous train before the Bridal March started up, and in they went. Lizzy was fussing over the train that seemed to have a mind of its own and getting it to follow Liz around the corner to go up the aisle.

She looked up and saw Patrick Shepley-Botham, all dressed up in his fancy uniform to be one of Jim's guard of honour, which had become an essential part of all their classmates' weddings. Her heart and her face froze. He looked heavenly, godlike.

*Why? Why was I so stupid? I should have made my move when I had my chance.*

She quickly looked away but for the rest of the service was distracted by the thought of him behind her. As they processed out, she made a point of looking at the bride's side of the church so as not to catch his eye.

The reception was at Wadhurst Castle, recently refurbished as a wedding venue and smelling of new paint. Lizzy had never been there before, hadn't even realised that such a grand house was hiding behind the high street. Getting older meant that you saw your childhood environs with new eyes.

For the first couple of hours, she managed to keep away from Patrick. They stood around, having the customary drinks and canapes between endless photographs directed by the bossy photographer. Lizzy didn't fancy the nibbles; they all looked very high carb and she was reluctant to drink empty calories. She kept having to waft away on pretend missions to escape being anywhere near Patrick. He seemed to have her in his sights and was circling around her, clutching a glass of bubbly in his hand.

*Why? Where is his fiancée – or is she now his wife?*

They were called in for the wedding breakfast and Lizzy found her table and sought out her place card. Standing there, to the left of her seat, was Patrick.

*Liz has bloody well put me next to him. How could she? Not kind, she knows how I've always felt about him.*

He leant towards her conspiratorially. "I swapped the cards round."

Lizzy was flustered and looked at him, more like a glare. He winked, drew out her chair and helped her to sit.

"Which is your fiancée?" Lizzy asked rather pompously and made a point of looking around the table.

"I am now very single. She wasn't for me. Red or white wine – or perhaps orange to go with your most fetching dress?"

**Lizzy gave an enigmatic smile on the outside while on the inside her soul whooped.**

# Lizzy 8

**She couldn't help it.**

He just enchanted her and when he asked her back to his cosy cottage in Chelsea for a nightcap, how could she say no? They had been out together so many times and he hadn't yet made a move. She had made sure that she wasn't always available, but it was hard not to say yes to every invitation.

Covent Garden, Trader Vic's in the basement of the Hilton, intimate restaurants in Shepherd's Market in revered Mayfair, and the fanciest of places, like Bibendum, the Steward's Enclosure at Henley, and Number One Court tickets at Wimbledon.

"I'm so sorry they aren't Centre Court."

He didn't seem to mind that she held back on the booze, full of sugar, and picked at her food. She just wasn't hungry. It must be love. He laughingly finished off the bottles of wine, "All the more for me."

She worked hard to maintain her ethereal persona, deliberately holding back, being careful not to gush, not to appear impressed by the ever more amazing places that he took her to. She knew how to do it. She could stay cool. Here she was. The time seemed right now.

At least he went through the motions of offering her a drink before guiding her to the bedroom. He slowly helped her undress. She didn't say anything, just complied and made it easy for him to pull her dress over her head, to unroll her tights and unhook her bra.

In total silence, he ran a finger down her face along her cheekbones, touched her lips softly and tracked down to her collarbones stroking the prominent hollows. He brought his other hand into play and let his fingers trail across her nipples. She shivered with delight.

He continued down her sides and over her thighs.

"I just love that gap between your thighs, so inviting."

She trembled as his hands swooped into the gully and couldn't help but gasp. Patrick laughed.

He was tugging at her pants and she wriggled to help him.

*Oh my God, oh my God. Is this it? Is it going to happen?*

He looked her up and down, a greedy look on his face, and hesitated for a moment.

"So, no matching collar and cuffs?"

She daren't look at his face. She blushed, mortified.

"I match my eyebrows," she was able to squeak.

He laughed.

"Well, my darling, I think the time has come. Don't you?"

She nodded, her eyes tightly closed, her lips clenched.

"You do know…"

*Oh God, how do I say this…?*

"Um, it will be my first time…"

He stopped dead.

"But I'm… I do want to… you know…"

He unexpectedly roared with laughter.

"Oh, Elizabeth, I can't believe it! That is amazing…"

He kept laughing. She blushed and felt the urge to cover her body that had been so unreservedly exposed. As her arms crept up to cover herself, he took her hands.

"Elizabeth, my virgin queen, I think I'd better marry you!"

He engulfed her and dragged her to the bed, his eyes alight with glee.

It wasn't quite how she thought it would be, but it was okay. It was with Patrick.

*All this fuss about sex and it's actually quite easy and perhaps a bit disillusioning.*

# Lizzy 9

**It is part of the whole getting married thing.**

The meeting of the parents. An awkward occasion all round. Lizzy and her parents had been invited to the Shepley-Bothams for drinks through Patrick. "Very informal, just a chance for the parents to eye each other up and make arrangements."

Lizzy dressed very carefully, wanting to make a good first impression. Neat, understated but chic. She was itching to direct her mum what to wear when she was shown the chosen outfit, she didn't want Mum to show her up.

Dad was easier. Somehow his usual dress of casual sports jacket, tie and cords were suitable for anywhere, but Mum's dress was too showy. It may be okay for Mum's Wadhurst friends, but it was a bit cringe making – trying too hard.

She had carefully briefed them on the Shepley-Botham family: Colonel George Shepley-Botham, retired soldier, had Parkinson's; Margaret, his mum. She couldn't think what to say about her.

*Would it be rude to say that she was a stuck-up stuffed shirt? Perhaps best not.*

The other family member they needed a good briefing on was Jeremy, Patrick's elder brother, sadly born with Down's syndrome. He was living in sheltered accommodation but rarely mentioned by George, Margaret or Patrick.

Sitting in the drawing room, perched on the edge of ancient settees that were lacking in stuffing, they were all politely gripping delicate sherry glasses. Mrs Shepley-Botham insisted very firmly that they all sat because of her husband's Parkinson's. He couldn't stand easily.

*Fair enough, poor old chap.*

Colonel Shepley-Botham was sitting in a winged armchair, his left hand gripping the arm rest for dear life. Lizzy assumed that at least it would stop it trembling like his wayward right. A tumbler was placed at his right hand. It couldn't be sherry, there was too much of it. Perhaps it was apple juice.

Every time he attempted to take a sip it was a major event and, although she tried very hard not to stare, the lifting in the trembling hand and wayward progress to his mouth was compelling.

*Poor man.*

Despite his terrible disability, he was extremely jolly and asked her parents lots of questions. A very charming man. He regaled Dad with tales of his life in the army and "how proud I am that Patrick is a chip off the old block, what?"

In contrast, Patrick's mum was as stiff as the polished fire irons that gleamed by the hearty fire, with a poker face to go with it. She gave clipped answers to all of Mum's friendly enquiries and managed to be snide at the same time.

"That's a lovely dress you are wearing, Margaret. Did you get it in Tunbridge Wells?"

"No, London. You can't get anything decent in Tunbridge Wells."

*She must know that Mum's dress came from there, everyone round here shops locally.*

"Have you had any nice holidays this year, Margaret?" Mum tried again.

"Of course not. Can't you see that my husband is very frail?" Not even a reciprocal question to keep the conversation going. Mum soldiered on.

*At least she is a trier. Good for you, Mum.*

"Now Margaret, has Elizabeth told you the plans for the wedding?"

"No." Mum looked taken aback but kept going.

"Oh. Well, we are definitely thinking Wadhurst Church. There will be plenty of room for our family, but what about your side? Do you have many relations and friends that you would like to ask?"

"Plenty enough, thank you."

Another awkward pause.

"Is Jeremy coming? Will he be an usher? Obviously not the best man…"

*Mum, please. How tactless.*

Margaret bristled visibly.

"We'll have to see."

Mum changed the subject awkwardly. "We were thinking about somewhere like Wadhurst Castle for afterwards, it being just up the hill." It came out as a question.

"Don't be ridiculous. You don't want to waste your money on something so ordinary. It has no soul. Ghastly place. You will, of course, have the reception in the garden here. A proper wedding. A marquee will fit splendidly on the croquet lawn. Much better, don't you think?"

"Well, Elizabeth thought…"

"Of course, Patrick and Penelope were going to get married from here." Margaret then managed somehow to engineer in some unstinting praise for the elusive Ploppy, who had been engaged to Patrick. "Such a good family. Such a charming girl with effortless, exquisite taste. Such a shame that she broke things off."

*It's funny how you have managed to say that I'm from a crappy family and try too hard all in one go. Cow. I don't think we are going to get on very well.*

Lizzy tried to keep her best enigmatic smile pinned to her face. Mum tried again. "That's very sweet of you dear but…"

"I won't hear another thing about it. Let's take that as an agreement. Now, I do think that George is getting a little tired." With that, she rose obviously dismissing her guests. Mum looked furious.

*George looks as if he is having a whale of a time, if you ask me. He is getting increasingly jolly by the minute.*

"Come on, Dad, time we were on our way," Mum said through gritted teeth.

"Don't go, don't go. Stay and have another drink do," interjected George waving his arms about.

**He tried to get to his feet, levered himself up using the arms of his chair, swayed and promptly fell flat on his face.**

# Lizzy 10

**Lizzy was in her childhood bedroom having her hair piled into an amazing creation that would look fantastic with her dress.**

The cascade of vibrant curls created from her reluctant locks would offset the simple lines of her dress. Simple straps showed off her thin, graceful neck, her collarbones prominent. The bodice, carefully padded in all the right places, clung to her body. The skirt flowed silkily from her clinched waist and flowed out into an unadorned, sleek train. Lizzy knew that she looked amazing.

Lizzy was deliriously happy to be marrying Patrick and couldn't believe her luck. Their wedding was going to be quite the occasion with every bell and whistle you could possibly imagine. Liz was a maid of honour, of course, with sister Prune as a bridesmaid.

"I do wish you would stop calling me that!"

Their dresses were going to be slinky but Prune was a bit on the chunky side for anything clinging. They compromised on an empire line style, which floated over tummies, in a peach silk.

The only fly in the ointment was Mum, who was in a bit of a sulk. She had moaned over breakfast, "Why do we have to get married from their house? You may be 'marrying well' but it is the bride's prerogative to marry from home, or at least her family are meant to be the hosts. That Margaret is crowing about it as if it were her wedding not ours. And she hasn't put a penny towards it."

"Mum please, not today. Let's just be happy. Their garden is enormous and where on earth would we have put a marquee in ours?"

"That isn't the point. Anyway, off you go and start getting ready. At least you will look fabulous wherever we hold your wedding."

Lizzy was quite sure that Mum had then added something under her breath.

**"Put that in your pipe and smoke it, Margaret."**

# Lizzy 11

**Lizzy was catching up with Liz over lunch.**

"Have you got your wedding photos back yet? Honestly, you looked so amazing. A bit thin but I always say that."

Liz pointedly looked at Lizzy's plate. She was picking at a starter.

"What a fabulous day it was, I'm just so thrilled that you married Patrick after all those years of infatuation."

Lizzy couldn't help but give Liz a sharp look.

"I mean… Well, you know how pleased I am for you. How was the honeymoon?"

"Antigua was fantastic. There was loads to do at the resort and we had a go at wind surfing and water skiing. The weather was glorious and I have managed to get myself a good tan without having to resort to a sunbed. The sea was so warm and we swam every day."

"What was the thing about Patrick getting arrested?"

"He wasn't actually arrested, because he and this crazy guy that he hooked up with, Roddy, managed to outrun the police. I suppose it was more hilarious than anything. All a complete misunderstanding. They were as drunk as Lords and didn't realise that there was anyone on the super yacht when they clambered aboard. Boys will be boys."

**Actually, Patrick seemed to spend a lot of our honeymoon pissed.**

# Lizzy 12

**Lizzy and Liz met up for lunch in Covent Garden to celebrate Lizzy's thirtieth birthday, and to compare notes on married life.**

Liz was drinking tomato juice, a current craving, and Lizzy just fizzy water. Both were finding it difficult to get near the table, their baby bumps were getting so big.

"You are so lucky that Patrick was only on a short service commission. I hadn't realised quite how nomadic life would be as an army wife. I quite liked Shrivenham, lots of white horses carved in the chalk and good country pubs, hated Fallingbostel – just too Germanic, but I do like Wilton – it is a cosy community, and Salisbury is fabulous, although our married quarters are pretty dire. Why do they have those godforsaken metal windows? I would love to be in a cottage in Chelsea, like you two."

"It is great being just down the road from Peter Jones, but there isn't going to be much room when this little thing arrives. I would love to move out to the country, but Patrick isn't so keen, he likes the easy commute to the city. I keep saying that, if we sold our little house, we could get a mansion in Sussex, probably as big as his family home and that is cavernous. It could happily house the Addams Family. In fact, it probably did – it is so old fashioned and dark."

Liz laughed in agreement.

"What does he do in the city?"

"Something very clever with loads of money – a 'merchant wanker', he says. It obviously requires a lot of long lunches and late-night dinners with important clients.

He often creeps in when I am in bed and falls over the furniture because he has had a few too many. I worry for his liver."

They laughed. They compared notes on where they had been for city breaks. Lizzy regaled Liz with trips that she and Patrick had made to Amsterdam, Berlin, Vienna and skiing holidays to Val d'Isere and Courchevel.

They reminisced about the last summer when a whole bunch of them from the original City University course had taken a fantastic villa in Sicily, although Patrick had only been able to stay for a week because of his job. They had partied hard and had outrageous evenings playing drinking games late into the night. Patrick proved the champion and could drink all of them under the table.

"No chance of drinking these days," laughed Liz, patting her belly and sipping her tomato juice. "When do you give up work?"

"At the end of the week. I will miss it in a way, but I can't wait to become a full-time mum. Patrick has bought me a new VW Golf for my birthday as my yummy mummy car. It is the very latest fourth generation model, apparently. Very smart. Isn't that sweet of him? I love it."

"Listen to you. You really have fallen on your feet, haven't you? Who'd have thought it when we were at school that our lives could have turned out like this?" Lizzy laughed, content with her lot.

"By the way, sorry to hear of your loss."

"Oh, George. Sad, but he has been unwell for years. He will be missed, I don't fancy having to cope with Margaret without him as a buffer."

Their happy lunchtime ended with them both agreeing to be godmothers to their respective offspring, whichever sex they turned out to be. Liz reminisced, "William, if it's a boy… do you remember our mad conversation that day at school all those years ago? Look at us now, happily married to the loves of our lives… and gone up in the world… I wonder how the others have fared."

When Lizzy arrived home, she updated Patrick on a gossipy lunch, but he interrupted.

"This can't wait. I have some excellent news for you. You have been saying that we should move to the country, preferably before the new addition arrives and so we are."

"But we would have to put this place on the market and find somewhere else and all in two months. Is that feasible?"

"Ah – none of that is a problem because I have come up with the perfect solution. We are going to move into the family home."

"What do you mean? Your mother's? Why can't we buy somewhere for ourselves?"

"For heaven's sake, darling, what is the point of buying somewhere else when that enormous family home is there, with masses of space and just mother rattling around in it now that pa has died? As the only son, well, only proper son… it is mine in any case, for all intents and purposes."

"But where will Margaret live?"

"With us, of course."

Lizzy tried hard not to grimace.

"It will be fantastic for the children having their granny there; they can get to know her much better. She can help you out – it is a fabulous house and she will love having us there…"

*Except it is freezing cold and like a Victorian museum… a bit like your mother.*

"And, my darling, as you were at school there, you can pick up with all your old chums and we can entertain, it is a fabulous house for entertaining."

"But why so suddenly?"

"It isn't sudden, you've been asking to move for ages and here we are, I have made it happen. Aren't you thrilled? You should be."

"But…"

"No buts, my darling. Let's open a bottle to celebrate."

"But I can't drink, Patrick."

**"I'll just have to have a drink for you too."**

# Lizzy 13

**The Millennium.**

What an extraordinary moment in history to be alive. *But it hasn't turned out how I was expecting at all.*

She had been so gleeful, marrying the love of her life, the long sought-after Prince, lunching with girlfriends, popping into galleries, shopping in Peter Jones and going to the gym. Now she was in a bleak, stale-smelling house, shovelling goo into Olivia's adorable little mouth. All under the eagle eye of Granny.

She had thought that they had agreed that they would have an au pair to help out, like all their friends in London, but Patrick had said that there was no point with Granny on hand and her not working. "Just how many adults does a baby need to look after it? And she will be off to school before you can blink."

They hadn't been anywhere since Olivia was on the way. No skiing in the winter, the Continent or Cornwall in the summer. She had mentioned it to Patrick.

"Patrick, it would be lovely to get away. I crave a bit of sunshine."

"Living in the glorious countryside of Sussex every day is as good a holiday as Cornwall or anywhere abroad."

The only place she ever went was to stay with her sister, still affectionately known as Prune because Lizzy knew it annoyed her, who lived with her rather boring husband and gaggle of kids. Prune was never invited to come and stay with Lizzy. "Mummy just couldn't cope with a house full of visitors."

If she wanted to see her own mother, she always went over to her. "Mummy and your mother don't seem to have hit it off so it wouldn't be fair. Why can't your mother just be an ordinary grandmother and not be so competitive?"

*Mum would just like to see her granddaughter a bit more often, that's all.*

She had hoped that they would have friends round for dinner and fun events in the enormous house that was a perfect size for entertaining. "I think that Mummy finds it too much and it isn't fair on her to disturb her quiet way of life. After all, she has to put up with you and the baby every day."

*The baby has a name, Patrick. She is Olivia.*

She had hoped that she would be able to turn her hand to updating the mausoleum of a house and making it a bit more New Millennium than 1900s. "It would break Mummy's heart to change anything. Can't you just wait? It is as if you were trying to hurry her to her grave."

She did at least get a generous allowance from Patrick for running the household, buying her clothes (he liked her to look good), and maintaining her long blonde hair.

She had thought that having won the love of her life, her fairy tale come true, they would live happily ever after in their castle, but she hadn't accounted for having Granny there every hour of every day with her list of complaints: "No dear, that is not how we do things in the Shepley-Botham family" as Lizzy poured the milk into her cup before pouring the tea. "Can't you just prepare some honest English food? Even you won't eat the foreign muck that you churn out".

*Everybody eats spaghetti bolognaise and lasagne in this day and age, for Christ's sake, and I daren't eat too much, Patrick likes me thin. It's so hard when you have to lose baby weight.*

Feeling a bit stir crazy and caught on the hop, she had accepted Liz's invitation to make up a party to go along to the Millennium celebrations on Lamberhurst Down. She could snuggle Olivia into her baby carrier and they could go and have a fun time. Without Margaret.

Perhaps if Patrick was with his old mucker, Jim, he might be a bit more amenable and make a fun evening out of it. It was a Sunday and there was the usual bank holiday the next day so he couldn't come up with too many excuses.

*Cross fingers.*

# Lizzy 14

*So far so good.*

*Patrick's in a great mood despite the eternal complaints about sleep deprivation, even though he never gets up for Olivia.*

Patrick and Jim, laughing and bantering in the glow of the most enormous bonfire, seem cheerful. Lizzy could relax. She and Liz were sharing notes on their babies, giggling about bulging boobs, empathising about lack of sleep and reporting on all the latest fads to get the little buggers to sleep. The babies being discussed were strapped to their chests and both happily asleep.

Lizzy and Liz were wondering how their babies, William and Olivia, would manage with the upcoming fireworks, but both had well-covered ears. There were loads of feral children running about of all ages, even tiny toddlers whose parents obviously thought they would cope with the noise. It's a once in a lifetime event, after all.

They sipped at their soft drinks, as designated drivers, while their husbands, tucking into the local beer, were getting increasingly jocular.

"Who fancies a hog roast? Smells good," asked Jim, sniffing the air.

Liz declared that she fancied one but the thought of that fatty, oozing, carbohydrate-laden cardboard bread was completely out of the question for Lizzy. Obviously, Jim didn't mind the extra weight that Liz was carrying these days. Patrick was happy with his beer, so Jim headed off to the hog roast tent and Patrick to the beer tent.

"Patrick doesn't change," exclaimed Liz.

"What do you mean?"

"Well, he's always liked a drink, hasn't he?"

*What is she getting at?*

Lizzy felt a bit prickly.

"Don't worry, just an observation. I shouldn't have said anything. Jim says, 'like father like son'."

"I thought George had Parkinson's?"

"Oh, is that what they always said to explain his shakes. Anyway, here comes Patrick now…"

Patrick was coming over towards them, clutching two pint glasses.

*Yes, he is unsteady and he's stumbling a bit, but the ground is slippery and uneven and it must be hard to see in the dark.*

He passed a group of burly blokes who seemed to be mocking him. Lizzy blushed. As he motored on, he suddenly fell flat on his face.

*Like George.*

A burly chap picked him up and put him back on his feet as his posse of friends openly roared with laughter.

Lizzy flinched.

**Can't a bloke have a drink or two to celebrate the Millennium?**

# Lizzy 15

**Lizzy knew immediately that she was pregnant again and knew exactly when it had happened.**

There was something rather historic about conceiving a child on the first day of the new Millennium.

*Not so much the first day but the early hours of the morning.*

She giggled to herself. It was the first time that they'd had sex since Olivia was born, it had been a long time, and the first time ever that Lizzy had initiated it.

*Very brazen.*

She had felt so sorry for Patrick, the humiliation of those yobs laughing at him. He was very surprised but seemed happy to go along with it, managing to stay the course despite the few beers.

Patrick seemed delighted with her news when she coyly revealed her condition. "Perhaps we might get a boy this time." In an extraordinary turn of events, he said that he would stay off the booze all the time that she was pregnant. It had obviously hit him hard, the whole tripping over and mortification thing.

It was lovely to be spending quality time with him, very much like the old days when she had been so preoccupied with her fantasies of married life with Patrick. She resurrected the Elizabeth he had chosen to marry, demure and accommodating. He liked her that way. He managed to get an earlier train home from work and came out for walks with Lizzy and Olivia at the weekends.

*I really must make more effort to be the dutiful and kind wife he wants.*

They were genuinely happy again.

Margaret didn't seem very pleased about it; her nose was definitely out of joint. She scowled when Lizzy placed a casual hand on Patrick's arm, ran her fingers through his hair and planted a kiss on his head. She couldn't help but catch Margaret's eye.

**Ha!**

# Lizzy 16

***Giving birth to their son turned out to be a nightmare.***

Lizzy went into labour just after Patrick had left for work. It was fine for the first few hours, but the contractions felt different this time. Instead of building up like a musical crescendo, they seemed to be random. Just as they were getting going and she thought she was well on her way, they would just as suddenly stop. It made it difficult to know quite what to do.

It was Margaret's day to go and visit Jeremy so she wasn't there, and Olivia was oblivious to her mother's predicament.

*I'll just have to wait and see.*

Lizzy phoned her mum and between them they decided that things were only just starting and maybe it was just Braxton Hicks contractions. Mum offered to come over, but Lizzy thought it unwise with Margaret's current disposition. She would be wrathful if she came home and found Mum there. She wasn't welcome at the best of times.

It went on all day and all night, on and off. Patrick was most solicitous and even rubbed her back.

After another day of weird contractions building and fading, but exhausting all the same, she insisted on going in to find out what was happening. Patrick took her in once he got home from work. Margaret was left with Olivia. She didn't seem to be too pleased but was adamant that Olivia shouldn't go to Mum's.

In the maternity ward there seemed to be a lot of shaking of heads and stroking of chins, listening to baby through old-fashioned Pinard horns, monitoring on a machine attached to her belly, endless taking of blood pressure.

"I think it best if we go for an unplanned caesarean. Baby seems to be getting distressed."

Suddenly she was being undressed, pricked and prodded, dressed, shaved and wiped before being laid on a hard bed in an operating theatre, a cuff placed on her arm, electrodes stuck to her chest, fed oxygen through a rubbery mask and shrouded like a sacrificial virgin. It was gruelling.

The sensation of having your stomach torn open, the slurping sound of amniotic fluid being suctioned out, and the rummaging around to extract the baby, all of it was disgusting. The thought of what was happening was revolting. She lay there in distress, a sheet hiding the activity, when suddenly, really quickly, a messy, bloody, roaring child was placed on her breast. It was hard to accept that this was her own baby, the baby she had been nurturing in her womb. It could be anybody's.

"Your son, Mrs Shepley-Botham."

*Was it? At least Patrick will be thrilled. He has his boy. He will be so happy now.*

Patrick was. He was deliriously overjoyed and bellowed over the vigorous cries of his healthy son, "My clever, darling. You really have come up trumps."

The doctors put in a drip, explained that the placenta was being delivered. She felt queasy. They took the baby boy away for his Apgar scoring. He passed with flying colours. "Of course he has, he is a Shepley-Botham," crowed Patrick.

They then started stitching her poor, damaged belly back together again. A boned and stuffed lamb leg popped into her mind. After being tidied up she was then wheeled into the Recovery Room, where she felt terrible. She was suddenly really cold as well as worn out to the point of delirium.

Patrick gave her a resounding kiss on her weary face. "I have something for you." He rummaged in his pocket and triumphantly pulled out a jewellery box. "For you, my darling."

He thrust it towards her. Lizzy managed a weak, "Thank you." It was all that she could manage, she felt so dazed and woozy and light-headed. She fumbled at the box.

Patrick took it from her and opened it with a flourish to reveal a beautiful circlet of diamonds.

"Thank you." It took a lot of effort to repeat it, she really just wanted to rest.

Patrick's face dropped. "You could sound a little bit more grateful, darling. I do try to make you happy." Patrick hurried away in search of his precious son. Lizzy tried to make things right, but she just didn't have the energy. She managed a pitiful, "I'm sorry."

It was a relief when they took her up to a ward. She could relax at last and try to sleep.

Lying there, Lizzy wasn't sure who had invented the term "too posh to push" but Jesus Christ the searing pain as a result of being cut open and having your baby ripped out seemed far more extreme compared to pushing it out of your vagina. The pain when the anaesthetic wore off was awful. She wanted to cry every time she moved and searing pains shot through her abdomen.

**Patrick celebrated Guillaume's birth with days of partying, involving bubbly, wine and copious amounts of whisky.**

# Lizzy 17

**Lizzy was so bored.**

She thought that married life to Patrick with two children should be fulfilling and was feeling a bit guilty. It was all she had ever wished for.

She felt sorry for herself. Lizzy had hoped that, being so close to London, she would be able to pop up to the capital to see friends, visit theatres, have fun like she used to, but this only happened when she could persuade Margaret to have the children for the day. "Darling, please don't take advantage of Mummy. She is getting on and you can't expect her to keep having the children all day while you gallivant around." Lizzy gave up.

She felt sorry for Olivia too. Guillaume was the apple of her daddy's eye and ever since the day he was born, one of the multitude of celebratory babies born after the Millennium, Olivia hadn't had a look in. Olivia had long ago given up racing to her daddy in the hope of being swooped up, whizzed round and given smacking kisses, which was what happened with her little brother.

Even when they were having fun playing in the vast mausoleum that was their home, all joy was squashed. "Please keep the noise down, dear, your children are just so unruly and undisciplined," Margaret complained. She thought she had married Patrick not Granny Margaret, but she hardly saw Patrick these days. As time marched on he seemed to be getting later and later trains home. She had suggested that she found herself a job, she was itching to get her teeth into something, but Margaret and Patrick freaked out. "A Shepley-Botham wife does not work."

*Married life most certainly has not turned out to be what I was expecting at all.*

Patrick left every morning to catch the train from Wadhurst station. His routine was set in stone. After busily getting himself togged up in his city suit, with clean shirt ironed by his doting mother, eating a plateful of bacon and eggs lovingly cooked for him by his mother, he would drop a kiss on Guillaume and Olivia's heads, kiss his mother and then leave a damp kiss, smelling of toothpaste and an underlying odour of yesterday's booze and cigarettes, on Lizzy's cheek before marching out of the house with a cheery goodbye, clutching his father's old briefcase. No more conspiratorial husband and wife moments. They were long gone.

They would hear the door slam, the engine growl and the tyres of his Volvo scrunch on the gravel as he whizzed down the drive and through the network of lanes to the station. The daily ritual.

She didn't expect him back until late nowadays, usually not until she had already gone to bed. She heard him come in, he didn't seem to make any effort to keep the noise down as he slammed the front door, clumped across the tiled hall, followed his nightly habit of going to the sideboard in the dining room, pouring himself a nightcap and returning to the study, a bottle chinking against a glass. He was drinking too much.

She knew that he would soon be ensconced in his favourite chair, lighting up a Rothmans, ashtray at hand, crystal tumbler in the other, telly on. Like clockwork.

She would wake as he flopped heavily into bed beside her, rolled on to his back and started snoring after only seconds. He reeked of booze and stale smoke.

She could see that he needed to unwind after a hard day's work with a scotch when he got in, but she wasn't entirely sure that he needed to continue this throughout the weekend. Granny didn't help, "For heaven's sake, Elizabeth, get your poor husband a drink. He slaves away all week for you so it is the least you can do." He routinely popped out to get the papers on a Saturday and Sunday morning and retired to the study to "read them in peace."

The children wanted to see their daddy and play with him, but they were banned from his sanctuary. So was she. Lizzy took them out for long walks to keep them happy and out of his way.

She could smell alcohol on him when he came through to join them for lunch, locking the study door behind him. When he pushed the food around his plate, complaining that he was used to decent fine-dining cuisine, not nursery fare, he would leave it and return to the study on unsteady legs, locking them out behind him. "It's the only way I can get peace and quiet."

Every Sunday morning was the ritual of sex. It had become perfunctory and to Lizzy somewhat pointless as they now had their two children, but she let him get on with it. It seemed the easiest thing to do.

Once in a blue moon, they would get asked out for dinner. Granny would babysit as long as Lizzy had the children bathed, settled with a story, and put to bed before they left. At the dinner party, Patrick was the life and soul of the party, getting more and more expansive as the evening progressed. It was usually his friends who would encourage him to more and more outrageous pronouncements.

He seemed to be asked as the after-dinner entertainment, and they would laugh at his antics. Lizzy cringed. They were definitely laughing at him not with him.

Patrick insisted on driving home, frantically sucking on a cigarette to make up for the dearth all evening. The combination of impaired senses and fiddling with a lighter filled Lizzy with terror, but it was easier to go along with it than make a scene in front of Patrick's friends as they jockeyed into the driving seat.

He insisted on using all the back lanes to "avoid the pigs", which made it even more terrifying as they raced along, getting so close to the hedges that the branches scraped down the side of the car. He didn't notice.

They never asked people back, "Mummy can't cope with an invasion of strangers", and the invitations to dinner tailed off. They hadn't seen Liz and Jim for ages. Fair enough, they had been posted to Germany for a tour, but they seemed to have forgotten to pick up again when they returned to the UK.

She was genuinely concerned about his drinking. All his friends drank a lot too, they always had, but she was certain that it wasn't quite as excessive as Patrick's.

She decided to test his mood and casually caught him before he had settled in for the evening with something a little less controversial.

Lizzy had for some time thought that it would be a brilliant time to get a dog. All children love dogs and she would love an excuse to get out more, keep out of Margaret's way. Olivia was always banging on about it, she was aching for a puppy to play with.

She broached it gently, but Patrick most certainly did not agree. "Mummy is allergic to dogs and they make a terrible mess. Horrible flea-ridden things and, if Olivia wants to be entertained, then I think that it is high time she went to prep school."

"But she's only just turned seven."

"I went off to school at seven. It did me the power of good."

Lizzy thought it best not to argue. Patrick was in one of those incalcitrant moods.

*Best not to broach the bigger elephant in the room just now.*

She crept away.

**Poor Olivia, but in truth she might actually prefer school to this atmosphere at home.**

# Lizzy 18

**She tried again.**

*Things can't go on like this.*

She tried to broach the subject, gently and in a sympathetic way, bringing him a pre-luncheon scotch into the study to soften the tone, recognising the irony of her offering, but it gave the excuse that she needed to enter his hallowed space.

Hesitantly, she tried to explain her point of view. "Darling, I am worried about your health. You work such long hours, get very little exercise, you smoke like a chimney and… we want to keep you alive and kicking until you are an ancient old man… we love you so much…"

*Actually, do I? Do I anymore? I can't remember when I stopped… what happened to that God that I worshipped for so long?*

"Perhaps you could think about quitting the cigarettes and…"

*Here goes, I have to try…*

"Maybe you shouldn't be drinking quite so much."

Patrick immediately started one of his lectures, his voice growing louder and angrier as it progressed.

"I have to entertain for work, you surely realise that. It means schmoozing the clients and keeping them sweet with fine wines and boozy outings." Lizzy nodded. She did understand that. "It was all very well when you were pregnant, but those days are gone aren't they? They'd better be."

Lizzy couldn't think what to say.

"It isn't easy, you know, keeping up with such a high-pressure environment. My job is very stressful with new whipper-snappers baying at my heels to steal my clients. I have to give them the best – champagne, caviar and cigars. I can hardly sit there like a total dick and watch them imbibing, can I?"

She wondered how safe he was driving his car from the station if he was drinking so much during the day and tentatively suggested, "Why don't you get a taxi from the station, darling? I wouldn't have to worry about you driving when… when… you are tired."

His response had been explosive. "For fuck's sake, didn't you listen to a word of what I have just said? What do you want? You just can't let me relax for one moment. You are turning into a nagging shrew, making your snide little remarks in front of Mother, trying to show me up in front of the children, always wanting more."

*I never nag… what snide remarks?*

"No wonder I have to have the occasional drink. It is to cope with you. You are such a disappointment to me… and to Mummy. And you are such a hypocrite; look at you serving me with drinks as if it would ingratiate yourself with me… for fuck's sake."

He struck out with his arm and the crystal glass went flying, shattering against the hearth, the whisky spattering everywhere. He leapt up, roughly shoving her out of the way, and she stumbled and nearly fell into the fireplace. He marched out. "I am going to the Old Vine. At least I can get peace and quiet there."

Lizzy stood rooted to the spot, heard him slam out through the front door, the violent acceleration as he sped away, the smell of alcohol hanging accusingly in the air. It was his first physical outburst.

**She went to get a cloth from the kitchen.**

# Lizzy 19

**It was a Wednesday and Patrick arrived home early.**

For the first time in living memory, he came in through the back door. He hollered for his mother. Lizzy went running, wondering what on earth was going on, but as she opened the door into the back porch, he pushed against it, barked at Lizzy not to come in and to go and get his mother.

She was reconciled in her mind that it was easiest in these circumstances to do as he asked; he could get tricky if crossed, particularly if he was already drunk. His mother was allowed through and they whispered as if plotting. Lizzy sat in the kitchen, listening carefully and trying to work out what was happening. Margaret wriggled out awkwardly, so that Lizzy couldn't see Patrick through the open door, went upstairs without saying a word to Lizzy and returned bearing a set of clothes.

She could hear Patrick scuffling about, presumably changing his clothes, and then the sound of the washing machine being started. Patrick and his mother opened the door wide and stepped through looking defiant, obviously hoping that this would stop any questions from Lizzy. It didn't.

"What is going on, darling? Why are you home so early?"

*Why on earth do I still call him 'darling'? Fallacious.*

Granny and Patrick glanced at each other conspiratorially. Patrick then stated, as if practicing for a judge, "Nothing to worry about, darling. I hit a deer on a bicycle. Sadly, it died at the scene, so I had to drag it off the lane and out of the way. As a result, my clothes were messed up with his blood. I didn't want to distress you or the children, you can be rather squeamish about that sort of thing, so Mummy has kindly sorted it all out for me. All taken care of. Nothing more to be done."

The whole effect was rather spoiled by his swaying. He was obviously blotto, saying stupid things about a deer on a bicycle, for God's sake.

"Poor little creature…"

"For fuck's sake, I'm sure it didn't feel a thing. It was over in a flash. Now, after all that kerfuffle, I need a drink."

*I bet you do. But what about the poor deer? I hope it was killed outright.*

"What about the car? Any damage?" But he had already left the room, escorted by his mother.

*Why is he home so early? Most unusual.*

He spent the weekend in his study, drinking and smoking, she assumed, although he had the TV turned on and she could hear excited sports commentators bigging up various events that he claimed to be watching avidly.

*Thank heavens Guillaume is at school and Olivia isn't out on an exeat.*

At one point, she heard an enormous crash. Should she go and check up on him? He had made it quite clear that he didn't want her in his study. The mood that he was in, it seemed unwise, and he was increasingly falling into the furniture and sending it flying, destroying lamps and ornaments in the process. She left it to him and his mother to clear up the mess.

Normal routine resumed. Sunday morning's increasingly perfunctory sex, Monday's leaving after breakfast, returning late, a nightcap in the study, rolling into bed stinking of booze and fags.

**Nothing more was said.**

# Lizzy 20

**The Bursar at Vine Hall collared her when she went to pick up Olivia for an exeat and had a word about the school fees.**

She assumed that Patrick had forgotten to pay them, but it was odd.

Her allowance, a weekly divvy of a bundle of cash ceremoniously handed over with extreme unction, had dried up to a sporadic fistful of crumpled notes left on the kitchen table. She would get up the courage to ask, when Margaret wasn't in listening range. His excuses were varied. "I haven't been to the cash machine, darling", "Don't keep nagging, darling. I will sort it out next week", "Of course I have paid, the idiotic fools have messed up."

So many explanations and always so feasible, difficult to contradict. She had even resorted to doing her own hair with the cheap dye they sold at the Wadhurst chemist, not a good look and pounced upon by Patrick. "You look like a whore, darling."

"Oh, she does, Patrick, doesn't she?" Tinkling laughter from Margaret.

Giggles from Guillaume, who clearly didn't understand but thought it would please Daddy.

**Alarm bells.**

# Lizzy 21

**Mum called and they made a last-minute arrangement to visit her sister in Wiltshire together.**

It saved Mum driving. They were going for the weekend, a bit of respite for her and the kids, she thought, a fun filled weekend with no tension or drama – no Patrick or Margaret.

Rather than let him get home and be told where they were by Margaret, she thought it polite to let him know so rang him at the office, a rarity because he hated to be disturbed during working hours. She hadn't done so for years.

She was surprised to be told that "Patrick Shepley-Botham doesn't work here anymore."

Perhaps she had used the wrong number, or it had changed – it had been so long since she used it. She tried his mobile but that gave a number unobtainable.

*Sod it, I will leave it to Granny to explain our absence.*

They arrived back on Sunday evening, the children sleepy from the long car journey and ready for bed. They hugged Patrick, who squeezed them tight and gave each of them a resounding kiss accompanied by a loud smacking sound. It made Guillaume laugh with delight. He loved his daddy. Olivia was less impressed, wriggling out of her father's clutches and heading upstairs.

They settled easily, too tired for the nightly story, a kiss and a hug for each of them, and were soon sound asleep. She tiptoed downstairs.

Lizzy remembered that she ought to have Patrick's correct number in her records in case she needed to get hold of him urgently. Supposing something happened to his mother? Or the children? It seemed an inconsequential request.

"By the way, darling, could I have your new work number please? I couldn't get hold of you on Friday."

He went ballistic.

"So you are checking up on me now, are you? I can't even go to work without you hunting me down. How dare you. I told you that I had moved offices, you just don't listen. Use my mobile if you have to, but I don't expect you to go snooping around checking up on me."

"I tried your mobile and it was unobtainable…"

"You can't even dial a number correctly. You are becoming totally impossible."

*I wonder who is becoming totally impossible here.*

"Just stop banging on. I am going to the study. It would be sincerely appreciated if I could be in my own home without being nagged and interrogated. And don't even think of prying in there."

She stood there not quite knowing what to say. Margaret glared at her. "For heaven's sake, Elizabeth. You have only been down for five minutes and already you have started on at poor Patrick again." She bustled into the study after her son.

She didn't see either of them again that evening. He came to bed very late but still managed to get up in the morning and go off to the train at his regular time. Routine was resumed. She had a nagging thought.

***What had he meant by 'don't even think of prying in there'? What did he have to hide?***

# Lizzy 22

**She resisted going into the study for weeks.**

If he wanted to make it his private den that was up to him, but she needed to dig out Olivia's passport for an upcoming school trip. She wasn't very surprised to find the study door locked.

She had no idea where he might be keeping the key. Did Margaret have one? She didn't even know if there was a spare one. Her curiosity was piqued. Margaret was on her weekly visit to Jeremy so she decided to see if she could get in. She felt all around the door frame. Nothing. She looked in the drawers of the hall table. Nope. She went outside and looked at the windows, but they were firmly closed and the curtains were drawn. She went and made a cup of coffee and pondered.

*He most definitely doesn't want me going in there.*

"I am an idiot," she said out loud as she remembered that there was a two-way cupboard between the study and the dining room. It took ages to pull out all the rubbish from the bottom of the cupboard, endless heavy cutlery canteens, old decanters with tarnished silver necklaces, glass bowls with spider skeletons in them. She checked her watch. She still had time before Margaret reappeared.

She wiggled across the dusty shelf, her face tickled by cobwebs, and pushed the door on the other side.

*Phew, not locked. They didn't think of this!*

She heaved herself up and looked at the study from an unaccustomed viewpoint and immediately kicked a bottle, which chinked alarmingly. It was hard to see with the curtains closed, they were such thick brocade. The atmosphere was stale and smelt of an old pub, acrid and dank with musty alcohol and stale smoke. She tiptoed over, turned on the light and looked around her.

It was a mess, papers higgledy-piggledy all over the desk and cascading on to the heavily stained carpet, discarded empty bottles unashamedly on show, brimming ashtrays. It looked as if a burglary had just taken place, with no effort made to close doors and drawers, replace books on the shelves, and no attempt to create any semblance of order. No attempt to hide the fact that Patrick was a total, out and out, rock bottom alcoholic.

*Oh my God, this is bad. Really, really dire. No wonder he locks it and won't let me in. What must Margaret think?*

She tentatively crossed over to the bureau, its leather top, the small bits that she could see under the mess of paperwork, was stained with concentric rings from the bottoms of damp bottles and overflowing ashtrays. She glanced at the proliferation of letters and roughly torn envelopes and picked one up at random, turning on the lamp so that she could read it. A bank statement.

*Jesus Christ, overdrawn by £20,568.*

She was shocked. She rifled through the other letters strewn across the desk. Credit card bills. Credit card slips, loads of them. Letters from the banks and credit card companies. All demanding payment. Solicitor's letters. County Court Judgements. Letters from Guillaume and Olivia's school about unpaid fees. She worked her way through them.

*Why is Patrick in debt? Surely his salary must cover his outgoings. What has happened to all the money from the Chelsea house sale?*

She was so wrapped up in the horror of the financial mess spewed across the desk she forgot the time. The sound of Margaret coming back sent a dart of shock through her. She snapped the light off, scuttled back to the cupboard and tunnelled back through. She met Margaret's legs.

"What on earth are you doing?"

Lizzy couldn't decide what to say. She felt a total idiot. She could hardly say that she was clearing out the cupboard as she was half inside it.

"I think we need to talk, Margaret."

"After you could explain why you are in the cupboard."

*There is only one thing for it. It is the only way that I am going to get to the bottom of all this. I'm a grown woman. I'm his wife, for fuck's sake.*

"I was trying to find Olivia's passport. This was the only way that I could get into the study. The door is locked."

"Of course it is. Patrick knows you like to go snooping about and you have rather proved his point."

"But Margaret... the money... the bottles... have you seen... have you any idea..." Lizzy wriggled up from the floor.

"I don't think that it's any of your business."

"But Margaret... the debts... why... do you know what is going on? I knew about the drinking but not the overdrafts..."

"Patrick takes care of us. Why can't you be satisfied that you live in such a luxurious home with such a devoted husband? You don't lift a finger to help out, just make unreasonable demands. You are just so... so selfish."

**She marched out leaving Lizzy gobsmacked.**

# Lizzy 23

**Lizzy waited for Patrick to get home, sitting bolt upright in the hall chair.**

He fell in through the front door. He was plastered.

*Am I surprised? No.*

She stood up and he noticed her. "Hello, darling. What a lovely surprise." She couldn't help notice that he put a sneer into the word 'darling'. He was slurring and swayed towards her.

"Patrick, I am going to come straight to the point. I have been in the study and know what the financial position is."

"You nosy cow. How dare you?" He was working himself up to shout but suddenly said, in a surprised normal voice, "How did you get in?" He looked exaggeratedly puzzled, like a ham actor. It was almost comical.

"I have seen the letters, the demands for money, the whole mess. The bottle collection wasn't a surprise, but I wonder if you could explain to me just what is going on."

He lurched towards her, his voice turning nasty. "Keep your nosy nose out of my business, you nosy cow."

She sidestepped and he crashed into the hall table. An ominous sound of breaking glass came from within his father's briefcase.

"Fuck."

"Patrick. Talk to me."

"Fuck off."

"No, I won't, Patrick. I need to know what is going on."

"For fuck's sake, you idiot. It is all your fault. You wanted the high life, nagging about getting the children into a good school, demands for fancy holidays, your high maintenance living, expensive hair dos, your airs and graces. Nothing is ever good enough for you. What do you expect? It all has to be paid for."

"But Patrick, surely the money from the Chelsea house... your high-powered job..."

"What fucking money? I never owned that house. That is why we had to move out when the owners came back from abroad. Why else do you think we moved out to the godforsaken country to this ghastly house? I hate it. I hated commuting. I hated the whole fucking thing."

"But you seem to enjoy your job. I know you work long hours but...."

"My fucking job! My fucking, fucking job. What fucking job? The bonuses dried up. They kicked me out and you didn't even care. I couldn't even tell you because you just want me to spend, spend, spend – that is all you care about. That night when I got back from having been fired, all you cared about was the fucking, fucking deer. Do you remember that? Do you? 'Poor little creature...' That is what you said... poor little fucking creature." He said it in a ridiculous high-pitched voice.

"But Patrick, you leave the house like clockwork..."

"Oh yes, I do, don't I? Got to keep up appearances, don't you know? I get off the train at Tonbridge. There are lots of cafes... and the library... you get free newspapers there, you know... the cinema... passes the time..."

*And pubs and off licences...*

He lumbered over to the study, took the key out of his pocket and opened the door.

"Come in, come in, why don't you? Have a good nose around at your leisure… have a fucking drink… Oh no, of course, Miss High and Mighty, you don't drink, do you? Then just fuck off. Fuck off, you nosy cow bitch wanker."

**Lizzy realised that it was time to leave.**

# Lizzy 24

**She loved her new home.**

It was tiny but had three bedrooms, each very small but enough for the three of them. It was cosy and surprisingly warm downstairs, with the Aga and the enormous log fire in the giant-sized inglenook fireplace. Upstairs was freezing and there was only a feeble bar heater in the bathroom and hopeless storage heaters for the bedrooms. The whole of the downstairs would happily fit into the kitchen at Margaret's, but it was perfect for her, Guillaume and Olivia.

Lizzy had discovered the feeling of being lighthearted and free from the enormous weight that had weighed down her soul. It made her want to whoop and dance and sing. The only irritation was that Patrick still came to take the children every other weekend. Guillaume still seemed to be eager to go. Olivia tried to make all sorts of excuses not to.

The only thing that she had taken away from her marriage to Patrick, apart from a few lessons learnt, was the VW Golf and her clothes – and her lovely innocent children of course. She had a roof over her head, the wherewithal to get about, and she had her children with her. She was okay. She would manage.

She was satisfied with her new job as PA to a solicitor in Tunbridge Wells. The job didn't pay much and it had been sad to have to take Olivia out of Vine Hall. Secretly she was delighted to have her at home to chat to every day, to hug and to cuddle, instead of packed off to a boarding school. She had put up with it because it seemed to be 'the thing to do' and kept her away from her drunk father.

It turned out that Olivia was very happy to have moved schools. She confessed that she squirmed with embarrassment when Patrick had insisted on coming to see school plays or attend parents' evening at Vine Hall. It is a strange and difficult position to be in, standing alongside your father who is patently drunk and trying to pretend that you haven't noticed and that you haven't observed that everyone around is clearly aware of his inebriated condition. The English are exceptionally good at ignoring giant, trumpeting bull elephants in the room. It also turned out that she was teased endlessly by all the kids and called 'I've a Shapely-Bum'. She didn't like it.

The children were young enough at seven and nine to not even realise the difference between the private and state sector, and their new school, St Mary's Lamberhurst, was fabulous, newly built and receiving outstanding ratings from OFSTED.

*What is the point of paying for education when you can get into such a fantastic school for free?*

They had settled happily into St Mary's, restyled as simply the Bothams, and had made new friends easily. They had at least inherited their father's gregarious nature and charm, she just hoped to God that they hadn't inherited the drinking gene.

Guillaume hadn't seemed to have perceived the state of his father. Perhaps he didn't want to – he was the only daddy that he had. He acted as if he was the most perfect parent in the whole world, was very affectionate and responsive towards him, receptive to his over enthusiastic hugs and smacking kisses. The look of hurt on his face when Patrick wasn't in the mood for playing at being paternal was wounding. I wonder why he doesn't recoil from his pervasive smell. Perhaps he thinks that is what all daddies smell like.

She dreaded the days when he came to pick up the children for his 'every other weekend'. He didn't even bother to knock or ring the bell, just strode in, ducking under the low lintel before coming to full height on the mat, dominating the kitchen.

*He's not bloody well coming in any further.*

Guillaume was delighted to see him, rushing to him with a cry of "Daddy!" Patrick picked him up and looked to twirl him around, but he couldn't because there wasn't enough space. Olivia held back.

Patrick claimed to have been to rehab and 'dried out', he promised that he had reformed and that his drinking days were over: "never again… I have learnt my lesson… Come home… Guillaume, Olivia, don't you want Mummy to come home?"

He was lying. It was so obvious, the dank sweatiness, the jumpy eyes, the over hearty speech, the careful one foot in front of the other. She couldn't accuse him outright – it didn't work.

"I swear to God that I am completely sober. I do rather resent the way you keep accusing me. It isn't good for the children that you persist with these allegations. What more do you want me to do? Take a breathalyser? Would that prove it to you? Come on, Guillaume, Olivia, let's go along with Mummy's silly accusations. Test me."

He stood there with his chest puffed out, arms wide, and a supercilious look on his face, glaring at her. She only wished that she did have a breathalyser kit. She would bloody well call his bluff.

**At least God knows.**

# Lizzy 25

**It was Patrick's weekend with the children.**

It was Lizzy's weekend alone. She was using it as a chance to have a supper party, just local friends, mostly girls and their partners that she had met over the last five years, and an old friend from schooldays who she had met up with again. It was a passing nod to her birthday but mostly a celebration of her divorce from Patrick. She had 'won' her decree absolute at last. Finally she was free of any liability for his burgeoning debts.

The bastard had refused point blank to get a divorce on the grounds of his unreasonable behaviour and made her wait out the full five years. When they met with solicitors he was a different person, back to his old charming self. He convinced them that he wasn't drinking any more, that he was a lonely man who missed his wife and children and wished they would come home. He managed to make her out to be the wicked witch in all of this.

*At least I can see why I fell for the charm all those years ago.*

"You were the one who walked out, not me. I am not the one who has removed the children from their wonderful home and made them live in a hovel. I am not the one who has taken them out of a fantastic school and put them into the State system. You are the one who has totally ruined their prospects… deprived them of a safe, secure and happy home…"

*Rant, rant, rant. No point in even trying to say anything.*

She was sure that it had nothing to do with his dignity, sense of hurt and especially nothing to do with the children, but to avoid having to pay up anything in the way of maintenance. Mind you, there wasn't any money to give her, he only had debts. The bailiffs had been unable to get anything out of him because everything was in his mother's name, even his car.

The children were upstairs getting their stuff together while she happily prepared tonight's celebratory menu. She liked to experiment and be creative with food, while still serving up something healthy and light, and she was busy de-boning a chicken. She heard him draw up, his Volvo had a distinctive growl but seemed to have developed a new squeaky rattle. She was surprised that it was still going after all this time.

Her mood sank. She shouted up to the children, who were fiddling around upstairs, distracting her from her sharp knife. She stabbed herself.

*Bugger.*

She grabbed a tea towel off the Aga rail, wrapping her bleeding hand as she opened the door before he burst in in his usual ostentatious way.

He stood there, looking horrified, a complete look of surprise on his face. He splayed out his hands. They were covered in blood. "May I wash my hands? I have done it again. Bloody deer. They just jump out at one." He was clearly plastered.

Lizzy wasn't sure what to do. She didn't want him to come in, this was her place of sanctuary and sacrosanct, but neither did she think it very appropriate for her children to see their father with blood on his hands. She stepped aside and waved her hand towards the sink. He dwarfed the small space. She was at a loss as to what to say. She certainly wasn't going to offer him any sympathy.

*Poor creature. Do I dare ask if it is okay? Clearly not by the amount of blood. Best not say anything after last time.*

It made her think of that pivotal day five years ago, the beginning of the end of their marriage. It made her shudder but, more than anything, she was terrified to think that he might harm Guillaume and Olivia by his erratic driving and his evident inability to react in an emergency situation.

As he ran his hands under the tap, swaying gently, she couldn't help but ask, "Are you in any fit state to take the children in the car?"

"Now what? What are you accusing me of now? For fuck's sake…" He was interrupted by Guillaume and Olivia coming into the room, each clutching a rucksack.

His voice changed in a trice. "My darlings, how are you? I was just explaining to Mummy that I hit a deer in the lane on the way here. Let me just dry my hands and I will be with you and we can get off."

He could switch from angry tyrant to bountiful, cheery patriarch in a second. He virtually snatched the tea towel from Lizzy's hands and wiped his hands thoroughly. "Lovely to see you. The car is okay, just a few dents, fine to drive. Damned deer. It isn't the first time…" He shoved the tea towel back at her as if she were his slave.

*Arrogant bastard. Pissed, arrogant bastard. Are the children safe? What can I do?*

She had to let them go. She found herself wringing the tea towel, looking down at it and feeling his hands on it.

**Seeing the blood, she shoved it in the bin with disgust.**

# Lizzy 26

**Olivia was full of it when she got back from school on Monday.**

"A girl who used to go to our school, her mum was hit by a car. It was a hit and run."

"Poor woman. How dreadful. Is she all right?"

"Don't know, but the ambulance that picked her up found all sorts of stuff belonging to someone else right underneath her. Guess who?"

"I don't know."

*What on earth is she on about?*

"Well, the thing is it is such a mystery. The stuff was from a teacher from our school who disappeared five years ago. His bicycle, his rucksack and other stuff. Do you remember when that happened? It was before I started there?"

*I wonder why children nowadays speak in questions all the time…*

"I don't remember it at all. How old would I have been? I would have been nine? It is all so spooky."

Lizzy remembered vaguely only because they lived nearby but she was far too wrapped up in her own problems at the time to take much notice. It was in the days when she was trying to keep her marriage going.

*Why did I bother?*

Her hazy recollection was a man had taken his own life. There was a schoolgirl involved somewhere. It had been in the *Kent and Sussex Courier*. His wife had plastered the place with flyers. It was pitiful at the time.

*His poor wife. It must have been so dreadful for her. I wonder if he had kids. I can't remember.*

"Anyways, Mum – what's for tea?"

***Typical fourteen-year-old, always starving. I mustn't let her get fat.***

# Lizzy 27

**Lizzy didn't bother with newspapers or watching the news on TV.**

She had made a conscious decision to live in her own little bubble and let the troubles of the world float around her in the ether. She preferred to watch endless old feel-good movies on the DVD player with a comforting cup of tea by her side. She only had booze in the house when she had visitors. It made her feel guilty to have alcohol on show in front of the children at any other time.

Sharing the one and only TV worked out okay. Olivia insisted on watching *The Voice*, which she and Guillaume found appalling, but then Lizzy did have a sneaky penchant for *Call the Midwife* on a Sunday evening, which the children found cheesy. She let Guillaume take over the telly for *Fresh Meat*, which wasn't entirely suitable. She liked Jack Whitehall; he was funny, so she didn't mind. The give and take and quarrels over choice of TV – a cosy, normal family. Peaceful.

Olivia had been keeping her posted on the scandal of the lost teacher from school; she seemed to have a rather unhealthy obsession with the whole thing. Lizzy thought it gruesome. It was so sad that the poor woman who had been hit by a car had now died. The most extraordinary thing was that it turned out that she was the mother of the child that had been involved in the missing teacher episode.

*This is getting very complicated. Was it a coincidence? Could the two incidents be linked in some way? Very mysterious.*

They had the *Kent and Sussex Courier* at work and she idly picked it up to read the sorry tale on the front page. The main picture was presumably of the family bereft by their loss. He was a good-looking chap, with lovely crinkled eyes; he looked such a kind and loving husband. He had his arms protectively around a boy, the spitting image of him, and a girl who looked as if she was from a completely different family. She reminded Lizzy a bit of Olivia, perhaps it was the latest standard for long straight hair that was in vogue. The text gave more details about where and when the incident had taken place.

*Good God, just up the road, Sweetings Lane. Very close to us. It could have been one of us.*

Lizzy shuddered. She suddenly took an interest, so close to home. She went on to read a heartfelt plea from the poor victim's husband for any information about the incident. 'Did anyone see or hear anything at all on that Friday? Did anyone you know appear anxious? Someone must have met the perpetrator, who would have been covered in blood.' A stab of adrenalin shot through Lizzy's core.

*Covered in blood? Friday?*

She stiffened, horrified. She could feel her heart thudding.

*Oh my God, oh my God. Could it be...?*

Was she jumping to conclusions? Was it just a coincidence? She ran it through her mind like watching a DVD. She 'rewound' and 'watched' carefully again. And again.

*He said a deer? The blood... He was agitated when she first saw him... He would have come down Sweetings Lane if he was avoiding the main road... What was he wearing? It could be important.*

What on earth should she do? Supposing it had been just a deer, but it all fitted and he was such an accomplished liar. How could she find out? This was the father of her children she was thinking about accusing of a heinous and terrible thing.

*Perhaps it was a deer? But a second time… was it possible to happen twice so conveniently?*

There was also a nagging echo about a deer and a bicycle.

*A deer on a bicycle?*

She sat and listened to the thudding reverberating through her head, her fists gripping and crumpling the paper. She had forgotten to breathe.

*He dried his hands on the tea towel… I put it in the bin when he left…*

Her boss, Martin, came in. She looked up, startled.

"What on earth is the matter? You look as if you have seen a ghost."

"Please can I… I need to tell someone… I think… Patrick…"

She burst into sobs, her whole body shaking in anguish, and babbled out her suspicions.

"I'm afraid you must go to the police."

"But what if it was a deer?"

"I think that the police should be the ones to check that out, don't you?"

She got home at 6pm and the children were waiting for her. She hated leaving them home on their own, even though Olivia was fourteen and perfectly responsible enough to be left in charge.

"Are you okay, Mum? We were worried when you called."

She had concocted a story about having to see the police on a matter related to work. It seemed easier that way and close enough to the truth to get away with it. It turned out that she was quite a good liar too.

"I'm fine. I'm afraid it is confidential. What I need now is a cup of tea."

*Actually, I'd prefer a large glass of wine.*

The thought of that tea towel at the bottom of the bin was preying on her mind. It could be the evidence that the police needed, but she couldn't make the children suspicious. She racked her brains for a reasonable explanation and crafted a cock and bull story about a ring that she had taken off to debone the chicken and not seen since. She needed to see if it had ended up in the dustbin. Thank God the main landfill bins didn't go until Tuesday.

She put on rubber gloves, pulled out the bin bags gingerly from the wheelie bin, found the one she was looking for and delved into it. She could feel the bones wrapped in newspaper and knew she was close. She found it, dragged it out, and looked at it. The blood had gone black and the whole thing stank of rotting chicken. It made her gag. She shoved it into a plastic bag – not quite the evidence bag she had seen in films – shovelled the other stuff back into the wheelie bin and walked triumphantly into the kitchen.

"You found it then, Mum?"

"Yes, I did, thank you, Guillaume." She clutched the carrier bag in her gloved hands, trying not to look guilty.

*Now what? I will have to wait until tomorrow to take it to the police. Or should I slip out now?*

# Lizzy 28

**The inquest of Elizabeth Arbuthnott had taken place at the Coroner's Court**.

Martin had explained that the purpose of the inquest was to determine the cause of death. It did not have to establish why the death occurred but only who the deceased was and how, when and where the death occurred. There would be no determination of any criminal liability for her death and no apportionment of guilt or blame. Any involvement of Patrick would not be considered at all. It all seemed to drag on.

Lizzy was on tenterhooks. She had thought that her evidence and the tea towel would result in a revelation for the police, but they were playing things very close to their chests. Her enquiries about the tea towel were met with, "It has been inconclusive. We only found your blood."

*Why didn't they find someone else's blood... or the deer's blood? Had he washed his hands that well? Perhaps I am just imagining the whole thing because I hate him and he has got away with so much crap over the years.*

She still hadn't said anything to the children. A team of forensic people came, fortunately during the day in school hours, and diligently inspected the path from where Patrick had parked the car, the doorstep, the kitchen floor. They delved under the sink and took samples from the drain. She knew that she must have washed up at least twenty loads since then, particularly all the dishes from the supper party, so she watched them knowing that they were unlikely to find anything, whether deer's blood or anything else.

It had rained too. She always washed the kitchen floor after it had rained because the children always made muddy footmarks as they stepped in from outside, despite endless nagging to wipe their feet. Rain would have diluted anything on the path and her diligent housework would have removed whatever might have been on the floor. It was all so frustrating.

*Am I wishing that it was him?*

She heard that Patrick had been interviewed, the house searched, but nothing had come of it as far as she knew. She assumed that they would have spoken to Margaret too.

*Do the children know that? What has he said to them? What do I tell the children? Do I need to prepare them for devastating revelations? Maybe it was just a bloody deer. Surely the police will have looked for a dead deer?*

She had to keep her fears, and any suspicions that the police might have, from the children but it was harder than she thought. Rumours were flying around at school. Olivia was horrified that somehow her father had become connected to this appalling situation.

"Mummy, people are saying horrible things. They are trying to say that Daddy is involved somehow. They have searched Granny's house and asked Daddy loads of questions. It can't be true, can it, Mummy?"

Guillaume took it all like a pre-teen and just called it a "whole lot of crap" before marching off to his bedroom.

*What can I say?*

It was going round and round in her head and she just didn't know what to think or what to do for the best. She was ninety-nine percent certain that he must have done it. But that one percent nagged.

*It could have been a deer...*

She couldn't say anything to the children other than, "I don't know why everyone is saying all these things. I'm sure it will get sorted out. The police will get to the bottom of it."

**At least she was being truthful.**

# Lizzy 29

**He came to collect them as previously scheduled on the Friday.**

There was absolutely no reason that she could think of that could stop him, and she thought that she would scream.

She noticed that Patrick seemed particularly shaky and she realised that, for the first time since she could remember, he appeared to be sober. He sounded different. It was strange to get a faint whiff of that different smell, how he used to smell when he was the young, handsome man she was besotted with. It seemed a lifetime ago.

Did he realise that she had told the police about that fateful visit? Did he know that they had taken samples from her plumbing? Did he know that she knew that they had interviewed him and searched his home? They were both pretending that nothing untoward was happening at all.

She pinned her usual polite smile on her face as if everything was normal.

He enfolded a happy Guillaume in a great big bear hug. "How are you, my favourite son and heir? Guess what I have got for you at home. No, you will have to wait and see."

*Home, he always referred to his place as home. It rankles.*

Olivia held back. She was reluctant to go with her father, probably for good reason.

She kissed her children goodbye, patted a reluctant Olivia on the shoulder. "Off you go love, have fun."

*What else can I do?*

# Lizzy 30

**Her boss told her that Patrick had been arrested and bailed pending investigation.**

He obviously tried to tell her gently, but it was like being hit in the face with a bucket of iced water. She went cold and didn't know whether to be delighted that he was being brought to justice or horrified of the effect that it was going to have on Guillaume and Olivia.

He calmly told her that Forensics had found scraps of paint from the Volvo and tiny fragments of glass. They could identify from these miniscule bits the exact make and year of a vehicle. They had found out where Patrick had taken the car for repairs. It had all stacked up and they had enough evidence to take him to a plea hearing.

"What happens now?"

"He will have to go to court. I assume that he will plead Not Guilty. The police file then goes to the Crown Prosecution Service who will decide if it is in the interests of the public to prosecute and assess the likelihood of a conviction. It won't be until then that there will be a date set for a trial, if there is one."

Lizzy sighed.

"After his plea hearing, he won't be allowed any contact with the witnesses, so he will have to know if you are going to give evidence. You do realise that you will be required to give evidence?"

Her head swirled. She thought she was going to throw up.

*What am I going to tell the children?*

Lizzy frantically searched the internet to research the possible impact on Guillaume and Olivia. She ascertained that there was professional help available and made a note of numbers for Victim Support and the NSPCC. She found herself reading a piece of advice on how to intervene if they were panicking, keep asking "What are the facts?", get them to breathe in and out deeply.

There was another horrifying idea about filling a bowl with cold water and sticking your face in it to calm you down. It sounded weird. The suggestion just to listen and let them talk about it made more sense and she hadn't thought that she might need to reassure them that they were in no way to blame.

*How could they be? Why would they think they were?*

She wondered what they had heard at school. All the kids had mobile phones these days and access to the internet. Everything was so instant, particularly the bad news. She left the office early to make sure that she was at home to greet them from the school bus. Her heart was thumping, as was her head.

*Funnily enough, I can see why sticking your face in cold water might seem to be a good idea.*

Olivia seemed to be much older than her fourteen years, and she seemed philosophical. She had long ago lost respect for her father and was clearly aware of his weaknesses – or especially his one all-consuming weakness. Lizzy could see that she was not unduly surprised by the revelation of her father's arrest after all the rumours that had been flying around. It didn't make it any easier for her. She looked crushed.

*Poor darling girl.*

Guillaume had absolute hysterics and screamed the place down. Twelve was a difficult age to find out that your worshipped daddy, who you refuse to believe is an alcoholic, has killed someone, or at least smashed them up with their car and dragged them into a rubbish dump to die.

Lizzy decided that the best thing to do was to let it all come out. She tried hugging him but Guillaume thrashed about wildly yelling, "Daddy's right – it's all your fault. Everything is your fault."

It didn't seem to be quite the right time to tell them that she was required to be a witness for the prosecution at this trial.

*My poor babies. How did it come to this?*

# Lizzy 31

**Lizzy had never been in a courtroom before, let alone a Crown Court with its enormous air of importance.**

The whole process wasn't at all what she was expecting. She had given the police a statement telling them about that fateful evening frame by frame, she knew it in the minutest detail in slow motion.

She tried to tell them about the time before when he had hit a deer, but they weren't interested and dismissed it as irrelevant. They seemed so disinterested that she thought it would sound stupid to mention the whole "deer on a bicycle" remark. They were so dismissive that she wondered if she made it up, she found herself almost whining in the hope of making them listen.

She signed her statement and that was the last she had heard from them. They weren't at all interested in the tea towel either. That remained a mystery.

She then found herself with some lawyers who asked her to repeat it all again. Apparently, they were acting for the prosecution. In films, this had always seemed to involve a great deal of discussion and an element of coaching on what to say, and what not to say. There was nothing of the kind. She realised that, at the end of the day, she had very little to say about just a few minutes out of a long challenging lifetime.

They listened carefully when she told them about the time before, but she noted that they didn't write anything down either. They weren't interested in anything that happened in the years before and, in fact, despite the impact it had on her and the children, they were right – the past didn't actually have anything to do with it.

Now that it came to it, it was the effect on them more than anything else that was tearing her apart. She sat Guillaume and Olivia down and told them as calmly and factually as possible that she was obliged to take the stand as a witness and what she would be saying and why. She had rehearsed it over and over again beforehand for all their benefit. To her ears it did seem very subjective. Was he drunk? Was it relevant whether he was or not?

*I am absolutely certain about the precise time and exact day and completely adamant that he had blood on his hands. But whose was it?*

She had to wait outside the courtroom until she was called. She sat on a bench alone, not sure what to do and too scared to go and get a coffee or go to the loo in case they called her. No-one spoke to her. She waited all day. There were other people hanging around too. She daren't speak to them in case she wasn't meant to and got into trouble or invalidated her evidence. They might even be witnesses for the defence. A bewigged barrister came out at four o'clock and told her that she could go home.

She returned the next day and settled on the same seat. She'd brought her Kindle with her this time to pass the time and to stop herself from getting into a state. She had downloaded a new book and, because she couldn't think what to buy, she just went for the Booker Prize winner as everyone was saying how brilliant it was. At the time it completely passed her by that *Bring Up the Bodies* was ultimately about a trial.

She reread the same pages over and over again and couldn't get into it. She looked up every time someone walked by or emerged from a door. One of the other people whispering would send a tingle of adrenalin through her.

Someone she hadn't seen before appeared calling "Mrs Shepley". It made her jump, and he invited her to follow him through a big imposing door. She followed him up a short flight of heavy stairs and it was like walking out onto a theatre stage.

*Why Mrs Shepley? What happened to the Botham?*

There was a stereotypical judge, just like in the films, looking old and wrinkled and dressed in fancy robes with a ridiculous wig. He was flanked by a cast of players who presumably each had their part to play. The jury sat in two tiers of seats, looking at her with interest as the newest character in the drama. A whole audience sat in a gallery gaping down. For the first time in her life she understood the expression 'stage fright'. She was centre stage.

She was ushered into the witness box on wobbly legs. It was terrifying. She didn't know where to look to avoid the array of eyes that were staring at her. She suddenly spotted Patrick. He looked smart, cleanly shaven, his hair tidy, quite the gentleman. He stood out for being handsome amongst so many ordinary-looking people but he was glaring at her, she could feel the malice from here.

*I mustn't look at him again. I can't. Oh God, I feel sick.*

Like a zombie, she took the oath. The barrister that she had seen briefly the day before began asking her questions. She tried to answer but her voice came out in a squeak.

"Take a deep breath, Mrs Shepley, and take your time." She tried to.

***Why** Mrs Shepley?*

"Would you prefer to sit down, Mrs Shepley? Perhaps have a sip of water," enquired the judge.

*How embarrassing.*

The barrister that she had met the day before started asking questions. "Please could you describe the day when Patrick Shepley came to your house..." It was easy enough to answer his questions.

*Why Patrick Shepley?*

She realised that she actually had very little to say but had practiced it in her head like lines. Once she started, she was able to tell everyone about his arrival, his drunk appearance, his agitation, his explanation, the blood, his washing and drying his hands.

*Nothing about the deer on a bicycle.*

Suddenly another chap in a wig bobbed up. The defence barrister, she could only assume. He questioned her aggressively in a sing-song voice, a ham actor. Each question came out with barely a chance to answer the one before.

"What is the nature of your relationship with the defendant? Would you say that **your** observations were objective? Who else witnessed the arrival of the defendant? What evidence do you have that the defendant was 'distressed'? Did anyone else 'see' the blood that you **claim** was on his hands? Why do you think that there was no evidence of any blood on the tea towel, other than yours, that you **claim** that he used? Can you be definite that the defendant was inebriated? How can you be certain? Are you sure that **any** of this happened as you are claiming? Can any of this so-called evidence be corroborated? It seems to me that you could be saying anything at all..."

He paused and posed like Henry VIII. "There is something I don't quite understand..." Another pose. "You say that Major Shepley was inebriated and in some distress. You knew that he was planning to drive the children to his home. Why, but **why**, did you therefore let your children go with him?"

She thought she was going to cry. It was horrible. Had she imagined the whole thing? Was she exaggerating? Was it a deer?

Suddenly the barrister turned to the judge. "No more questions, m'lud." He abruptly sat down in his seat. She was 'dismissed' and left the room, her head all over the place. She wandered out into the quiet corridor, shell-shocked, and wasn't sure where to go. Did she want to stay and hear any more?

*Too exhausted – physically, mentally and emotionally. I need a drink. Ironic.*

# Lizzy 32

**The trial had been going on for days as the defence made their case.**

She had become resigned to it going on and on and to the insatiable appetite of everyone round about for more sensational revelations. The *Kent and Sussex Courier* were having a field day. Wherever she went, the billboards yelled the latest juicy detail.

She found herself reading every column inch avidly. It transpired that the Shepley-Botham family weren't double-barrelled at all. George was Shepley and Margaret was Botham and they had simply joined the two up to make themselves sound more posh.

*I'm such a fool to have been taken in by those ridiculous airs and graces.*

She was astonished to read that Margaret had stood up in court and stated that she and Patrick had just had a cup of tea together and a digestive biscuit when he left to pick up the children. She poo-pooed the idea that he had been drinking, other than tea. It's funny how those little details of a particular brand of biscuit make a difference to whether you are believed or not.

*Perhaps he had had a snifter, or ten, in the car as he drove along. Who knew? He was definitely, definitely drunk by the time he arrived on my doorstep covered in blood.*

It turned out too that, according to Margaret, Lizzy had been a most haughty, profligate wife and mother. Margaret somehow made out that Lizzy was untrustworthy, vindictive and obviously a liar. There didn't seem to have been much point in giving her version of events after all.

Everyone continued to stare at Lizzy wherever she went. She couldn't bear to be recognised as Mrs Shepley and associated with the whole circus as if it was her fault too or that she was the "vindictive, lying wife."

*Thank God, I chose the Botham bit for the children to use at school.*

She decided to dye her hair the colour it used to be before she started her masquerade of a life as a blonde. She cut it much shorter than it had been for twenty-five years in the hope that together it would disguise her identity. At least the colour was how she imagined it had been, it was hard to tell after over twenty-five years and her roots were looking distinctly greyer than they used to be.

The transformation looked okay, but it was taking a time to get used to it. Guillaume and Olivia were astounded and gawped at her as if she was a stranger. Well, at least that aspect had clearly worked. She caught herself in the mirror and kept getting a shock herself. The darker colour seemed to reflect as shadows under her eyes, or perhaps it was just the stress.

None of her clothes seemed to be quite right with the new look but that was the least of her worries. They were hanging off her too. She was thinner than she ever had been. Even she could see that she looked like a skeleton, but trying to eat was impossible. She just couldn't swallow.

Being back at work was a solace. Her boss, Martin, after getting over the surprise of her new appearance, was being very supportive and kept reminding her that she had simply told the truth and the whole truth and that she had been obliged to do so. She had tried to concentrate on her bulging in-tray but it wasn't working very well.

"They have reached a verdict." Martin had crept in. She hadn't heard him. She flinched and stared at him, a wave of nausea made her swallow hard.

"I thought that you would want to know. He has been found guilty and convicted of causing death by careless or inconsiderate driving under the Road Safety Act 2006."

*Oh Jesus.*

"What does that mean? Will he go to prison?"

"It depends on what level of culpability the Judge decides. It appears that he has concluded that it has not been proven that Patrick was drunk at the time, which would make it a longer sentence. It could be anything between one to fourteen years in prison."

Lizzy gasped. It was suddenly so real. The father of her children in prison.

*Oh God, oh God. Poor Guillaume and Olivia. How are they going to cope with this?*

"But do bear in mind that if he is given a determinate sentence, where the Judge fixes a length of time, that he would spend the first half of it in prison and the second out in the community on licence. I'm afraid you will have to be patient."

*In honesty, I rather hoped that they would just put him in prison and throw away the key, but the children... oh God, the children.*

"Thank you. I will just have to wait and see, I guess."

He patted her tentatively on the shoulder and left her to her spiralling thoughts.

*So it really wasn't a 'deer'. But what about last time? Was he involved in that? A deer on a bicycle? But they found a deer with Elizabeth...*

She buried her head in her hands.

**What am I going to say to the children?**

# Lizzy 33

**How come she was still getting the death stares?**

Would it ever end? She had nothing to do with it, but good old rural England was thriving on the outcome of the whole trial and the juicy revelations. She wanted to up sticks and move, but would it be right to do that?

Guillaume and Olivia were going through hell at school. Someone had found out that they were Shepley-Bothams – or just Shepley, in truth. How does a child cope when their loved parent is vilified for causing someone's death? It might as well have been premeditated murder.

*It was not their fault.*

Speculation was still rife. Being found guilty for the death of Elizabeth Arbuthnott had only whetted their appetites for even more supposition. It was impossible for the police to prove Patrick's involvement in the whole mystery of poor Andrew MacLellan, but there was endless tittle-tattle making the connections that forensic science and reasonable doubt could not prove.

She was so tempted to pack them all up and move away. Just get away and start again.

But would they want to go and visit their father in prison? They might, Guillaume particularly. HM Prison Elmley was miles away on the Isle of Sheppey and not exactly a relaxing little day trip even from here.

The Judge had picked on a figure of six years as his sentence. It seemed pathetically meagre for killing someone, but they could never prove that he was drunk at the time. How could they? It turned out to be her word against Margaret's. They chose Margaret's.

He would be out on licence in three years. Would the children want to build a relationship with him then? They would still only be fifteen and seventeen, still minors, still at school. Perhaps in prison they might be able to treat his alcoholism. Some hope. He would probably end up on drugs instead.

*It is so difficult… I could scream. Why am I caught in the middle of all this?*

Lost in her maelstrom of agonised thoughts, Lizzy nearly died when she looked up to see that James Arbuthnott had walked into the office. It was weirdly reminiscent of those surges of alarm that she used to experience when seeing Patrick unexpectedly.

Martin hadn't warned her that he had made an appointment, which she felt was a bit insensitive. There wasn't any reason that James would make a connection between her and Patrick, but he caught sight of her as he walked into Martin's office and obviously recognised her from the trial. He looked at her hard for what seemed several minutes and then stared at the nameplate on her desk. She averted her gaze immediately. She caught sight of him as he shook his head.

*What did that mean? Disgust? I'm so sorry but it was nothing to do with me.*

On his way out, he appeared to veer towards her desk, slowed up, stared at her again quizzically. Lizzy felt herself blush and was terrified that he might try and say something to her.

*What can he want?*

He appeared to change his mind and accelerated away and out through the door, muttering.

**Lizzy breathed.**

# Lizzy 34

**It was such a relief to be somewhere completely different, away from all the stares, the pitying looks and the sneers.**

It was like coming alive again being far, far away from Kent in the sleepy comforts of a completely new county, Wiltshire, chosen to be close to her sister who had moved there years ago.

It was only possible because of Mum dying so soon after Dad. It was sad but it had left her and her sister with the proceeds of the family home to share between them. It was enough to buy the most miniscule little cottage ever seen. She couldn't get a mortgage. No-one would countenance lending money to a Shepley-Botham or indeed a Shepley or a Botham with a string of CCJs.

She had thought that their rented home in Lamberhurst was minute, but this was miniscule, a black and white dolls' house in the historical little village of Bishops Cannings, bang smack opposite the church and a stone's throw from the Crown Inn pub.

*But I promise I won't be throwing any stones.*

Before moving in their stuff, she took the opportunity to give her new cottage a good clean. It wasn't dirty, the previous people had done an excellent job, but it was cathartic. Not only was it a way of washing away all traces of the previous incumbent, like an animal spraying its territory, but a way of getting to know all the nooks and crannies, the intimacy of getting into all the corners, creating a satisfactory introduction for them both. It made it feel like hers.

The previous incumbent had partitioned off the main bedroom to make it into two so, on paper, it had three bedrooms. Her sister declared them "not so much bedrooms as loose boxes." She was spot on – but it was home with a capital H.

Being a house owner for the very first time was a novel experience but very satisfying. She had total freedom to do anything she liked with it and she was so looking forward to investigating the old lathe walls and curious higgledy-piggledy beams and had plans to put a wood burning stove into the ridiculously oversized fireplace. She was so excited to find an old bread oven hiding in the depths and was determined to make a feature of it.

She knew that, at some stage, she should do something about the rather mundane, utilitarian bathroom tacked on to the back of the house. It was time to get into the modern age and have a shower… and it was going to be bloody freezing in winter.

The garden was a mess. The last incumbent clearly was not green-fingered. A stand of nettles was growing vigorously from a muddy stream. She itched to get her hands on it.

The pub was proving handy for the first night in their new home. Lizzy was knackered from the move, both physically and mentally, and also feeling just a bit isolated and alone. Olivia had pleaded to be able to help her move in, but she had wanted to slap some paint on the walls and get to know it on her own.

She had left Guillaume and Olivia's own boxes in their rooms to unpack when they arrived so they could take possession of their own spaces, although she wasn't entirely sure how they would find anywhere to put anything, the bedrooms were so tiny.

After so much activity she was actually hungry, very unusual for her. She hadn't anticipated cooking so headed for the pub. It was a lovely, homely place with a cheerful landlady who made her feel instantly welcome.

"Hello, I'm Dee and you are the lady that has moved in opposite, aren't you?"

"Yes... Elizabeth Botham."

The only oddity was a strange man who was sitting at the bar when they walked in. As he turned to look at her, he dropped his pint of beer. It hit the stone tiled floor with an explosion and a wave of beer and glass spread like the debris from a bomb.

"Don't worry, Alan, I'll mop that up when I've settled this young lady."

He shimmied out of the door and vanished. Odd man, he must have been terribly embarrassed.

Dee showed her to a table, where she settled, seeking out comfort food on the menu, supping her half pint of Wadworth 6X, the local brew made only a few miles away apparently. It was delicious, she could taste the hops and wondered if they had been grown near her old home.

They certainly didn't grow anywhere round here on the treeless, chalk downland that rolled its way along the Pewsey Vale.

**You couldn't get a more different countryside from Kent if you tried.**

# Lizzy 35

***Thank God I made the decision to move.***

The sense of freedom was fabulous. For the first time since she could remember she could be herself, act how she wanted, wear what she wanted, and with no-one to judge. She had decided to let her hair go 'au naturel' and was quite surprised to find how much grey had crept in under the years of dye.

Her 'Mrs Shepley-Botham' wardrobe of fancy clothes and tweedy outdoor garb rarely saw the light of day and she was happy to slop around in jeans and comfy fleeces. No make-up. No jewellery. No upmarket scarves to make a statement and create a place in the hierarchy of society. The children didn't notice, she was just Mum.

The children seemed relieved to be away from all the speculation and engineered scandal. They slotted into the local schools where they made new friends and quickly adapted to a different accent. There was a bit of confusion when Olivia complained that she didn't have the right daps but Guillaume, now firmly calling himself Will, translated and identified them as trainers.

Without consulting Lizzy, both Guillaume and Olivia told people that their mum and dad were divorced and that Dad lived in Kent. Kent was an alien concept to local people in Wiltshire; it could just as well as have been a different country. A casual reply of "no, we don't see much of Dad" was enough to satisfy people's curiosity and it seemed not unusual enough to invoke further enquiries.

Patrick was out of prison on licence in three months' time. It may be mentioned in passing in the *Kent and Sussex Courier*, it was old news, but it was never going to be of interest in this neck of the woods, so they were well protected from any rekindled interest.

Hopefully it would be difficult for Patrick to create further chaos in their lives and he would have to behave himself impeccably to comply with his licence conditions. Margaret was still going strong. She could look after him.

*Perjuring bitch.*

There are solicitors wherever you go and it proved simple to slot into a new job in Devizes, only a few minutes' drive from home in her faithful VW Golf, which she managed to keep going on a wing and a prayer and a bit of sticky-backed plastic.

She had discovered that the walks around the village were incredible and that you could walk for miles across the most amazingly old historical sites. She and the kids popped up the road to a UNESCO site, Avebury, where they ran round ancient stones, older than Stonehenge, and scampered up and down the deep ditches that surrounded them.

Everywhere she went, she saw people with dogs. Perhaps they could have a dog now with no Margaret and Patrick to complain. What had been a spur of the moment thought turned out to be a long and official process. The people at the Bath Cats & Dogs Rescue Home were very thorough. It was quite frankly rather scary and felt like being judged all over again. The questions were well meant but felt stupidly threatening.

A man came to assess their home for suitability, which was terrifying. He was terribly tall and her ceilings were terribly low, which wasn't a good combination. Would he think her home too small and not good enough? The garden was tiny, but she explained in a rather pathetic squeaky voice all about the walks nearby. She made sure that he realised that she wasn't stupid enough to think that the current fencing was adequate to keep a bouncy dog from the dangers of the road. She found herself almost pleading with the man that she was acceptable. Pitiful.

The visit to the home to meet the dogs was heart wrenching. She wanted to take them all home. All the dogs seemed to be either fierce little terriers, big guard dog types or Staffies. Her visions of a cuddly little scruffy mongrel were soon dispelled.

She ended up with a Staffie crossed with something indeterminate, possibly Labrador, for no other reason than she felt that he was most in need of a home. Guillaume and Olivia argued endlessly about what he should be called, their arguments continuing well into the night through the paper-thin partition between their bedrooms.

"Manhugger."

"Alexander, Alistair, Alan…"

"Bonecruncher."

"Bill, Bob, Ben…"

"Butcher Boy."

"Charlie, Chris…."

"You are working through the alphabet Olivia – and they are all people names, that is stupid."

"Not as stupid as your giant names… he is far too cute. David, Donald…."

Olivia reached J in the alphabet. "John, Julian…."

"Julian," Guillaume echoed in a ludicrous, high-pitched voice and burst out laughing. Olivia joined in and they spent the next half hour saying "Julian" in silly voices and giggling hysterically.

*It is so good to hear them so relaxed, carefree and happy.*

Julian it was. Julian just seemed so contrary for such a butch-looking dog with a bullet head and such a strange mixture of colouring that it was difficult to describe it. He ended up being called Jules.

Jules was a real sweetie, incredibly lovable and cuddly and very good on the lead. He seemed delighted to meet other dogs and grinned at them while waggling his not inconsiderable bottom. He was very chubby and she had been given strict instructions to put him on a doggy diet, which she was following to the letter in fear of the officious field officers who were to check up on her. As a result, he was always on the hunt for any morsel that he could get his tubby little paws on.

He had settled in well, was immaculately clean and house trained, and he turned out to be very affectionate. The only fighting and aggression was between Guillaume and Olivia as they each tried to sneak him into their beds.

Lizzy had reached the point of feeling that she should trust him enough to try letting him have a bit of time off the lead. She took the footpath down to the Kennet and Avon Canal, it was fun to see all the colourful barges pottering along, and there was also an open field, a caravan site, where she was going to see how they got on with this big experiment. She was suitably equipped with a bag of treats so that hopefully he would come back to her.

She unclipped him casually and carried on walking along the path. For a few seconds, he seemed to be unaware of his freedom. Suddenly, he stuck his nose in the air, caught a whiff of something and took off.

*Bugger.*

Lizzy yelled at him, feeling like the ineffective man on the Fenton YouTube hit as he shot off towards the canal.

*Bugger, bugger, bugger. Stupid idiot. Far too soon.*

Lizzy stomped after him, trying to decide whether it would be better to run or whether it would make things worse if he felt he was being chased.

She caught up with him at the canal, where he had boarded an immaculate narrowboat, clearly uninvited, and was being held by the collar by the resident, who was clutching a sandwich in his other hand, held high to keep it out of Jules's reach. It was the man from the pub. She remembered Dee calling him Alan.

"I am so sorry, so very sorry, Alan. He is such a pig and he must have smelt something delicious and…" She trailed off, hugely embarrassed.

Instead of berating her, he simply stared at her piercingly. "Do you know me, Elizabeth?"

"Um no, no I don't, I'm afraid. Should I? I mean, I think I saw you in the Crown and Dee called you Alan."

*Is he someone famous that I'm meant to recognise? He's certainly very good-looking in a bohemian sort of way. He must have heard me telling Dee my name in the pub.*

He seemed a bit confused. "I am sorry. I am indeed Alan. Alan Callender. Pleased to make your acquaintance. Now would you like your dog back?"

He spoke with a funny mongrel accent, with an overtone of Wiltshire burr.

"If I can get him away from your sandwich. I will try and entice him with a biscuit."

She scrambled down the bank to the boat and passed over the lead, which he clipped on without hesitation, and handed back. Lizzy pulled, Alan pushed and Jules was eventually persuaded to disembark.

It took a lot of effort.

On her subsequent walks down to the canal – a useful circle that happened to take this in – she waved at Alan and hung on for dear life to Jules to stop him repeating his misdemeanour.

**Jules definitely remembered the enticing source of food. Alan waved back laconically.**

# Lizzy 36

**"Do you only walk this way, Elizabeth?"**

Alan enquired after yet another round trip and another wave.

"No." She looked baffled and embarrassed at the same time.

"I mean, have you not been to Morgan's Hill, Oliver's Castle, the Ridgeway, the Harepath, Wansdyke?"

He might as well have been speaking Double Dutch.

"Um…"

"You need your eyes opening, lassie! I know 500 miles of walks around here and 500 more."

She couldn't help but laugh. She got the reference.

"If you don't think it very presumptuous, I would be very happy to show you and your kids a bit more of the place. If you don't mind?"

"Thank you. That would be nice."

*Nice, what sort of word is nice. I'm an idiot.*

She felt a blush spreading up from her chest.

*Please don't show on my face.*

"How about Saturday? Pack up a picnic, something the kids would like. I'd do it myself but I don't have much experience with kids. Come down here to my humble home about ten o'clock and we can head for the hills."

"Thank you. Yes. Okay." She blushed again.

*What is all this blushing? Stop it, you stupid cow. Nothing can happen if I am chaperoned by the children.*

*But what if he's a mad axe murderer? I know nothing about him at all.*

**I'll pop into the pub and let Dee know so she knows who we were with if we disappear mysteriously.**

# Lizzy 37

**They went and gathered up Alan.**

Lizzy had wasted a ridiculous number of hours fretting about what to wear. Did she need to impress this man, or would she be better just being herself? Whatever that was. She plumped for her usual dog walking ensemble of scruffy jeans and a fleece jacket that had fast become a comfortable favourite.

Guillaume and Olivia were excited to be allowed to see inside Alan's narrowboat, *Red Squirrel*. It was spotlessly tidy and painted a foxy red with neat navy-blue lines.

After their tour they all piled into Lizzy's old VW – Jules squeezed in the boot and the picnic in the front with Alan for safekeeping – and headed towards Marlborough. Lizzy felt a bit uncomfortable to have Alan in such close proximity.

*What am I feeling here? Is this a date? Keep cool. Relax.*

She tried to act unconcerned and at ease as she reached to put the car in gear within inches of his knee.

They parked by The Sanctuary, a boring-looking so-called monument of concrete posts. Guillaume and Olivia looked a bit puzzled, even disappointed.

"Close your eyes kids and listen." Guillaume and Olivia glanced at Lizzy who nodded. They obediently closed their eyes.

"5,000 years ago a Neolithic family built their home just here. A round hut four and a half metres across with a central post. Can you see that? Wattle and daub walls, whips of wood filled in with clay and animal hair, a reed roof?

Maybe Mum sitting outside stirring a pot of lunch, Dad off across the hills keeping an eye on his cattle and chopping down trees with a flint axe for firewood. Remember we are talking 5,000 years ago."

Guillaume and Olivia nodded.

"Farming must have been very profitable all those years ago, because they extended their home and created a ring of new posts six metres across. Things were still going great and then they extended their home again growing it to eleven metres across. It would have been very large. They must have been pretty rich, I would say."

Guillaume and Olivia nodded again. Even Jules seemed to be listening intently.

"But it wasn't enough. They added a third ring of thirty-three posts, in a circle twenty-one metres across, and at the same time they decided to make things a bit more solid with sarsen stones. Can you imagine Mum saying to you 'Go get us sixteen big stones from the hills over there Guillaume and carry it back and put it just here'? I bet they were heavy."

Guillaume and Olivia giggled. Jules wagged his tail.

"You have to wonder how they managed that with no tractors and machinery."

Guillaume and Olivia tipped their heads, obviously thinking about it.

"But that family were on a roll. For the final phase, they made their kids go off and get another forty-two sarsen stones, forming a ring forty metres in diameter. That is huge. They must have been pretty chuffed with themselves.

"Meanwhile, their neighbours just up the road at Avebury built themselves their very fancy stone circle. You've seen it, I know. It is enormous. 330 metres, eight times the size of our family's offering. Very impressive.

Our family here couldn't have been too offended by this outrageous one-upmanship because they made an avenue of stones running the full two and a half kilometres from The Sanctuary to Avebury. Perhaps they were going to the Red Lion pub!"

Guillaume and Olivia laughed, opened their eyes and strode round the posts with new understanding and imagination.

"Thank you so much, Alan. You have no idea how good this is for the children…"

*Being with a normal sober man…*

"You are so brilliant with them."

"Ah, I had a daughter who used to lap up my long explanations…" He looked thoughtful, a bit sad.

Lizzy wasn't quite sure what to say, then left it too long and missed the moment.

"Anyway, let's go you lot. We're now going to head up a road that has been used by people from around here, farmers, soldiers and even our family of home builders here, for over 5,000 years. It's called the Ridgeway. Let me tell you about it as we walk along…"

He saw them safely across the road and they set off at just the right pace to meet Guillaume's stride.

That evening, a supremely tired but exhilarated Guillaume and Olivia had crawled into bed. Jules was flat out and hadn't moved for hours. Lizzy was sitting in front of the fire, a small glass of red wine in her hand, thinking about the day she had just had.

*That was nice. Bloody hell, nice… risible word… but it was nice.*

# Lizzy 38

**It became a regular weekend thing.**

Collecting up Alan, piling the children and Jules into the car, they headed out to find fascinating places to walk. They spent hours in each other's company and Lizzy felt very comfortable with Alan. She felt that she could be herself and not try to conform to what she thought he might want her to be. He was a gentle soul, undemanding, thoughtful.

*Handsome. Smells of wood smoke and fresh air. I like him. A lot.*

She couldn't work out where this was going or what he was thinking and the conversation never went beyond what they were seeing. Nothing personal was ever discussed. She could hardly tell her life story with Guillaume and Olivia listening in. Perhaps he felt the same. She had gleaned odd snippets… he was married… he had a daughter. He loved the simplicity of life without the "evils of technology".

*If this is going to go anywhere at all, I need to see him on his own.*

"Alan, the children are both off with their mates this weekend. How about we meet in the pub for supper?"

*Neutral territory. That shouldn't be too scary for either of us, although everybody would gossip about it.*

He looked aghast.

*Oh shit – blown it. How embarrassing… What will he think?*

He seemed to manage to pull his face together into a more relaxed pose. "That would be nice."

*Nice… ironic!*

# Lizzy 39

**Alan had arrived first and was ensconced at a table.**

He was nursing what looked like a whisky. He politely stood up, helped her sit down, and popped up to the bar to get her a drink from Dee. They were like complete strangers on a blind date.

*Awkward. Oh God. It is obvious that he isn't at all happy about this.*

They sat at a table facing each other but using their menus as barricades. Alan looked like a rabbit caught in the headlights.

*Or a deer… For God's sake, don't go there…*

Pulling herself together, she started, "Tell me…"

At exactly the same time, Alan asked, "Tell me…"

They both laughed. It broke the ice.

"After you," Alan gestured politely. "Tell me what brings you here to Wiltshire, so thin and forlorn with that sad look on your pretty face…"

*Sad? I look sad? And he thinks I'm pretty.*

It was very cathartic to tell him a somewhat tailored version, he wouldn't want to know all the details. He wouldn't recognise the names of places even if she said them.

It felt good to vent about Patrick's alcoholism, the lies, Margaret's maliciousness, facing the fact that your husband had killed someone and the worst of it being that it was a hit and run, not even an honest accident. No remorse. The guilt of association.

Alan hung on her every word, his face expressing shock, disgust, horror, sympathy in all the appropriate places. He stretched out a hand and tentatively covered hers.

307

She knew that she was giving a very one-sided version of her marriage, but it felt good to play the martyr and have someone see her side of the story. She kept perfectly still.

"I just don't get it. What a bastard. I am so sorry, Elizabeth, for what you have been through. Such a disappointment, but at least you have Guillaume and Olivia. They are wonderful kids. You must be so proud of them."

"I am and I love them to bits. But we can't spend all evening talking about me. What about you, Alan? What is your story?"

Their food arrived, breaking the spell. Alan took back his hand. They started to eat.

"Well, Elizabeth. It is difficult to say. I was married to a wonderful girl. She was clever, sophisticated, witty and fun. 'But to see her was to love her, Love but her, and love forever.'"

He looked at her straight in the eye. It was a bit uncomfortable and she looked down at her food, poking at a carrot with her fork.

"We drifted apart. So sad. Entirely my fault. So stupid. I suppose that I am married still. I have never done anything about it. I just couldn't face it." He worked away at his steak with his serrated knife, took a mouthful and chewed solemnly, took a swig of his drink and continued.

*I wonder what happened to the daughter. I daren't ask, it might be some awful tragedy.*

"I lived the usual life, work, work, work. It turned out that I wasn't that good at it, which was a bit of a disappointment all round. 'The best laid plans of mice and men often go awry.' I changed tack and became a teacher for a while."

"Ah, that is where you get your amazing storytelling skills from," smiled Lizzy.

"I guess so. It turned out that I wasn't so good at that either. I moved on." He took another bite of his steak.

"I decided to go for the simple life. Put it all behind me. I happened on Wiltshire. It has been so easy to find odd jobs, gardening, mending, all wholesome, down to earth things. 'Dare to be honest and fear no labour.' I work for cash, it makes it easier. I only spend what I earn and my needs are very modest."

Alan, set to at his steak again.

"The only problem is that I have become a lonely old man – until I met you…"

Lizzy blushed.

"…and your children," Alan added hastily.

"But where did you live? You have a real mish-mash of an accent. What did you do for work? Why did you give up teaching? You must have been excellent at it."

"So many questions. Now, my steak was delicious, but Dee is renowned for her amazing puddings. What are you going to have?"

Lizzy was a bit taken aback. She had laid her soul bare, but Alan seemed to be holding back. Did he have something to hide?

"No pudding for me, thank you. I am not a fan, never have been." She paused. Waited. Couldn't resist going back to it.

"Alan, I don't wish to appear pushy but… what did you do? Where did you live? They aren't very personal things really…" She looked at him. He was staring into space, avoiding her eyes. He looked tense. She waited.

He closed his eyes, screwed up his lids, opened them suddenly and looked directly at her. "I don't think you realise how hard that would be for me."

"What do you mean? I don't get it." She was beginning to feel alarmed.

"Honestly, I can't. I just can't. I have told you everything that is important."

"What are you withholding? Why? It's making me nervous."

"You just have to take me as you find me."

"I tried that once but look how that ended. I need honesty, Alan."

The atmosphere had turned from soft and conspiratorial to spiky and dangerous.

They sat, rigidly, in difficult silence, both looking down at the table.

Dee came up, oblivious to the atmosphere. "Can I interest you in a dessert? The special is your favourite bread and butter pudding tonight, Alan." She smiled warmly at him.

"And you, Elizabeth. What can I get you?"

Lizzy was close to tears. She wasn't sure why. She had been so happy and full of anticipation when she'd walked in, the prospect of this friendship blossoming into something special, but now…

*I can't stand this.*

"Not for me, thank you, Dee. That was delicious but I am a bit worried about leaving Jules on his own for too long. I dread to think what he will get up to."

As she burbled on, she reached for her purse, drew out a banknote, stood up, put the note on the table. "Thank you so much for dinner, Alan. See you." Grabbing her coat, she scrambled out through the door.

**She daren't look back because the tears had started.**

# Lizzy 40

**The next morning, she took Jules up the lane in the opposite direction of the canal.**

She stomped along, feeling a total idiot. Once she had started her march, she just couldn't stop. She followed the farm track up to the Wansdyke and followed the path along the ridge of the ancient ditch, breathing in the invigorating air.

The air was clear and she could see for miles and miles south across Salisbury Plain, north to Roundway Hill, west towards Westbury and east to Marlborough. It had the therapeutic effect of making the world large, inviting and innocent and herself small and insignificant. Realisation dawned.

*Oh, what a twit I am. I've made something out of nothing. I've got everything out of proportion. I'm an idiot. I did rather over-egg my terrible life when it was my choice to marry Patrick. There were some good parts. I did have amazing experiences that I would never have had if I'd have married someone else. I wasn't to know that he was an alcoholic.*

Lizzy strode on. The air and the chill soothing her heated thoughts.

*Oh God, I am an utter fool. I think I owe poor Alan some honesty and an apology. Talk about hypocritical. Talk about drama queen.*

The thought of how ridiculous she must have appeared was calming. She headed down the Harepath, another ancient track that Alan had brought to life for her and the children.

She picked up the towpath of the Kennet and Avon Canal and followed it to where Alan was moored. She was shaping her apology in her mind as she almost skipped along.

The *Red Squirrel* was not there.

Lizzy stopped, abruptly jerking Jules on his lead. She looked at the other narrowboats that were moored up, their little black chimneys belching smoke, each painted with its own livery of playful bright colours. She looked again at each in turn. The *Red Squirrel* was definitely not there.

*Perhaps Alan has had to move. He's probably gone up to The Bridge Inn... or into Devizes or perhaps to Honeystreet... Somewhere close by... he can't have gone far...*

She was shocked, panicking and stood there just looking for ages. She wondered if she had the courage to ask one of his fellow boaters, but they always looked a bit alarmed when they saw Jules and she didn't know any of them by name. Should she go further up the canal to look for him?

Total indecision.

She looked at the time. She ought to be getting home as the children were going to be delivered back from their various friends at lunch time. She had to be there. She slowly, reluctantly, took the track towards home, looking back questioningly.

She arrived to find a piece of paper on the doormat.

It turned out to be a poem written neatly in blue biro:

*Farewell, thou stream that winding flows*
*Around Eliza's dwelling;*
*O mem'ry! spare the cruel thoes*
*Within my bosom swelling.*
*Condemn'd to drag a hopeless chain*

*And yet in secret languish;*
*To feel a fire in every vein,*
*Nor dare disclose my anguish.*

*Love's veriest wretch, unseen, unknown,*
*I fain my griefs would cover;*
*The bursting sigh, th' unweeting groan,*
*Betray the hapless lover.*
*I know thou doom'st me to despair,*
*Nor wilt, nor canst relieve me;*
*But, O Eliza, hear one prayer-*
*For pity's sake forgive me!*

The 'forgive me' was underlined.

*The music of thy voice I heard,*
*Nor wist while it enslav'd me;*
*I saw thine eyes, yet nothing fear'd,*
*Till fears no more had sav'd me:*
*Th' unwary sailor thus, aghast*
*The wheeling torrent viewing,*
*'Mid circling horrors sinks at last,*
*In overwhelming ruin.*

It was signed with a flourishing 'A' with what could be interpreted as a kiss... or maybe just a cross.

*What the hell is that all about? I don't get it.*

She reread it several times. It definitely looked as if it was saying goodbye, but it also seemed to be a sort of love poem – or perhaps she was reading things into it. She sighed. Baffled, a bit hurt but realising that she had blown it. He had gone.

There was a knock at the door. Lizzy jumped up wondering – hoping? – if it might be Alan. It wasn't, it was Dee.

"Hi there. I saw you get home. Alan left his hat in the pub last night. You couldn't give it to him could you, please? Save me a trek down to the canal."

"Yes, yes. Of course."

*What else can I say?*

"Must dash, veg to prepare, floors to clean, glasses to polish… See you." Dee thrust the hat into her hands and scarpered.

Lizzy looked down at the hat. It was Alan's favourite one, a black bobble hat. She couldn't help but put it to her nose to smell the hint of wood smoke and fresh air that she associated with him.

It was a bit damp so she thought she should dry it on the Raeburn. For safety, she turned it inside out so it didn't scorch. She had lost too many jumpers that way already. Stitched inside were initials A.A.M. How odd. I thought he said he was Alan Callender, not something beginning with M.

**I wonder what the second A stands for.**

# Lizzy 41

**Lizzy was pouring out her heart to Prune over a skinny latte.**

Prune had a cappuccino and a blueberry muffin. Lizzy couldn't help but think that was why Prune was rather overweight, but she held her counsel.

She told Prune about the walks with Alan. The unsatisfactory dinner date. The fact that he'd seemed to move off without saying goodbye, the odd poem. It was difficult to describe it all in answer to Prune's incessant questions.

"Was it a date? How did you meet him? Was he safe to be allowed to hang out with the children? Do you like him? Will you see him again? Where has he gone? Is he coming back?"

*Dear Prune, she didn't get it, the heartache, the sadness, the sense of loss after such a tentative endeavour. I wish I could turn back the clock and make things different. Not just this but my whole life. I'd better change the subject.*

"You sound like a dippy teenager, Prune. Which reminds me. There was an invitation to a school reunion on Facebook today. Years and years ago, Liz made a speech wondering what we would all be up to when we were fifty and she thought it would be fun if we all got together to find out. They've set a date for the end of October, Halloween weekend, only a few months' time." She paused and had a sip of her coffee. "I can see Liz now, in her far too short skirt taking the stage, and she was so skinny then, we all were." Prune froze, Lizzy realised she was waiting for a dig about her weight, but she continued without verbalising the obvious remark. "It was funny because she was so serious speculating who we would have married, where we would be and even how many children we would have."

"For some reason, I can't remember why now, we all decided that the ideal name for our children would be William and Oliver. Quite ridiculous, but that is why Liz's children are called exactly that. Her William was born first and then Oliver, but I had a girl, so she is Olivia. Then I had Guillaume which is a variation on the name William. Clever, eh?"

"That is bonkers. You are all quite mad." Prune chomped another bite from her muffin.

"I know, but we were only seventeen years old. I can even remember her portentous pronouncement: 'be careful who you marry, girls.' At the time, I only had eyes for Patrick. She paused. Sighed. "Just think of all the other people I might have married. One of the local Young Farmers, someone on my course, like Liz. Anyone else at all. Who knows what would have happened if I had somehow met and married Alan years and years ago?"

Prune raised her eyebrows in sympathy.

"Are you going to the reunion? You should go. Cheer you up. See how everyone else turned out. We all have our moments behind closed doors, believe me, even me."

"No, I can't. After all that 'unrequited love' nonsense with Patrick I would feel a complete idiot." She shuddered. "They're sure to be laughing behind my back – all those airs and graces, the dyed hair, they wouldn't recognise me now, all that effort I made to be what I thought he wanted me to be. Jesus, I was a total sucker."

Prune put out a comforting hand. "Hey, you couldn't have known. Anyway, these are your friends, they'll understand."

"Yes, but they're meeting at the Old Vine in Cousley Wood. I know that I'm being ridiculously sensitive but even after all this time I just can't show my face there. Far too close to home." She shivered. "The thought of it makes me feel sick. Everyone would know, and supposing I should bump into Patrick or Margaret…"

"Fair enough. You'd better make sure that Liz is sent on a mission to extract all the juiciest bits of gossip and take loads of pics. She is, after all, the only person from school that you have stayed in touch with."

*Liz? I am barely in touch with Liz nowadays. Oh, but she'd been so right all those years ago.*

**Be careful who you marry.**

# Lizzy 42

Lizzy was walking Jules on her own along the Harepath, enjoying the feel of the autumn wind and a friendly sun on her face. The school reunion was going to take place this weekend but here she was hiding in Wiltshire.

She allowed herself to feel just a little bit sad regretting her choices that had brought her here. As she strode, she couldn't help but remember Alan's imaginative descriptions of the ancient path, the many people over thousands of years who had trodden this same route.

*Life does go on. It has done for centuries, millennia before now.*

She had made a real effort to pull herself, her whole life, together. She had decided, resolutely, to just be herself, as she was, true to her roots. She had joined the tennis club and was getting her eye back in. She had been very good at tennis at school. It was a bit like riding a bicycle – you never completely forget, and she was loving it. The other members of the club were so friendly and they always invited her to join them for a drink in the clubhouse afterwards.

She had really made an effort to meet Olivia and Guillaume's friends' mums and was chuffed to be included on outings with them all to the cinema and the pub. They didn't turn a hair that she was on her own and relegated her past to where it belonged, ancient history.

*As old as these glorious hills.*

She had reached the canal and was on the home stretch.

*In more ways than one.*

Lizzy followed Jules as he sniffed his way along the canal towpath, turned right towards the church. He knew his way off by heart, ritually lifting his leg on the same posts and clumps of vegetation that he always did. He knew to sit when he reached the pub so that he could cross safely under supervision.

"Good boy, Jules." Lizzy smiled down at him.

She looked up and a movement caught her eye, a figure standing at her door. She was intrigued.

*A delivery?*

She couldn't remember ordering anything. She crossed cautiously and walked steadily towards home straining to see who it could be.

Suddenly she realised who it was and stopped abruptly.

*Oh my God. He's back. What shall I do?*

She felt frozen to the spot. Her hair prickled. A wave of adrenalin swooped through her. She took pathetic half steps forward. She wanted to cry.

*What do I do? What do I say? How do I feel? Can he forgive me?*

He met her at the gate, standing, staring at her fixedly.

"Elizabeth?"

*Was that a question?*

"Elizabeth. I think I might have forgotten something."

She stared blankly. Her heart thumping.

*Has he come back for his bloody bobble hat?*

"Elizabeth." He swallowed hard, looked at the ground and then back at her. His eyes seemed to be brimming with tears. "My heart is sair-I dare na tell, my heart is sair for somebody."

He sighed then fell silent. She looked at him. Jules pulled at his lead breaking the spell. She flinched.

Alan shuffled and looked awkward. Lizzy looked at his face for clues to what he meant, held her breath, waiting for him to make more sense.

He sighed deeply. "I do need to face up to reality… 'some great lies were never penn'd'… I've a messy, complicated story to tell you…" He screwed up his eyes, grimaced and looked at the sky. "But are you willing to hear it, Elizabeth?"

He looked at her intently, beseechingly.

*Am I reading this right?*

"Oh, Alan, of course. I'm so sorry. I don't think I've been completely honest either. I don't think I have been totally genuine since I can remember." The tears ran down her face.

Alan opened his arms entreatingly. Elizabeth dropped Jules's lead, stepped towards him, wrapped her arms around his waist, squeezing him tight, and pressed her face into his coat.

"Please help me find my way, Elizabeth."

*It feels right. I don't know why, but this feels familiar and right.*

**"I'm so glad you came back."**

# Epilogue 1

**The Old Vine pub was crowded with middle-aged women all talking at once.**

Schoolgirl laughter whirled them back in time below a banner hanging haphazardly from the ancient beams reading "Reunion Upland Community College 1987". Squeals of recognition ricocheted around the room.

A woman in casual trousers, no make-up and white trainers sauntered up to a tall lady who was standing, quietly observing the gathering from a corner. "Hey, Nikki, it's me, Tina. Do you remember me? You look great, not a day over fifty."

"Tina! I do remember you very well. You don't look so bad yourself for our mature years. How come the American accent? Are you living there?"

"Me and Pete got married twenty-five years ago and moved to California, right after we both graduated from Imperial College, to work in Silicon Valley. I guess I hadn't realised that we would still be living and working there now. All four of our kids were born there. We love it, but I'm really glad I made this trip. It's great seeing everyone after all this time." She caught her breath. "What about you, Nikki?"

"I met my husband, Graham, up at university too. I went to Edinburgh. Afterwards we headed for London where Graham climbed to exalted heights in Reuters and I qualified as an accountant, which suits me very well. Far, far away from that horrible, pokey council house of my youth."

Tina chipped in, "Awesome. Do you have kids?"

"Yes. We've got two girls, twenty-three and twenty now. Let me bore you with pictures." Nikki rummaged in her handbag for her phone.

"Talking of husbands reminded me of that great pronouncement from Liz. You remember?"

Nikki laughed. "Be careful who you marry. How could I forget? I do think she was right. It seems to have made an enormous difference to how things have panned out."

Tina looked at Nikki questioningly. "We both seem to have done okay, right?" They nodded. Tina took a hearty swig from her glass of wine and looked candidly around the room as Nikki sipped tentatively at a fizzy water, looking gratified before she continued.

"It seems that was quite a pivotal point in our lives, though, that moment in time."

"What do ya mean?" Tina's attention came back to Nikki.

"It isn't just who we married but all the other choices that we made leading up to it, right from that Young Farmers' Disco at the Commemoration Hall."

"The Halloween Disco? You're kidding. That made a difference?"

"If you remember, it was soon after that that we all disappeared off on study leave then took our A Levels. Every choice we made set up a chain reaction: the grades we achieved; accordingly, where we went for university; who we met as a consequence and who we married; our careers; the children we had. It brought us to where we are now. It's funny how life turns out."

A blonde woman, smartly dressed, hair meticulously styled but a bit plump, bounced up to them, interrupting Nikki's flow. "It's Nikki and Tina, isn't it?"

"Yes, I'm Tina. Hi, it's Liz, isn't it? You look exactly the same as you did thirty-three years ago, Halloween 1987. Except for the outfit and the black tooth of course." Liz laughed. Nikki murmured agreeably and laughed, instinctively knowing not to mention the weight gain. Tina and Liz joined in.

"Hey, Liz, we were just talking about your great pronouncement: 'be careful who you marry.'"

Liz chuckled. "Good grief. I don't know about you, but I did okay. I married Jim, an army officer, no less. Very much going up in the world. Apart from trailing around the world after him and moving every five minutes, I've had a great life. Although I think, to be honest, all marriages have their moments."

Nikki ran a hand through her hair, still just as bushy after all these years, and looked at the floor. Tina agreed heartily. "Oh, yeah!" Tina nodded in accord.

"Now, this is going to make you laugh... I did have two boys. We actually called them William and Oliver. Do you remember that bit too?"

"I do but really, Liz, you're crazy. I can't believe you actually did that." Tina and Nikki dissolved into youthful giggles. "Honestly, we were really childish back then. Look at us old folks now."

"What? Stop laughing. They are nice names. They are lovely boys. Really, please."

Nikki pulled herself together and interposed, "I know that Elizabeth called her little boy William too. But did you hear what happened to her?"

"Which Elizabeth?" enquired Tina. "There were several of them."

"Five foot six, mousey brown hair, nice girl. It is an absolute tragedy. She was out horse riding and was killed in a hit and run five years ago. She was only forty-five."

"No…" Collective gasps.

"It was heartbreaking. Do you remember she had a baby just after our A Levels? I'm sure it was conceived at that Halloween Disco. She was determined to have it. She married the father, a nice local farmer, James Arbuthnott. In the end, I do think she was exceptionally happy."

"That's good, right?"

"Yes, but I lost touch with her. I feel a bit guilty, but we just went our separate ways."

"Mum told me all about the tragic accident. It was plastered all over the *Kent and Sussex Courier*."

"That is really sad."

Tina interrupted suddenly. "Now hang on a mo. I thought you meant the Elizabeth that was sporty, good at tennis, quite quiet?"

"Yes, she was."

"But she came to Imperial with me. I have every suspicion that she had an abortion soon after that infamous Young Farmers' Disco. No-one looks quite so distraught over having their wisdom teeth removed, and it gave her a funny attitude to men. I never said anything, though. It was her secret."

"What happened to her?"

"After a false start, when she jilted a perfectly nice boy, I've no idea why, she married an amazingly clever, geeky scientist and moved to the States. They became quite the talk of the town in LA, some fancy stuff with the Space Shuttle Programme."

"Wow, very illustrious."

"We met up with them for a vacation. It was a bit tricky because they didn't have any kids and we had so many." Tina paused, then she grimaced, looking embarrassed. "They also moved in very different echelons of high society than us. He had a meltdown after the dreadful Space Shuttle Disaster in 2003 and they hoofed it back to the UK, back here to this neighbourhood. Then an extraordinary thing happened. He disappeared, just totally disappeared. Elizabeth kept phoning me, really distressed."

Nikki and Liz simultaneously said "No..." in horror and looked aghast.

"She blamed it all on the whole not being able to have children thing. They never did find him and I kinda lost touch since then. Like you, Nikki, I feel bad about that. I invited her to this reunion via Facebook but she said she had her hands full with two young kids, which was a total surprise."

Nikki looked questionably at Tina.

"I am guessing that she must have remarried and things worked out okay for her. Clearly not **her** fertility problem then." They laughed conspiratorially.

Liz butted in. "Hang on. This can't be right. I think you both must have the wrong Elizabeth."

Nikki and Tina looked at her doubtfully.

"No, most certainly. I'm sure it was that Elizabeth who came to City University with me. Five foot six, we played hockey together. She was obsessed with Patrick Shepley-Botham. You must remember that? She was drooling over him at the end of the Young Farmers' Disco."

"Not really."

"What do you mean?"

"At university she totally reinvented herself, became what she thought he wanted, posh clothes, even a posh accent. She lost loads of weight and became borderline anorexic. Quite amazingly, with a little bit of help from me and my husband Jim, she ended up marrying Patrick. To my regret."

"Regret?" Tina looked askance. "What do you mean, regret?

"For all his charm, his double-barrelled name and fancy schooling, he turned out to be a boozer. It didn't end well. I don't suppose it is possible to sustain an alter ego for your whole life…"

Nikki nodded in agreement.

"It ended in a messy divorce. In fact, I heard he went to prison for killing a woman in a driving incident.The last I heard, she moved to Wiltshire to get her two children away from the scandal."

All three paused in silent introspection. Nikki ran a hand through her thick hair.

Liz sighed. "I don't think she wanted to come to this because of how things turned out. I just hope she finds her true self and someone sympathetic to share her life with."

Nikki added, "You were right though, Liz. It does seem your life is defined by who you choose to marry." They all nodded thoughtfully, each reflecting on their own marriages as they sipped at their drinks.

Tina suddenly burst out. "But this is crazy. Come on, girls. We can't be talking about the same Elizabeth, can we?"

They looked at each other blankly.

"Come on. Can we?"

**Could they? Perhaps your life really is defined by who you marry. Be careful who you marry…**

Printed in Great Britain
by Amazon

67886375R00199